T0106113

THE CRAFT

FREEMASONS, SECRET AGENTS, AND WILLIAM MORGAN

THOMAS TALBOT

iUniverse, Inc.
New York   Bloomington

The Craft
Freemasons, Secret Agents, and William Morgan

iUniverse books may be ordered through booksellers or by contacting:

iUniverse
1663 Liberty Drive
Bloomington, IN 47403
www.iuniverse.com
1-800-Authors (1-800-288-4677)

Because of the dynamic nature of the Internet, any Web addresses or links contained in this book may have changed since publication and may no longer be valid. The views expressed in this work are solely those of the author and do not necessarily reflect the views of the publisher, and the publisher hereby disclaims any responsibility for them.

ISBN: 978-1-4502-3929-5 (pbk)
ISBN: 978-1-4502-3927-1 (cloth)
ISBN: 978-1-4502-3928-8 (ebk)

Library of Congress Control Number: 2010908950

Printed in the United States of America

iUniverse rev. date: 8/4/10

PROLOGUE

THE WOMAN WAS DESPERATE. SHE had traveled to Philadelphia to send her sons to live with new families. The half brothers were seven and four years of age. Her first husband had died from a fever, and her second was killed in the recent War for Independence. She could no longer afford to raise the two boys, and the prospect of what she was about to do tore her apart. Fortunately, she had relatives with some means who had made arrangements for them to be raised by families who would give them decent homes. The older son was going to England to live with distant relatives, and the younger boy was sailing to Boston where he would be raised by a proper New England family. She knew she was doing the right thing, but the guilt was overwhelming.

She was in Philadelphia to turn the boys over to the guardians who would see that each boy reached his new family safely. She was already late. Both boys were dressed the best she could manage, but they looked shabby in spite of her efforts. They cried and begged her not to separate them. As she entered the building near the waterfront, she began to have second thoughts. Maybe she could find suitable employment and keep her sons with her. She did not need to do this. They may never see each other again. Neither family taking in the boys would ever know each boy had a half brother.

Reluctantly, she pushed those thoughts out of her mind. She hugged and kissed both of them and assured her sons that they would be better off in their new homes. They had heard their mother tell them this for the past two months. The last she ever saw of them was as they turned their heads to look back over their shoulders as the guardians led them to the wharf and the ships that would take them to their new homes. It broke her heart and her spirit.

A few days after she returned to Virginia, a neighbor found her body hanging from the limb of a tree near her small house.

PART 1

CHAPTER 1

SPRING IN WASHINGTON WAS SUDDEN and pleasant this year. The warm, fragrant air drifted over Georgetown down to the former swamp that was now the nation's capital. The sound of birds and the soft greens of new leaves made the recent departure of winter distant and nearly forgotten. The rider, Matthew Prescott, was a good-looking man in his thirties with sandy blond hair, blue eyes, and a medium build. He let the horse find her own way around the mud and pools of water scattered along Pennsylvania Avenue. He had made excellent time from the Baltimore waterfront. With the new capitol building far behind him, he was only a few minutes from the President's Mansion. The warm sun lightened his mood as he reflected on why President Adams had sent for him.

The letter he received a few days ago, hand delivered by military messenger, said it was urgent that he meet with President Adams today. It was a good thing he did not leave for Boston when he had originally planned; otherwise, the message would have missed him. His shipping business would have to wait until he discovered the nature of this urgent matter.

Matthew was a well-known Boston shipping entrepreneur with offices in Boston, New York, and Baltimore. After his father died from a brief illness, Matthew successfully took over. Hard work and

3

New England ingenuity had improved the business and brought him a substantial profit. During the War of 1812, he had fought at the Battle of New Orleans. He single-handedly rallied his men to hold their position against the British regulars and prevented them from breeching his part of the defensive line. The ragtag collection of frontiersmen, pirates, and soldiers fought heroically. Matthew took a bullet in the leg that left him with a star-shaped scar.

Washington appeared to have recovered from the British attack in August of 1814. Repairs had been made on most of the public buildings that were damaged or burned, and little evidence of the attack remained. New buildings were under construction using solid Vermont marble and obviously were meant to last many generations. The little town on the Potomac that became the capital at the turn of the century certainly looked better. The streets were being paved with cobblestones, and L'Enfant's plans were apparently being carried out with a good degree of faithfulness to the original.

When Matthew reached the White House, a servant took his horse, and he was directed to wait in an antechamber. As time passed, he considered the Georgian chair in which he sat and smiled at the irony it represented. Here he was sitting in a piece of English furniture that symbolized everything the new country had fought against—twice. It was only twelve years since the English had put this building to the torch. Adams really had a strange sense of history.

"The president will see you now, Mr. Prescott."

Matthew Prescott acknowledged the announcement with a slight nod and followed the thin, angular man into the adjoining room where he was announced to the president. John Quincy Adams rose from behind a huge mahogany desk to greet Matthew. President Adams was nearly sixty and had been in government service most of his life. Matthew wondered if the story about President Adams swimming nude in the Potomac last summer was true. Apparently, his boat, which contained his clothes, overturned. His servant had to return to the White House for dry clothes, and President Adams hid in some bushes on the riverbank.

"My apologies for detaining you, Mr. Prescott. I hope you have not been inconvenienced."

"Not at all, Mr. President. It was good to rest a few minutes after the ride from Baltimore. And, please, Mr. President, call me Matthew."

President Adams offered Matthew a chair. His manner was very pleasant, not at all what Matthew expected. The secretary poured two glasses of wine, left them on a silver tray, and took his leave. President Adams offered Matthew a glass, and he accepted it with thanks. The ride that day had been long and warm, and he was thirsty.

"Matthew it shall be. I realize you must find this request somewhat of a surprise."

"Mr. President, you are absolutely right. I cannot, for the life of me, imagine why you would want to speak with me, or, for that matter, about what."

"Matthew, let me be frank with you. I have asked you here regarding a matter that may involve our young nation's security, as well as a man you knew during the last war. I would like your assistance, not only because you knew the man, but also because you have the ability to successfully complete a task I want you to undertake. Before I tell you what that task is, let me give you a little background."

"Certainly, Mr. President." Matthew wondered who the man could be and what the task would require of him. He was tempted to ask, but he waited for the president to continue.

"Our country has been tested on several occasions since we gained our independence from England. We have managed to take advantage of every opportunity available to enhance our diplomatic position with Europe. The Jay and Pinckney treaties in 1794 and 1795 helped keep us clear of military entanglements with England and Spain. We fought an undeclared war with the French from 1798 to 1800 and managed to survive. We purchased Louisiana from Napoleon when his plans for expansion in our hemisphere went awry. This expanded our nation's boundaries considerably to great advantage, as Lewis and Clark eventually proved. We had to deal with British incursions on our fur trade in the West and the Russians trying to attain a sphere of influence in the Pacific near our boundaries adjacent to Oregon. The British impressed our sailors and went so far as to attack the *Chesapeake* and forcibly take four men from her crew. This led to the second war with them in a thirty-year period. Incidentally, I regard Jackson's role in that conflict as critical and his contribution as significant. No one can dispute that." Matthew nodded in agreement. President Adams continued. "President Monroe just recently declared our hemisphere out of the European sphere of influence. Based on events in Europe after the Congress of Vienna, as well as the problems in the Spanish colonies to our south, this will prove to be a critical and important turning point in our nation's history. At least, that is my opinion. We are still a young nation, Matthew. Our fiftieth birthday is this year."

Matthew said nothing. He sensed that President Adams was not finished. The president continued. "The matter I am about to discuss with you may directly affect the security of this country, and it is known by only a few of my most trusted men. I know I will be able to count on your discretion as a gentlemen and a patriot."

"You may be assured of that, Mr. President."

"During the recent war with England, now being called the War of 1812 by some, the British infiltrated several agents—spies, if you will—into this country. These agents joined forces with others who had been recruited before the war and became established in several locations. Some of them were British, while others were Americans. We have been able to identify most of them. Many were captured during the war or within a few years after it ended. Some were executed for treason, and the rest were imprisoned or deported. One man in particular has eluded us. You knew this man, Matthew, but not as a spy. He served with you during the recent war and fought under your command at New Orleans. His real name is Andrew Fletcher, but you knew him as William Morgan."

"Morgan, a spy? I find this difficult to believe."

"There is a good reason. Fletcher came to America from England in the early 1790s. His relatives in London sent him to live with a loyalist family named Morgan in Virginia somewhere near Culpeper

County, we believe. The boy was legally adopted by the Morgans and given the first name of William. Andrew Fletcher ceased to exist. He led a fairly normal life. He was sent to school and then apprenticed as a stonemason. Not much else is known except that before the second war with Britain began, he returned to Britain to visit his relatives. The relatives, it was later discovered, had contacts with members of the British military assigned the charge of gathering intelligence from Europe as well as the Americas. The French had to be dealt with and Napoleon stopped from creating a French empire. Some of the British intelligence agents never gave up the idea, however, of regaining the colonies lost during the Revolution." Adams continued speaking as Matthew finished the last of his wine. "Morgan was recruited in England as an agent and given the task of gathering intelligence information when he returned to America as a British spy. He sent information to the British by means of a contact in Virginia. Another interesting part of this story is that the English relatives were Freemasons. I do not know what this means in regard to his spying, but we are trying to find out. When Morgan returned to Virginia, he resumed his work as a stonemason. Eventually, he became involved in several government projects. He helped build powder magazines, armories, and even worked on an expansion project at Fort McHenry in Baltimore. We think he may even have worked on several shore battery installations in the Washington area along the Potomac. Obviously his knowledge of defense installations around Baltimore and Washington would be useful information for the British. When war finally started, he enlisted in the army and served in various locations, including, of course, New Orleans. It was a good way to cover his tracks."

"Yes, Mr. President. Morgan was in my unit." Matthew had difficulty accepting what the president had just told him about Morgan. "Morgan and I knew each other quite well and even corresponded for a time after the war. Eventually, I lost track of him, but I did not consider that unusual. A number of people were moving about the country during those years."

"No, it was not unusual, but Morgan is no ordinary person. His knowledge of the defenses around Baltimore and Washington may have been very helpful to the British, especially in their attack on Washington."

"Yes, that would be very useful."

The president's eyes were watery, and he wiped them with his handkerchief. "After the war, our intelligence unit examined documents captured from the British. One document in particular was a major find. It contained a list of British agents working in this country during the period from approximately 1800 until the end of the war. Morgan's name was on the list. Attempts were made to find him. The search began in 1820, but as the years passed, we had no success. The document had been with lists of supplies and troop movements and remained unread until other documents had been cataloged and filed. By this time, Morgan had returned to Virginia, married the daughter of a Methodist minister from Baltimore, and left Virginia. He was traced to New York City and then to York in Canada. We could not extradite him from Canada even if we found him. Most of the knowledge we have regarding his activities was derived from interviews with his neighbors and an interrogation of a British spy who had been deported. This British spy was traced to England and then to France, where he was captured by one of our people and convinced that it was in his best interest to talk."

Matthew tried very hard to control himself. It was very difficult to believe what he had just been told. "My humblest apologies, Mr. President, but I am incredulous. Morgan was a good soldier and a good man. He gave no indication whatsoever that he could possibly be anything else."

"He apparently was good at his work. By serving in the army and removing himself from the area where most of his intelligence gathering occurred, he succeeded in his deception quite skillfully."

Matthew wanted to steer the conversation to his role in all this. "Mr. President, what do you require of me?"

"It is really quite simple, Matthew. You knew Morgan. He trusted you and considered you a friend. Find him for us and bring him back to Washington."

"Why now, Mr. President, so many years after the war?"

"We recently obtained information that leads us to believe that Morgan has been in recent contact with British agents. Something is being planned—an event, a staged occurrence—that could prove to be embarrassing to this country at a time when we have just begun to consolidate our position with Europe. Morgan may be a key to this plan. Unfortunately, we do not know what the plan is, but we believe it will take place this year and that British sympathizers are behind it. We have come too far to allow those conceited individuals to interfere in our affairs again."

Matthew was skeptical. "With all due respect, Mr. President, how can they possibly do anything now? It is 1826; the war ended more than ten years ago. The British have other more important interests."

The president sighed. "Old men never give up dreams of power and conquest, Matthew. There are former government officials, military officers, and even a few of those presently in power who would do anything to destroy what we have here. I realize not many people know this, but maybe it is just as well. They probably would not believe it."

President Adams dabbed at his eyes again. Matthew's thoughts raced. If he agreed to pursue Morgan, how could he accomplish it? He was no spy or special agent. His military experience would be helpful, but that was several years in the past. "What is your plan for me, Mr. President?"

"You are an American civilian. Travel to Canada on the pretext of business. Locate Morgan and make arrangements to accompany him back to Washington. We will promise not to execute him if he returns. We need to find out what he knows, and we feel you are the one person who can convince him to return. I do not mean to sound overly melodramatic, Matthew, but your country does need you. Will you accept our request for your services?"

Matthew was very tempted to say no. He was very reluctant to become involved in this since he knew something the president and his agents did not. A few months before his father, John Prescott, died, John told Matthew he had an uncle. Matthew's uncle was his father's half brother. His father had found this out from the contents of a letter that had been sent from Virginia. He sent a private investigator to try to find out the truth. The investigator checked local records and interviewed people who might have some knowledge of the relationship. He found that two boys had apparently left the area around 1784 or 1785. The older boy came back and was adopted by the Morgan family.

A neighbor remembered talk in the village that the other boy had been sent to New England, probably by ship from Philadelphia. A check of passenger lists and legal records from the period revealed that a boy from Virginia had been adopted by Matthew's grandparents in Boston. Matthew's father made contact with Morgan in Virginia, but Morgan wanted nothing to do with him. His father thought it odd but did not pursue the matter. It was only when he was dying that he decided to tell Matthew.

Matthew made a quick decision. He had to say yes. It was his patriotic duty, but he also had to agree for a personal reason. Morgan was his uncle. He needed to accept the president's request in order to make sure that no harm came to Morgan. "Mr. President, logic tells me to say no, but the opportunity is too challenging to refuse. I accept."

"You have made a wise decision. I have arranged for you to meet one of my agents who will provide you with more background and details. I must inform you that if you are discovered or if your mission is compromised in any way, we must disavow any knowledge of you or your assignment. Our relations with the British and the rest of Europe are too delicate at present."

"I understand, Mr. President. Where do I meet this agent?"

"You will be contacted this evening by Mr. Cardwell. A room is reserved for you at the Constitutional Tavern in Georgetown."

"Out of curiosity, Mr. President, what would you have done if I had refused your offer?"

"That possibility was never considered, Matthew. Godspeed and good luck."

CHAPTER 2

MATTHEW FOUND IT DIFFICULT TO accept the revelations of President Adams as he left the mansion and walked toward the stable to retrieve his horse. President Adams made a very strong case against Morgan, and he obviously had the proof to substantiate it. He still found the possibility of Morgan being a spy hard to believe.

The long ride and the meeting with President Adams had taken most of the day. He was tired. One of the grooms at the stable had rubbed down his horse, watered and fed her, and put her in a clean stall according to his instructions. He thanked the groom and offered him a tip. The groom refused. "No, sir. My pleasure, sir. No need for any money."

Matthew faced a difficult decision. At some point, he needed to tell Mr. Cardwell that Morgan was his uncle. If he said anything now, they might suspect his motives and refuse to work with him. On the other hand, if he said nothing and then told them later, they might feel the same. He could only hope the relationship would not become an issue. He wondered if President Adams and Mr. Cardwell knew this already. He decided not to say anything until he met Mr. Cardwell and took his measure. When the time was right, he would tell him. God, he hoped this didn't turn out to be a very bad decision.

He made his way through the late afternoon along the Washington streets and eventually found his way to the Constitutional

Tavern in Georgetown. It was a pleasant enough structure with its neat brickwork and stone trim, a type of structure that in the next century would be referred to as "Colonial." The tavern was frequented by lobbyists, government officials, political hangers-on, and businessmen. It offered excellent food, comfortable rooms, and, most important of all, an atmosphere of discretion. Matthew left his horse with the stable boy and climbed the steps to the front porch. Several groups of gentlemen conducted animated conversations from their rocking chairs. The sharp smell of cigar and pipe smoke as well as kitchen odors met him as he entered the tavern. A short hallway led to the common room and the innkeeper's station just behind the bar, the common room decorated and furnished in the current style. Comfortable chairs were arranged in conversational groupings with several more private areas scattered around the periphery. Matthew identified himself to the taverner, and with a look obviously well practiced, the man became very deferential.

"Yes, sir, Mr. Prescott, we have a room ready for you. You are expected. Is there anything I may obtain for you?"

"Not at the moment, ah, Mr. … I didn't catch your name."

"Johnson. Jacob Johnson, at your service."

"Well, Mr. Johnson, thank you kindly for the offer, but all I want to do at the moment is go to my room and rest for a while before I have some supper."

"Of course, Mr. Prescott. I'll have Ezekiel bring your bag to your room immediately. Ezekiel, come over here and help this gentleman with his bag. Take him to room 27."

A black servant of about fifty with gray hair, a slight limp, and a practiced subservience to whites hurried over and took Matthew's bag. Matthew had not brought much in the way of luggage—just a change of clothes and a few other items. He liked to travel light and did not plan to stay in Washington very long. Events were soon to prove him correct.

"Follow me, Mr. Prescott."

Matthew followed Ezekiel through the bar and up the stairs to the second floor where the tavern's sleeping rooms were located. There were more on the third floor, but he was glad his was on the second.

His leg bothered him a little, and the prospect of the extra stairs did not appeal to him at all. Ezekiel showed him the room and put the bag on the bed. The room was furnished quite well. He gave Ezekiel a generous tip, and Ezekiel politely thanked him. Ezekiel took his leave, and Matthew removed his boots and coat. With a sigh of relief, he fell on the bed. It felt good to relax after the day's events.

As Matthew relaxed, he mentally reviewed the recent events that had put John Quincy Adams in the presidency. Adams had been secretary of state for two terms under James Monroe from 1817 to 1825. The election of 1824 was a hotly contested one. Adams had the greatest competition from Andrew Jackson, as well as Henry Clay and William H. Crawford. Crawford suffered from a paralyzing illness during the campaign and was no longer a serious contender. Adams was considered by many, in spite of his brilliance as secretary of state, to be a cold and distant man. Jackson was popular among the common people, especially in the newly developing West. He had been in Congress as a member of the House of Representatives from Tennessee and was a senator by 1824. He was a military hero with national prominence, but to some people he appeared to be a crude and short-tempered frontiersman. Jackson was a self-made man. He had been raised as an orphan in the Carolinas but had managed to become a very well-to-do planter. He was considered to be a gentleman by his contemporaries in Tennessee. His famous home, the Hermitage, was a center for social and political gathering near Nashville.

When the votes from the Electoral College were counted, it was clear that John C. Calhoun was the winner of the vice presidency, but the presidency was far from clear. Jackson had the most votes with ninety-nine, while Adams had eighty-four. Clay had thirty-seven votes, and Crawford had forty-one. Crawford, due to his paralysis, withdrew from contention, and the election was thrown into the House of Representatives based on the provisions of the Twelfth Amendment to the Constitution. The top three were now Jackson, Clay, and Adams. Jackson was Clay's rival in the West. Clay threw his support to Adams because they shared similar political views regarding domestic policies.

Prescott remembered the deal that had been struck. Adams had selected Clay as his secretary of state. Jackson was disgusted with the events and resigned from the Senate after the inauguration and began his campaign for president in the next election of 1828. Jackson wanted to make sure Adams or Clay would not win the next election. Prescott had supported Jackson, but it did not do much good in New England.

He reviewed the meeting with the president. President Adams did not seem to hold it against him that he was a Jackson supporter. Also, he did not appear to know Morgan was his uncle. He would have to be very careful with this Mr. Cardwell.

Matthew was awakened by a knock on the door. "What is it?"

"It's Ezekiel, Mr. Prescott. I have a message for you, sir."

"Wait a moment. I'll be right there." He opened the door to find Ezekiel standing there with a folded piece of paper in his right hand. "The man who gave me the message, Mr. Cardwell, said to be sure I delivered this to you in person."

"Did he request a reply, Ezekiel?"

"No, sir. He said the message was all I was to give you, and I was to go back and tell him that I had given it to you."

"Thank you, Ezekiel."

"Is there anything else I can do for you, Mr. Prescott?"

"No, Ezekiel, that will be all."

"Yes, sir. Good evening, sir." Ezekiel turned away and limped down the hall.

The note was written in a bold script and addressed to Matthew Prescott, room 27, Constitutional Tavern. The note read:

Prescott,

Meet me for supper at seven in the dining room of the tavern. A table has been reserved.

Your servant,

Zebulon T. Cardwell, Esq.

Matthew checked his timepiece. It was 6:15. He had better start moving if he was going to clean up and change before going downstairs.

The main dining room of the tavern was not crowded when Matthew entered at five minutes before seven. Apparently, most of the guests had eaten. Cardwell may have planned it this way to decrease the chances of someone overhearing their conversation. The head waiter, who expected him, met Matthew at the entrance and led him to a table at the far end of the room near the fireplace. Just as he was in the process of sitting down, a man appeared. Startled, Matthew immediately stood up.

The man was tall, over six feet, and of medium build. He had dark brown hair, brown eyes, and looked very fit. He appeared to be in his early forties.

"Matthew Prescott, I presume."

"Yes, that is correct. Then you must be Mr. Cardwell."

"Yes, I am. Shall we sit down?" It sounded more like an order than a request. "Please, call me Zeb. By the way, I see Ezekiel is still as efficient as ever."

"Yes, he gave me your message an hour ago."

"I know. Ezekiel has done many favors for me in the past. I have found him to be quite useful and discreet. Prescott, let me give you some of my thoughts before we begin our business. I do not know who decided to advise the president to include you directly in this search. I am not an enthusiastic proponent of using civilians to do our kind of work. Apparently there are good reasons, but I wanted you to know how I feel before we continue."

"Please call me Matthew. Frankly, I am as surprised about this entire matter as you. I know why I was selected, but I believe there must be someone else who could do the same thing much more expertly and efficiently than I. There has to be someone with more experience in these matters. I must admit, though, I do find it intriguing."

Zeb grinned slightly and seemed more relaxed. "Matthew, do me a favor. Listen to what I have to tell you and then decide if you still want to stay with this endeavor. Let us order dinner first. The hard-shell crab is excellent, and so is the oyster stew."

"All right. I am a good listener."

Zeb signaled the waiter and placed their orders. "Matthew, there is a great deal more to this affair than the president has told you. I know he did not hold anything back out of any hidden motive. He merely wanted me to provide you with the details once he had your agreement to participate."

"I'm listening."

"President Adams is a very honest and sincere man. He is really more of a scholar than a politician. The president is a prolific writer who puts so much on paper that he gets cramps in his right hand. Because of this, he has learned to write with his left hand, as well. He often rises before four or five in the morning and even starts a fire so he can go about his scholarly pursuits without disturbing the staff at that early hour."

"I'm not surprised."

"He views this entire matter with some reservation. President Adams can deal with it in the abstract, but not as something he directly participates in. Do you understand?"

"Oh, yes. He told me that if I were to be apprehended or compromised in any way, the government would not protect or help me."

"That is true."

"But isn't a president required to make difficult decisions in the real world?"

"That is true up to a point. President Adams does not like to become bogged down in the day-to-day politics of the job. He prefers to deal with ideas and principles. That is why he has people like me to jump in the mud and get dirty. I am not being critical, mind you; that is just the way he is, and I have to accept it."

"I suppose I can accept it, as well."

"Let me get to those details I referred to a few moments ago. As you know, Morgan has been identified as a British spy based on records captured during the war but not read until much later. Also, we believe he was instrumental in providing the British with information concerning our defensive positions near Baltimore and Washington."

"Apparently," replied Matthew. He still found it difficult to believe.

"The president asked you to help us find him. Morgan was last traced to Canada, and we have reason to believe there is a plan to create an incident that could embarrass our country in diplomatic circles. Furthermore, Morgan is thought to be part of this plot."

"Yes, Adams believes that, as a civilian, I could travel to Canada, try to make contact with Morgan, and bring him back."

"All by yourself? Doesn't that strike you as being somewhat oversimplified?"

"Of course it does, but I thought I would have some help."

"Good thinking. At least you appear to have some common sense."

"Then how will this whole scheme be accomplished?"

"Before we discuss this, let me give you some more information. You have been given the general background, but not the details. First, there is an incident planned. We do not know what it is or where it will take place. All we know is that Morgan is involved and that the incident is scheduled for the last half of this year. We believe it may be in September or October, but it could be in late summer."

"How do you know this?"

"We have a good source. One of my people is in New York. After several members of a Masonic lodge had left a recent meeting and retired to a local tavern, they became talkative. By sheer coincidence, one of my men happened to be in the tavern and joined their conversation. The discussion turned to foreign matters, and one of the men, who had become quite inebriated, said he knew for a fact that one of the attachés at the British consulate was in a good position to gather intelligence for the British. The rest of the group laughed at the man. My agent remained after the others left to speak further with the gentleman. He was told by the brother in his cups that one of the attaché's assistants had bragged to him once about how the Americans were going to be very embarrassed one day soon.

We did some further investigating. One of my other people, who worked as a domestic in the consulate, found a letter referring to a plan called Machiavelli. The letter was not detailed, but it did speak of a plan that could mean a great deal to the British. It alluded to the possibility of great embarrassment and could possibly initiate a chain of events that could lead to Britain regaining her former colonies."

"How did she manage to get that letter?"

"That was fairly easy. The attaché liked the maid, and they had sex in his study. He fell asleep afterward, and she went through his correspondence and found the letter. Damned brave girl! She could have been killed if he had found her doing that."

"Who was the letter from?"

"There was no indication on the letter as to who had sent it. The document did come from England. That was clear enough. We don't think whoever is involved in this has the sanction of the British government; we think this person is a lone wolf operating with a group of like-minded friends and paid hires. We believe he probably has his people strategically located in diplomatic and commercial positions within our country."

"What can they possibly do? It is probably a group of old men trying to recapture the glory days of their youth."

"You may be partially correct. They probably are older men, but they have something else that is very important—money and power. We do not know who they are, but one thing is certain—they have been in touch with Morgan."

"How so?"

"The letter referred to him as their contact."

The waiter arrived with the food and a bottle of wine that Zeb had ordered. When the waiter finished placing the dishes on the table, they resumed the conversation.

"Matthew, this whole business sounds absurd to any rational man, but it is true. We do have evidence, and we need to find Morgan. We know he has gone to Canada, but whether he is still there or not is questionable. I would much rather send one of my own men, in spite of the diplomatic repercussions it could cause, but the president will not hear of it."

"How did my name become involved in this? I never asked President Adams this afternoon."

"You were recommended by Morgan!"

"The devil you say! You had better clarify that, Zeb."

"Don't get excited. It was not a direct recommendation. We know you corresponded with him after the war as a result of our recent investigations. Also, when Morgan applied for work, he used your name as a reference."

"Yes, that is correct. One letter I received did request a reference. I believe it was nearly a year after the war. How did you know?"

"We checked with some of the people who hired him after the war, and one of the individuals, an inveterate paper hoarder, had kept the letter of reference you wrote. We did some further checking into your background and decided to contact you in Baltimore."

"Now that you have told me, how do you plan to carry this off?"

"We would like you to go back to Baltimore and sail to Boston. From Boston, you will travel to Albany, take a packet boat on the Erie Canal, make your way to Lewiston, and then over the Niagara River to Canada. You will travel as yourself on the pretext of business. I am sure you can think of something that would take you to that part of the Great Lakes. Incidentally, York is at the western end of Lake Ontario. We burned York during the war before the British torched Washington. Washington was partly revenge for the burning of York. Morgan was last reported in York and may still be there. At least the trail should be warm there. You must be discreet in your inquiries. Use the fact that you are an old friend in the area on business and heard from relatives of Morgan that he and his wife were living there. In the meantime, I must travel to New York for a few days. I will meet you in Lewiston. Lewiston is on the Niagara River across from Canada, near Fort George. You must stop in Lewiston before going into Canada."

"Why?"

"I'll explain later."

"Fair enough."

"It is pretty straightforward. You will be on your own in Canada. I will have the proper papers drawn up for you, as well as provide you with a few other essential items."

"What do you mean by 'a few other essential items'?"

"Oh, a good pistol may come in handy. I hope you haven't forgotten how to use one."

"No, I have not, but why do I need to be armed?"

"You may not need one, but it is much better to have some protection than to travel around at the mercy of those who may be protecting Morgan."

"What do you mean?"

"You don't really expect him to be involved in some plot like this and not have assistance, do you?"

"No, I suppose not."

"Here is the timetable. Leave tomorrow and ride back to Baltimore. Sail your ship to Boston as planned. You must create a cover story for your business associates and friends to explain your trip. Leave Boston by the beginning of May and travel to Albany. It does not matter if you want to go overland to Albany or sail to New York and go up the Hudson. Once you reach Albany, you will be able to take passage on a packet boat going to Buffalo on the Erie Canal. A good packet boat with four mules can make twenty-five miles a day or more. This should put you in Lockport in about two weeks at the longest. From Lockport, it is a short ride to Lewiston. I will meet you in Lewiston before you go to York. I will be traveling under the name of Samuel Trapp, seller of sundry household goods. Stay at the inn on the main street and wait for me. Don't ask for me. I will find you and make contact. When I find you, I will give you any additional information you may need before starting the next phase."

"What if I find Morgan in Canada?"

"Leave him there, and I will draw up a plan to go there and capture him."

"What if I miss the timetable?"

"Don't."

Matthew looked directly at Zeb. What he saw was a resolute man, very professional, giving orders. There was a great deal more to Zeb than first appearances suggested. Matthew could sense it.

The meal was finished, and the waiter brought them brandy and cigars. As a haze of cigar smoke encircled the table, a shot rang out, and the decanter of brandy shattered, sending glass fragments onto the table and the two men. Zeb instinctively fell to the floor, but Matthew momentarily froze in surprise. A burly waiter near the entrance wrestled a man in the clothes of a frontiersman to the floor. Zeb rose and ran over to help the waiter. More help came, and the frontiersman, or whoever he was, was roughly removed from the room. Zeb had a brief conversation with the head waiter and returned to the table. He told Matthew to follow him quickly to the back entrance by way of the kitchen. Matthew started to regain his composure after the shot and shattering of glass.

"What the hell was that?"

"That was either some crazy frontiersman's idea of fun, or someone is trying to kill me. I am not sure, but I will know more after we question him. He's being taken to a location for that purpose. On the assumption that someone is very interested in what you and I are doing together, I think we had better get out of here quickly."

The two men went quietly and rapidly through the kitchen exit, down an alley, and over to the next street. They walked for several blocks at a rapid pace, with Zeb giving directions. Then they slowed a bit, continuing toward the waterfront. Eventually, they came to a tavern and went to a room in the rear. If there was a problem, they would be safe there until Zeb could learn more about the frontiersman.

CHAPTER 3

TWO MEN SAT AT A table. The dim light from a candle was the only illumination in the room. Zeb sipped his mug of ale, while Matthew stared at the flame. They had been waiting nearly two hours, and both men were lost in their own thoughts. The silence was interrupted by one of Zeb's men. John Richards entered the room without knocking and immediately sat down. He was breathing hard but able to speak clearly. He was in his midthirties, of slightly above average height, with curly brown hair and brown eyes.

"You won't like what I have to tell you, but here it is, anyway. The man from the tavern is not a westerner from Kentucky or Tennessee as his appearance would suggest."

"Damn it, Richards, who the hell is he? Don't embellish the story; just give it to me based on what you know." Zeb was relieved by the man's appearance but a bit perturbed by his manner. Matthew thought it probably was nothing new; they must have worked together for quite some time.

"We took him to the rooming house and questioned him."

"Jesus! Get to the point."

"When he first opened his mouth, we decided he was either doing a damned good imitation of an Englishman, or he was the real thing. He didn't say much at first. He wanted to know who we were and what we wanted with him. Said he was just on a drunk and didn't know what he was doing. He had been drinking, but he wasn't that drunk. He told us he was just visiting some friends in Washington who gave him the outfit as a gift. Said he was a Canadian who had emigrated from England last year. That sounded plausible, but when we started to get serious, he stopped talking. I asked him if he had ever heard of Machiavelli, and he looked like a man who just saw a ghost."

"What do you mean?"

"He just sort of went all white—like I'd said Old Scratch was sitting next to him, ready to poke his pitchfork into his ribs. He wouldn't talk at all anymore. I knew you wanted to know everything, so we started to persuade him to tell us more. He just broke a few minutes ago. We didn't kill him, sir, but he sure won't be socializing for a while—not with his new face."

"All right, Richards, you have done well." Cardwell was keenly attentive now. "What did he tell you?"

Richards's reply was soft, but it had the effect of the striking of a blacksmith's hammer. "He told us he had been hired by a man from New York City to follow you and, when the opportunity presented itself, to kill you!"

Zeb was stunned. "Why me? No one knows anything about this Morgan matter except Phillips in New York and the maid at the consulate."

Richards replied, "Well, he sure as hell knew, and somebody had offered him a lot of money to kill you. He was given five hundred dollars for the job."

"A good sum these days. Did he say anything else?"

"No. Only that the man who hired him said that he represented an organization that would pay a great deal to have you killed."

"Did you find out why?"

"No. He didn't know."

"How did he manage to miss?"

"That's the funny part, if you will excuse the expression. Just as he was squeezing off the shot, one of the waiters accidentally bumped him."

"Thank the good Lord for clumsy waiters. I want to talk to him. Since he was trying to kill me, I would like to know more."

Matthew had remained silent during the conversation. If what Richards just told Zeb was true, then this plot—whatever it was— needed to be stopped. If attempted murder was involved already, anything was possible. He rose quickly and followed the two men without even asking if he could join them. Apparently, Zeb didn't mind since he said nothing as Matthew walked with them.

The three men walked through the now quiet city to a boardinghouse. It was a nondescript structure with no special features. They entered the building and went down the hallway to a flight of stairs at the rear. Richards unlocked a door at the bottom of the stairs, and they entered the room. The man's face was the first thing Matthew noticed. His face was bloody and bruised. Zeb told Matthew to sit in the corner out of the light cast by candles hanging in the wrought iron holder suspended from the ceiling. Zeb approached the man, who was tied securely to a sturdy chair. His eyes followed Zeb's every move.

"You bastard! I could have you killed. I hope you realize that." The man did not reply. "We know why you came here. Who sent you and why?"

The man stirred slightly, shifting his weight to a less painful position. "You filthy scum, Cardwell. I should not tell you anything, but I want you to know what you can expect in the next few months—if you live that long. My life is worth nothing now that you have me. They will kill me no matter how much protection you provide for me. I'm not the only one. If I fail, others will follow. We will kill you sooner or later—and everyone else who finds out about us. Nothing is going to stop us from gaining our ultimate goal. You colonials think your new system is going to last forever."

Cardwell glared at him. "Why do you want to kill me?"

"I told your friends already. We know you have sources in New York who stumbled onto some information linking a former member of your military with our plans. We expected you to start looking for this man. My superiors sent me to kill you. With you out of the way, our major source of opposition would be gone."

"I'm flattered, but that is not true. I am only one man."

"A matter of opinion, dear boy."

"Why the frontier garb?"

"That should be obvious. If I had succeeded, they would be looking for a demented frontiersman, possibly a follower of your Jackson, who wanted to get revenge against Adams through you. We know how highly esteemed you are by that pudgy windbag."

"I've heard enough. Take him to the security cells and lock him up until we can question him further." He motioned to Matthew, and they left. The other men in the room began to prepare the prisoner for the transfer.

It was after midnight when Zeb and Matt walked the nearly deserted streets of the capital. Only a few people were heading home from taverns or other late-night business. Zeb started walking in the direction of Georgetown and the Constitutional Tavern. "I think it is safe to assume that no one knows of your role in this yet, Matthew, but in order to keep your participation unknown for as long as possible, you should return to the tavern and get a good night's rest. Leave early in the morning and follow our plan. Nothing has changed in that regard. The problem I now have is finding out exactly who hired that damned assassin."

Matthew was worried. Things had been happening very quickly since yesterday. If they were after Zeb, he could be next. This was suddenly turning into something more than expected. He thought about telling Zeb that Morgan was his uncle, but he decided to wait. "Look, Zeb, maybe I had better get out of this entirely. Maybe I should take you up on your earlier offer."

"There is no chance now, Matthew. Events have gone too far, too fast."

They both were silent as they walked back to Georgetown. Patches of fog drifted in from the Potomac and began to shroud the city in its embrace. The two men, if anyone had been observing them, appeared to be out for a late-night walk or headed to a favorite tavern for a drink. One limped slightly, and the other took long, steady strides. When they reached the Constitutional Tavern, Zeb spoke. "Get out of here at dawn. You should be relatively safe. I don't think they know about you yet. Go to Baltimore as planned, and take your ship to Boston. I'll see you in Lewiston in May. Good luck."

"Wait. What if I need to contact you?"

"That will not be possible, Matthew. You will not see me until we meet in Lewiston. I have a great deal to do before then. Keep to the plan, and don't worry. Just be careful, and you won't be in any danger. I am the one they are focused on right now."

Zeb left Matthew at the entrance to the inn and walked quickly away into the thickening fog. Matthew wondered if he would ever see him again. Well, if he wanted excitement, he sure as hell was getting it.

CHAPTER 4

MATTHEW'S LIMP WAS MORE PRONOUNCED as he mounted the stairs to his room. The old wound ached, and the day's events weighed heavily on him. All of it had happened so quickly. Yesterday he was merely a merchant on a trip to Baltimore. The next day, he had become a major part of an attempt to thwart a yet unidentified plot against his country. The president had convinced him that he should participate. Now he faced an uncertain future, and only a few hours earlier, someone had tried to kill Zeb.

Surprisingly, Ezekiel was still up when Matthew entered the Constitutional Tavern. Matthew gave Ezekiel instructions to wake him at dawn. He also told Ezekiel to see that his horse was saddled and ready to go as soon as he ate a quick breakfast. Ezekiel assured him that all would be done. Matthew fell into bed exhausted and went immediately to sleep.

However, the day was not finished for Zeb Cardwell. A carriage picked him up three blocks from the tavern, a prearranged location, and took him to a small maximum-security prison run by the intelligence service. The unsuccessful assassin was in a special security cell with Richards.

"Anything new?"

"No, he hasn't told us anything else at all."

"Let me have him for a few minutes. Let's see if I can get him to talk."

The prisoner was secured to the wall with heavy chains attached to iron rings in the wall that led to shackles on each wrist. His legs were loosely tied so he could sit or stand. A slop pail was in the corner.

"We have established a few things, haven't we? First, though, I do not know your name. What shall I call you?"

"My name is Harold Villineau."

"Well, Villineau, let's get started. Unless you want Richards here and his friends to work on you again, and not just your face, you had better start talking. Let's begin with the man from New York who hired you. Who is he?"

"Go to hell, Cardwell. I won't tell you anything more than I have already."

"Richards, bring me a poker from the coals over there." There was a small stove with a glowing bed of coals in the corridor. Embedded in the coals were several lengths of iron about three-quarters of an inch in diameter with thick wooden handles. Richard pulled one out and handed it to Zeb. He held the glowing tip of the metal inches from Villineau's eyes. Villineau pulled his head away from the heat.

"If you don't answer my question, you murdering son of a whore, I will shove this poker in one eye and out the back of your skull. Do you understand?"

Villineau began to sweat and started to tremble slightly. Zeb brought the poker close to his left eye and shouted, "Talk or burn!" Villineau moved quickly and lashed out with his legs, sending Zeb flying backward. The poker clanged noisily on the stone floor. Zeb got up, retrieved the poker, and shouted again, "Richards, hold the bastard." Richards grabbed Villineau and held him securely. Zeb took the poker and laid it against the prisoner's cheek. The flesh sizzled, and Villineau let out an ear-shattering shriek. He screamed, "Enough, enough! I'll tell you everything I know! Keep that damned iron away from me."

"Start now, or I'll give you a matching one on the other side."

"I was sent by a man who contacted me in York. It's in Canada at the western end of Lake Ontario."

"Yes, I know where York is."

"He approached me about two weeks ago and spoke of a group with a plan they called Machiavelli. He said the group planned to create an incident that would cause problems for the United States. All was going according to plan until someone started snooping in New York and found out about the plan and the existence of the group. They killed the girl in the consulate and dumped her body in the Hudson."

Damn, Zeb thought. "Go on."

"They know she had a contact, but they could not find him. She would not talk and died before they could make her reveal his identity. She was a tough girl. Anyway, this man called himself Robinson, and he told me he knew about my work with Napoleon in the past."

"Napoleon?"

"Yes, I was in his hire before Waterloo and performed several services for him as an independent."

"You mean you killed for him?"

"Yes—and some other tasks."

"What else?"

"Robinson knew me by reputation and recruited me. He offered a sum sufficient to ensure my services. He also told me that if I failed, others would be sent. He said that failure meant the forfeiture of my life. I am a dead man either way. Go ahead and kill me. If you don't, those bastards will."

"If the girl did not tell them anything, why did he send you to kill me?"

"He didn't say. All he told me was that you were very important to Adams. He didn't tell me exactly who you were. I found that out when I came to Washington and started checking into your background. That's when I found out how important you really are."

"What else?"

"That is all. I was hired to kill you, but the plot itself is a mystery to me. I don't really care. I only get paid to kill people."

"Richards, put some ointment on that cheek and let him get some sleep." Zeb left the cell and went to the room that served as a combination office and conference room. Richards joined him about ten minutes later. "What do you think, Richards? Is he telling us the truth?"

"Yes, I think he is. He has nothing to lose now. In fact, he is probably better off with us now that he has failed. We can't try him under normal procedures because the whole affair would become public. The only thing he has to do to remain alive is stay locked up."

"I agree. Keep him in that cell until you hear from me. I am going to bed and get some sleep. I need to travel to New York as soon as possible. If the maid is dead, Phillips could be in trouble. I haven't heard from him for several days as it is. I'll check with you in the morning before I leave. Put a double guard on Villineau just in case he is telling us the truth."

"Yes, sir."

The waiting carriage took Zeb to Georgetown and a comfortable town house near the Jesuit university that had been founded by Bishop Carroll in 1789. He had attended the university but never expected to find himself in his present occupation. It was an unsavory business, but his sense of patriotism helped him rationalize some of the things he had to do. Deep down, he knew the most convoluted logic couldn't justify what he sometimes did, but patriotism was a good enough rationale. He thought that it was odd how, after all these years, the high moral purpose and ethics that had been injected into his brain could be overcome by a baser and less ideal mode of living.

Thinking about ethics and his job reminded him of two things. First, he was Jewish, but no one in the government knew this, not even President Adams. The anti-Semitism of the Old World had crossed the ocean with many of the immigrants. Some of them held important positions in government and were not big supporters of

President Adams's secret organization of agents headed by Zeb. If they knew Zeb was Jewish, they would find a way to get rid of him. The second problem was his current standing with President Adams. Zeb was on probation. He had killed a man on his last mission in a fit of anger. The man deserved to die, but Zeb was supposed to bring him back for trial in Washington. If he failed this time with Morgan, he would be removed from the service.

He entered his house and found a note on the table in the entrance hallway. He took the note and went upstairs. The household staff was asleep, having learned long ago not to wait up for him. His occupation had left no time for marriage. His income was quite good, and he found some comfort in the books that lined the shelves of his library. Anyone looking at his collection would see works by Washington Irving, Wordsworth, Coleridge, Burns, Shakespeare, Defoe, Fielding, and Richardson. He was obviously an intellectual who worked very hard hiding it from his men.

A fire had been kindled in the library, and the embers still gave off some warmth. He sat in his favorite chair and lit a pipe. *Matthew will work out*, he thought to himself. The man was only a novice in intelligence work, but he had potential. Zeb was a good judge of character, and the file he had on Matthew confirmed this. He only hoped he could find what he needed to know before he met him in Lewiston. It was possible Morgan might not be found at all, but he could not tell Matthew. Yes, Matthew would work out, but he had other affairs to deal with before they met again.

He broke the wax seal on the note and read it. Just what he needed—a note from someone who did not have the courage to sign his name. The contents unnerved Zeb. The person sending the note threatened to reveal Zeb's Jewish identity to President Adams unless he resigned from his position. This could mean trouble for Zeb, but he had too much to worry about right now. He would deal with it later. Zeb tamped his pipe tobacco into the ashtray and leaned back in his chair. He sure as hell hoped it would all work out. Within minutes, he was asleep in his chair.

As Matthew slept in the Constitutional Tavern and Zeb dozed in Georgetown, two men crept silently along the wall of the prison. It was nearly four in the morning, and the foggy city was eerie and quiet in the predawn darkness. They picked the lock at the rear entrance and made their way down the hallway leading to the cells. The first two guards never saw them coming. They were quickly strangled and dragged into the meeting room. Two more guards were just outside the cell. One of the intruders tossed a hissing dark object into the cell, causing a muffled explosion and enveloping the guards in sulfurous smoke. Coughing and choking, they tried to see the intruders. Their throats were cut, and both men collapsed to the floor, where pools of blood formed around their bodies. The intruders picked the lock to the cell. Villineau screamed, "No! No, please! Don't kill me! I didn't tell them anything."

One of the men killed Villineau with a quick knife thrust under the ribs and directly into the heart. He died before he could scream again. The two assassins left as quickly as they came, melting into the darkness. Footsteps pounded down the stairs and into the cell area. Richards's voice rose above the confusion. "Get Zeb. Wake him up and get him here as fast as you can. Jesus Christ!"

CHAPTER 5

ZEB AWOKE WITH A START. Isaac, his butler, was gently shaking him by the shoulder. The room was cool, the fire was dead, and for a second, he did not remember the previous day's events. Suddenly, it all came rushing back.

"What is it, Isaac?"

"There is a man at the door, sir. Says you must come quickly. There has been a lot of trouble. He said you would understand."

"Thank you, Isaac. I don't have time to change. Get my luggage ready for the trip. After I see what happened, I'll come back and pick it up."

"Yes, Mr. Cardwell. I'll have everything ready."

Zeb went downstairs. When he saw the look on Daniel Sherman's face, he was fully awake. Dan was a newer member of his small unit, and he showed promise. He was only twenty-one and looked to be about sixteen. He had black hair, blue eyes, and was nearly as tall as Zeb. In spite of his looks, he was very good with weapons and his hands. "What is it, Dan?"

"Richards sent me. Someone broke into the prison. They killed the guards and Villineau."

"Judas Priest!"

"Richards sent me because he figured you would want to know as soon as possible and go down there right away."

"He was right. Let's get going."

They climbed into the carriage waiting in front of the house. Dan briefed him on the way to the prison. He described the attack as very professional, efficient, and very deadly. Five men were dead in less than ten minutes.

Richards was waiting in the meeting room when they arrived. The bloodstains from the guards that had been dragged there were still on the floor.

"How the hell did this happen?"

"I don't know for sure. I was on the second floor and had the guards all posted. The guards in the corridor were strangled and dragged in here. They must have used some kind of wire because their heads were almost completely severed from their bodies. The used a smoke screen to take out the guards in the cell area. The killers were gone before the rest of us could get here. They came in the rear door and left the same way."

"Why wasn't a guard posted at the rear door?"

"I didn't think it was necessary. The door has a huge bolt on the inside, as well as the heavy lock on the outside. The bolt can only be opened from the inside. Jesus, Zeb, that means the bolt must have been opened from the inside!"

"I want every man who was here tonight questioned thoroughly. If one of our people is involved, we really have problems."

"Don't worry, Zeb, I'll find out who it was."

"How did you discover what was happening?"

"The thing that alerted us was the screams."

"Whose screams?"

"Villineau. He screamed bloody murder before they killed him. He must have known who they were and why they were there. What do we do now, Zeb? This is a holy mess!"

"First, get the bodies to the morgue and notify their families. Tell them the usual. They died in the service of their country. For Christ's sake, don't let this get out. Make something up—anything. This must not become known beyond the people who were here tonight. Is that clear? I mean no one! The people we are dealing with are fanatics, but professional fanatics from the evidence they left here tonight. We have got ourselves one hell of a way to go before we can get the best of these people. It is more imperative than ever that I get to New York and try to find out more about this group. You clean up here, and I'll take Dan with me to New York. Remember, I want you in Lewiston by May 20. In the meantime, you can contact me through the usual procedure."

"I won't let you down, Zeb."

"You'd better not. You sure as hell did not do very well tonight."

Richards had a pained expression on his face. Zeb knew he had been too harsh and tried to smooth over the last remark. "Look, Richards, I know all hell broke loose here tonight, but professionals did it. It could have happened while any one of us was on watch. Get moving and clean up the mess. When you find out who slipped the bolt, let me know."

"Yes, sir." Richards looked a little less chagrined.

Zeb left immediately and returned to his house in Georgetown. He cleaned up as quickly as he could and left the usual instructions for Isaac. His butler did not know exactly what his employer did for a living, but he was not naive. Zeb was quite often gone for long periods of time and came back on several occasions with unexplained wounds and bruises. Isaac knew better than to ask questions. His loyalty was absolute. Zeb had always treated him with respect and kindness, which was far better than the treatment he had received on the plantation in South Carolina before Zeb found him.

Zeb and Dan checked their gear one last time and went out back to the stable, where another servant had two horses waiting for them. The horses were saddled, and they stowed their bags. They planned on bypassing Baltimore and Philadelphia and using the post roads and major trails. They would change horses at prearranged locations along the way. With any luck, they would be in New York in a few days.

Ezekiel awakened Matthew at the appropriate time. Matthew stirred lazily. He was tired and did not want to get up at all. Ezekiel shook him again and urged him to get up. "Mr. Prescott, you got to get up. It's time for you to go." Reluctantly, Matthew got out of bed.

"Ezekiel, what time is it?"

"About ten after six, Mr. Prescott. It's time you got yourself up and about."

"Thanks, Ezekiel. You certainly are good at following orders."

"Yes, sir, that I am." Ezekiel grinned.

Matthew dressed quickly, and Ezekiel gave him some food to eat on the way. The horse was saddled and ready. Ezekiel fastened Matthew's bag behind the saddle and saw him off. "Good luck, Mr. Prescott."

"Thank you, Ezekiel. I sure can use it."

Matthew wondered just how much Ezekiel knew as he rode off. He made excellent time through the city and entered the post road to Baltimore he had traveled only yesterday. His ship was waiting for him in the harbor and should be ready to sail tomorrow. If Zeb was right, he had nothing to worry about until he arrived in Lewiston.

CHAPTER 6

AFTER A SWIFT JOURNEY IN good weather, they reached New York. They left their horses at a stable in New Jersey and rode the ferry across the Hudson River. Zeb hailed a cab and told the driver to take them to South Street and Maiden Lane. They stopped in front of a rooming house next to McKibbin and Cayley Grocers on the corner. This section of the city straddled the border between the city proper and the more residential section growing northward. The port was a conglomeration of all types of people, and two men like Zeb and Dan could go about their business without standing out. Merchants, sailors, city dwellers, and stevedores all intermingled in the area. It was ideal for their purposes.

After they settled into their rooms and had something to eat, Zeb discussed their strategy over the next few days. "Dan, I cannot help but feel that the key to this puzzle is here in New York. Villineau was recruited in Canada by a man from here who knew about Mary in the consulate. I've got to make contact with Phillips and see what he has learned. I want you to wait here until I come back."

"All right, Zeb, but be careful. I don't like the feeling of this at all. After what happened in the prison a few days ago, it looks we are up against some pretty nasty characters. If they can murder four of our men and a prisoner in one of our own most secure prisons, there is no telling what else they are capable of accomplishing."

"I agree. That is why it is important for you to stay here. If they are still trying to kill me, then maybe with a little luck, we can draw them out and obtain some important information. I'm going to visit the Lion and Eagle Tavern at the southern end of the island. Phillips and I use it as a contact point when we need to talk. If I can find him, we will start from there. If I do not return by this evening, let's say around eight, come looking for me, but be careful."

Zeb left the boardinghouse and hailed a cab on the cobblestone street. As the cab headed toward the southern part of the island, the clatter of hooves and the noise of the metal-shod wheels on the cobblestones blended with the sounds of the city. Stevedores shouted to one another as they loaded and unloaded ships, and peddlers hawked their wares in the streets. Loads of freight and goods were being hauled away from nearby ships, and the furled sails on the tall masts stood out in the background against their rigging. The driver shouted and cursed at carts and wagons in his path as he made his way through the streets. Zeb never liked New York that much, but he was always impressed by its constant activity and growth. It was nearly one hundred fifty thousand in population and still growing. With the completion of the Erie Canal last year, the port would soon overtake Boston and Philadelphia in importance as raw materials flowed from the interior and manufactured goods were sent in the opposite direction. It was a rapidly changing city.

The cab jolted to a stop outside the Lion and Eagle. Zeb paid the driver and went quickly inside. The innkeeper was behind the bar and recognized Zeb right away. He had been very good at providing information in the past and proved to be reliable as well as discreet.

"Hello, Zeb. What brings you to New York this time?"

"Just a little business, Jim. How have you been?"

"I'm fine except for a little lumbago in my back. What'll it be? How about some of that Prussian ale you like so much? I just got in a fresh shipment last week."

"That sounds good. I'm thirsty as hell."

The innkeeper lowered his voice now that the public pleasantries were completed. As he gave Zeb the ale, he asked, "What can I do for you this time, Zeb? No trouble, I hope?"

"I'm not sure, Jim. Have you seen Phillips lately?"

The innkeeper noticed the anxiousness in his tone. "Yes, as a matter of fact. He came here yesterday and told me if you were to show up in the next few days to give you a message."

"What is the message?"

"Just a minute. Let me think. My memory isn't so good anymore." Zeb put a gold piece on the bar. With one quick motion, Jim swept the coin into the pocket of his huge apron. "He told me he would check for you here at the tavern every day around two in the afternoon. That'll be in about an hour. Have a seat over in the corner there, and I'll fix you up with some more of this ale."

The table offered an excellent view of the entrance, yet it was far enough away that one could remain relatively inconspicuous in the crowd. Zeb nursed his ale and waited for Phillips. The tavern's clientele was a good sampling of the seafaring world that came to New York. Several languages were spoken, including French, Spanish, German, and even Russian. Zeb could follow some of the conversations, and this helped pass the time. There was a variety of types in the tavern, including sailors, gentlemen of leisure, and men of questionable occupation, which probably included a pickpocket or two. There seemed to be an understanding among the customers that the tavern was neutral ground where all were welcome.

Just as the young Dutch barmaid with the nice cleavage served Zeb his third ale, Phillips walked through the entrance. He was casually dressed with an open-neck shirt and cotton trousers tucked into riding boots. He was a few inches over six feet with blond hair and blue eyes. He was in his early thirties, and he was one of Zeb's best agents. He saw Zeb at the corner table but did not immediately approach him. He went to the bar, exchanged a few words with Jim, obtained a drink, and walked casually over to where Zeb sat. Anyone observing him would see only a man going over to join a friend for a drink.

David Phillips sat with his back to the entrance without blocking Zeb's view of the door. They were only a short distance from a rear door. One of Zeb's rules was to make sure he had more than one way to get out of a building quickly.

"Jesus, Zeb, am I glad to see you. All hell has broken loose here. How about Washington?"

Zeb was startled. Villineau had told the truth. "What do you mean, Phillips?"

"Mary is dead. They fished her out of the river last week. She had three stab wounds in the chest, and her throat was slit. There were bruises over her entire body. It was not a pleasant sight. I've been trying to stay out of sight until you could get here. What about Washington?"

"I could say the same thing about all hell breaking loose." Zeb briefed Phillips on the recent events in Washington.

"Who the hell are we dealing with?"

"I wish I knew. This is what we need to find out. Before we do anything else, let's go over what we both know and then come up with a plan."

"Fine, Zeb. Let me tell you what I know."

"All right."

"Mary managed to read a letter that mentioned the plot and Morgan as being connected. She told me she would try to find out more—and she did, but I'm not sure what it means. The attaché practically drooled with lust whenever he saw her. She arranged her schedule so she could be in the building when he was there. The attaché is an inveterate womanizer and couldn't keep his hands away from her. He made love to her every chance he could, and she managed to encourage him to talk about himself and what he did at the consulate. This is the interesting part. The man is an avid Mason. You know the Masons—secret handshakes, rituals, passwords—all that nonsense. Well, this fellow takes it all very seriously. He told Mary he joined one of the lodges here in the city and was accepted because he had already attained several degrees of Freemasonry in England. One afternoon, the attaché—his name is William Melbourne—became very talkative. It seems that he is related to Lord Melbourne—a cousin, I think. He told Mary that he has traveled to Albany quite often to visit the governor."

"DeWitt Clinton?"

"Yes. I'm not sure why, but Clinton was the grand master of the New York State Lodge from 1806 to 1820."

"What does this have to do with the plot?"

"I really don't know. He may have gone there as part of his consular duties, but it would be interesting to check on it further. He also visited Stephen Van Rensselaer while in Albany. Van Rensselaer has an estate called Rennselaerwyck on the Hudson. He is the eighth patroon of the Dutch West India Company, as well. A very important man in this state."

"I know. Van Rensselaer is a supporter of Adams. I really can't see any connection here with Melbourne unless Melbourne was merely seeing him regarding diplomatic matters."

"That's not all, Zeb. The Patroon, as Van Rensselaer is called, is now the grand master of the upstate Masons."

"The grand master?"

"Yes. Melbourne has made several trips to Albany in the past few months. He has seen both Governor Clinton and Van Rensselaer. Melbourne's major function at the consulate, as far as I can tell, is to act as a goodwill ambassador. He makes social contact with many prominent businessmen and politicians in the area and tries to promote friendly relations between England and her former colonies. Anyway, Mary found out that Melbourne made a couple of trips upstate to Rochester and Buffalo. He told her he wanted to see the new canal for himself, so he took a trip from Albany to Buffalo and back. The second trip was by steamer to Albany and then by coach to Buffalo. That's all I know about these two particular trips."

"What about the connection with the Masons?"

"I'm not sure, but both Van Rensselaer and Governor Clinton are prominent Masons. In fact, there is a rift between the New York City Masons and their upstate brothers. There is a state organization called the Grand Lodge that sets policy and rules for all the lodges in the state. It also collects dues from each member lodge. The grand master is the head of the Grand Lodge. Right now, there are two."

"Why have they split?"

"As I mentioned, Governor Clinton was the grand master from 1806 to 1820. It seems that his political enemies helped engineer his resignation but could not control the division it created. Clinton is very popular upstate. The difference spilled over and eventually led to the formation of a dissident New York City Lodge that separated them from the Grand Lodge. The original Grand Lodge represented the entire state. Clinton has made quite a few enemies as a politician. He has been a state legislator, a U.S. senator, the mayor of New York City, and now governor. You don't hold all of these positions without making some enemies along the way. Apparently, the New York City Masons don't like Clinton very much, even though he has held nearly every important office there is in the Masons."

"I know you are going to tell me more," Zeb joked. They both laughed, and Phillips continued.

"In the 1790s, DeWitt Clinton was a junior grand warden and a senior grand warden. He has also been grand high priest and grand master of the Knights Templar. His father was General James Clinton and fought in the War for Independence. Hell, now that the Erie Canal is finished, Clinton's probably the most important man in the state right now. The New York City boys are on their own now, and a fellow named Hoffman is their present grand master. The funny thing is that, even though the upstate boys have about one hundred lodges and the city boys have thirty-one, the New York City Masons have all the records, archives, and the money from the dues that were collected over the years. All the meetings of the Grand Lodge were held in New York City, and even the upstate lodge—they call themselves the Country Grand Lodge—has been meeting in the city. Last September, the upstate lodge elected Van Rensselaer their grand master. Governor Clinton officiated at the ceremonies and installed the Patroon himself. They had a real fancy ceremony, from what I've been told. The two must be pretty close. Van Rensselaer worked very hard with Clinton to get the canal built."

"So what you are telling me is that the Masons have split off, city against upstate, and there are hard feelings between them?"

"That's right. Clinton and Van Rensselaer head the upstate group."

"Melbourne belongs to a New York City Lodge?"

"Yes. St. John's Number One—the same lodge that has the Bible George Washington used when taking the oath of office."

"Jesus, this is getting more interesting by the minute."

"All of this doesn't really mean anything at face value. We don't know what connection there may be between the Masons and Melbourne over and above his membership and the fact that he has seen both Governor Clinton and Van Rensselaer."

"Do you think there is a connection here? Are the Masons possibly involved in whatever it is Melbourne is planning?"

"I don't know. We don't have enough information yet, but it is certainly worth investigating."

"I agree. What else did Mary tell you?"

"Not much more. Melbourne has some rather expensive tastes. He gambles quite a bit and drinks heavily. He's a real dandy, but he's not stupid. Mary tried to find out more, but somehow she was discovered. Poor girl! What a rotten way to die. I'd like to get my hands on the bastards that killed her."

"Maybe you will, Phillips. Villineau said the maid had been discovered and killed. He was contacted by a man from New York in Canada and hired to kill me. What I wonder is how much Mary told them before they killed her. They are after me, so they must know she worked for me. The information we obtained from Villineau indicated that they had linked the girl to me, but they did not know the identity of her local contact. She didn't tell them about you, Phillips."

"She was one tough lady."

"I'll make sure the president makes arrangements for compensation to her family."

"I think they were guessing just like we are. I don't think they can prove a direct link to you. They only surmised that anyone trying to find out about their plan must be associated with your organization. Anyone familiar with the intelligence group President Monroe directed you to put together would know of your position.

If they wanted to cripple the organization, your death would serve their purpose quite well. After all, you brought us all together and trained us."

"I understand what you are saying, but why hire some assassin who worked for Napoleon to kill me in Washington?"

"Maybe this is bigger than any of us realize, and they believed killing you would keep us off their backs. The New York connection may be a key to this. Maybe Morgan was involved in recruiting him, or possibly York is important to their plan."

"I think New York is very important right now. What we need is more information."

"What do you want to do now?"

"If Morgan is an important figure in this plot, as we believe him to be, and Melbourne is the New York connection, then we may have something to work on. Melbourne's trips upstate could even have taken him to Canada. He certainly would not have told that to Mary. It is possible that Melbourne is in contact with Morgan and is the British agent directing the plot. The letter Mary found seems to point to this. Let's look into his connection with the Masons. This will give us a place to start."

"We need to keep you alive. If they could get that close to you in Washington and kill Villineau, they cannot be underestimated here in New York where they might have their base of operation."

"I will be careful, don't worry."

"This whole damned thing is getting crazy. They want you dead, and Mary has been brutally tortured and murdered. Four of our men were killed in Washington, and now we are talking about the Masons and a British attaché who might be a spy. There has to be a key here somewhere."

"There is, Phillips. All we have to do is find it. I think we have something more substantial to go on than we had a few days ago. The main thing now is to find out before I head upstate to meet Matthew Prescott."

"What can I do?"

"Let's find out as much as we can about Melbourne. I'll work with Dan on this. I brought him with me for two reasons. I want to see how he handles himself. Besides, no one knows him in New York, so he may prove useful. I want you to make a trip to Albany and see what you can find out. Check into the political situation and ask around about the Masons. Find out what you can about Melbourne's visits to Governor Clinton and Van Rensselaer. Make it quick, though; we don't have that much time."

"How long?"

"Well, I have to meet Matthew near the end of May. That gives me six weeks, give or take a few days. I'll need time to travel upstate. If for some reason Dan and I run into trouble and have to leave New York, we will go to Princeton and wait for you at the inn."

"Fine. I'll be back as soon as I can."

"We'd better leave separately. I'll go first. You wait about fifteen minutes and then get moving. Travel to Albany as quickly as you can."

"Don't worry. You know you can count on me."

A well-dressed man at the bar watched the two men leave. He left a generous tip and went outside to an awaiting carriage. He was taken to the British consulate.

CHAPTER 7

ZEB LEFT THE TAVERN AND hailed a cabriolet across the street. He really liked these two-wheelers with the covered sitting area. They had been in use in London and Paris before becoming popular in America. He gave the cab driver the address of the rooming house on South Street.

When Zeb arrived at the rooming house, he went directly to Dan's room, and Dan told him, "I just received a message from the courier. He must have been right behind us all the way from Washington."

Zeb took the note and started reading.

> We found who slipped the bolt on the rear entrance to the prison. One of the murdered guards had a message in his pocket that gave him explicit instructions in return for one hundred dollars. I don't know why he didn't destroy the message. Maybe he thought he could get rid of it after the attack at the prison. There was no signature on the note, and the paper is nothing special. The guard was hired only two months ago and had a pretty good security record. The only thing that may be of use to us is that he used to work at the arsenal in Harpers Ferry. While he was there, a shipment

of weapons was reported missing, but he was never linked to the theft. It may be only a coincidence, but I thought you would like to know. Good luck.

Richards.

"When did this arrive?'
"It was about an hour ago."
"Where is the courier now?"
"I told him to wait in your room."
"Good. I want to speak with him."
When they entered Zeb's room, the courier was asleep on the bed.

Zeb smiled and shouted, "Stevens, you lazy bastard! Get up!"

The man rolled off the bed and stumbled to his feet. Then he smiled when he saw Zeb and broke into a loud laugh. "Zeb, how the hell are you? I see you still don't want anybody to get any rest."

"You look good, Stevens."

"Oh, I'm as well as can be expected for a man of my advanced years, but I hope things will get better soon."

"How long did it take you to get here?"

"I made it in three days."

"You are still pretty good for an old man."

"Look who's talking. You're not so young anymore yourself, Zeb."

"None of us are, except Dan here." They all laughed.

They talked for several moments about recent events. "Thank you for bringing the message so quickly, Stevens. The information is important. You can take a message back to Richards for me. You should get started in the morning, but first, why don't we all have something to eat?"

"Sounds good, Zeb. I'm hungry as hell, and my rear end could sure use a nice chair instead of a saddle for a while."

"Good! Let's go."

The three men left the room and went downstairs. There was a tavern down the street that served decent food. They found an empty table and sat down.

"I heard about the trouble at the prison from Richards. What the hell is going on?"

"I wish I knew, but we don't have enough information yet. Don't worry about it. It's not your job now. You just make sure you keep those fast horses in good shape."

"I know it isn't my concern anymore, but I worry about you. You've been in too many scrapes before, and one of these days your luck will run out."

"Jesus, Stevens, you really are full of good news today."

"You know what I mean, Zeb. We've been through a lot together. Remember the war and all the action we saw then?"

"I remember."

The conversation continued through dinner, and the men recounted old times while Dan listened. Zeb and Stevens had served together in the War of 1812, and both were now in the intelligence service as they had been under President Monroe. Zeb had been promoted by President Adams and had made Stevens a courier in order to keep him out of harm's way. Stevens had nearly been killed by a crazy rebel in South America three years before. Zeb pushed Stevens out of the way at the last minute and killed the man with a shot that only an expert could have made. When they returned to the rooming house, it was getting late. They would make plans for the next course of action in the morning.

A few hours earlier in another part of New York, a carriage stopped in front of the British consulate, and the man who had been watching Zeb and Phillips in the Lion and Eagle stepped down. Henry Wollstonecraft was a very large man, about six feet two and weighing around 220 pounds, most of it muscle. He entered the building and went immediately to the library on the second floor, where a man in evening attire was waiting. The man's back was to him, and he gazed into the dead embers of the fireplace.

"Well, Wollstonecraft, what did you find out?"

"Your information was correct. He met another man at the tavern, and they had quite a discussion."

"What exactly were they discussing?"

"I don't know. I was unable to get any closer than the bar. At least we know he is in the city and can expect him to start snooping around."

"It is imperative that he does not learn anything more. I'm afraid he knows too much already. If that idiot Villineau hadn't failed so miserably, we would not have to worry about Cardwell any longer. Certainly no thanks to you, since you hired him."

"I am sorry about that, Mr. Melbourne. Villineau was a top man for Napoleon. He must have lost his touch. At least we were able to get our man to open the bolt and give us access to the prison so we could kill the scum."

"Yes, and nearly everyone else who was in the building. God, Wollstonecraft, do those animals ever control their thirst for blood?"

"It couldn't be helped. It was necessary in order to get to Villineau."

"I suppose so."

"What do you wish me to do now, sir? Now that we know that Cardwell is in New York, do you want me to kill him?"

"Not yet. We have tried that already. I don't want another fiasco on my hands so close to the consulate. No, I think what we will do is keep an eye on our Mr. Cardwell and see what he is up to. Do you think you can handle that for me? We do not have much time."

"No, sir, we do not. I need to see Morgan again before the final arrangements are made."

"Do you have everything you need?"

"Yes, sir. All I need to do is give Morgan his final instructions and make sure the rest of those involved are doing their part."

"Good. You realize, of course, that if anyone finds out about this, we will be dead men?"

"Of course I do."

"The Craft is very harsh when one of its members fails to do his appointed duty. Don't ever forget that. I have managed to keep you alive after the Washington debacle. I will not be able to do it a second time."

"Yes, sir, I realize that."

"Good. Find out where Cardwell is staying, and report back to me when you do. I will give you further instructions after that. Understood?"

"Yes, Mr. Melbourne. I understand. I had better be leaving."

"Of course. I have an engagement this evening with a very beautiful and very willing young lady. I do not want to keep her waiting."

After he was dismissed, Wollstonecraft went to his lodgings, drank a cup of rum, and crawled into bed. Before he fell asleep, he held out his right hand. It was shaking slightly. Someday, that pompous bastard Melbourne would get what was coming to him, and Wollstonecraft would be happy to be the one to make sure the job was done.

That night, he dreamed about the horror back in England. It was the same dream. His little sister fell into a nearby stream during the spring runoff, and he tried to save her. He saw the terror in her eyes as her tried to grab her. He never succeeded. His parents never forgave him, and he left home as soon as he was old enough. There were plenty of jobs in the underbelly of London for someone his size.

Melbourne walked down the steps of the consulate and stepped into his private carriage. He gave the driver directions to a private club in Harlem Heights. He looked forward to these excursions. The young lady he met last week promised to be there this evening. He anticipated a rather pleasurable evening.

The carriage pulled up in front of a large mansion with a circular drive and a huge lawn. The first floor was brightly lit by hundreds of candles, and music from a pianoforte drifted out the open windows. Melbourne told the driver to wait. The driver knew it would be a long wait, but at least he could catch up on some sleep. He resigned himself to another long night.

Melbourne entered the mansion and was greeted by Mrs. Medley, the owner and hostess of the establishment. Melbourne was a regular and a big spender.

"Good evening, Mr. Melbourne. It is so nice to see you again. I hope you have a pleasant evening and enjoy the hospitality of my little establishment."

"It is always a perfect joy to see you, Mrs. Medley. I cannot imagine being anywhere else this evening."

"Thank you, Mr. Melbourne. I wish all my guests were gentlemen like you."

"As always, you are quite welcome."

The lush interior was always a pleasant sight. He went immediately to a servant and took a glass of wine from a proffered tray. He went to the gaming room to try his luck at roulette while he waited for the lady to appear. Melbourne was in his element. He had several glasses of wine and then switched to the dicing table. He soon felt that he could beat anyone, but he lost most of the money he had won at roulette.

A hand gently grasped his elbow, and he turned to see who it was. *My God*, he thought. He had nearly forgotten how beautiful the girl was. She had dark hair and a body like Aphrodite's.

"Good evening, Penelope. You look as beautiful as ever. I must say, that dress is ravishing."

"Why, thank you, William. You are such a gentleman."

She actually thought he was a rake and a scoundrel, but he was sometimes very good in bed. She watched him play for several moments and drank a glass of wine. They soon went to a room on the second floor reserved for him by Mrs. Medley. After the door was closed, he took her into his arms and kissed her hungrily.

"William, please don't hurry. We have all night."

"Thank God. Let's get you out of that dress."

He started to undress her, but she had to help. He kissed her breasts as she helped him out of his clothes.

"William, don't be in such a hurry. You know what happens when you get like this. Penelope will take good care of you."

Soon they were both naked and under the covers. Unfortunately for Penelope, Melbourne had an orgasm within seconds of entering her. She was lucky he got that far. He fell asleep, and her efforts to awaken him, as usual, were to no avail. The alcohol had overcome his lust again. She gave up and snuggled next to him. He would eventually wake up, and they could do it again. She would make sure of that. Her husband was out of the city for several days on business, and she did not want her time to be completely wasted.

CHAPTER 8

ZEB WROTE HIS MESSAGE TO Richards the next morning. He updated him on what they had learned since coming to New York and instructed him to find out as much as he could about the guard who let the killers into the prison. *Jesus*, Zeb thought, *I hope he was the only one.*

"Dan, I want you to check into Mr. Melbourne. Find out what you can about him, but be careful. Find some pretext that would take you to the consulate and then ask for him. Tell him you are traveling to England this summer and need information. In the meantime, I'll go back to the Lion and Eagle to talk to Jim."

It had been his experience that when a meeting such as the one he had with Phillips yesterday took place, it would be worthwhile to backtrack and see whether anyone had been asking about him.

Zeb arrived at the Lion and Eagle before the lunch hour customers and found Jim behind the bar, as usual.

"Well, Zeb, it's a rare day when I see you here this early."

"It sure is, Jim. This time I'm not here for my thirst, though. I need to know whether anyone has been asking about Phillips or me since we were here yesterday."

The innkeeper thought for a moment. "No one has been asking about you, but there was a fellow in here yesterday while you and Phillips were here. He looked like a merchant, but he wasn't a regular.

I'd never seen him before, so I kept my eye on him out of curiosity. I noticed that he kept looking over at you two. After you left, he waited a few minutes and then left, too. I told Charlie, the little man that sweeps up for me, to see what he did. Charlie saw him get into a carriage that was waiting for him. Charlie overheard him say something about a consulate as he was leaving."

"Did you say consulate?"

"Yes, that's what Charlie heard him say."

"Thanks for the information, Jim. I appreciate it very much."

"Glad to be of help, Zeb. You know that."

Zeb left another gold piece on the bar. "By the way, Jim, do you remember what this fellow looked like?"

"Sure. He was here long enough, and you know my memory when it comes to faces. He was a tall, swarthy fellow. He had a powerful build. Come to think of it, he didn't look quite right in the clothes he was wearing. He was clean shaven and had a scar on his cheek."

"What did the scar look like?"

"It was shaped like a crescent moon."

"Thanks, Jim."

Dan approached the clerk at the reception desk in the British consulate. "May I help you, sir?"

"Yes, you certainly may. I was hoping that one of the staff could help me with some information. I would like to travel to Britain this summer and need to acquire the appropriate travel documents, as well as obtain some advice on what to see when I am there. Someone told me a Mr. Melbourne would be the man to see."

"Yes, sir. Please wait a moment while I check to see if Mr. Melbourne is in." The clerk left his desk and went down the hall to the last office. He knocked on the door and was greeted with a gruff reply. The clerk went timidly inside. In a few moments, he came out of the office and returned.

"Mr. Melbourne will see you now. Please follow me." Melbourne was sitting behind his desk with a tea service and assorted pastries in front of him. He was just taking a bite out of one. He put the pastry down, wiped his hands, and rose from his chair.

"Please have a seat. You must excuse me this morning. I have a beastly hangover—too much of an evening."

"I'm sorry to hear that. I was wondering if you could direct me to some of the more interesting places in your country that a visitor would find of interest."

"My staff usually takes care of that. Why did you ask for me?"

Dan suddenly realized he may have made a big mistake. He thought quickly. "A friend of a friend mentioned he had met you at a party and that you would be a good person to speak to about traveling to England."

"I'm really busy this morning, and both my assistants will not be here until after lunch. Why don't you come back then? One of them will be able to assist you. My clerk will make an appointment for you."

As Dan was about to leave, there was knock on the door. A very large man came into the office. "Ah, Mr. Wollstonecraft. I see you are up and about early this fine day." Wollstonecraft glared at him, and Melbourne coughed to cover the nonverbal exchange. "I will be with you in a moment, Mr. Wollstonecraft. Have a seat. I apologize for the intrusion, sir. I hope my assistant will be able to help you this afternoon." Dan got a good look at Wollstonecraft as he left the office. He did not like what he saw.

"Well, Wollstonecraft, what do you have in mind so we are able to find our Mr. Cardwell?"

"I really don't think that will be necessary. He will probably find us."

"What do you mean?"

"He knows that stupid maid is dead. Villineau probably told him that. She worked here and probably told them about you and your travels. I think he will be showing up here any day now."

"You know, Wollstonecraft, for once you are making some sense. We might as well sit back a few days and wait for the fish to take the bait. After all, we do have a few days before you need to visit your friend upstate again."

Zeb knocked on the door of the Georgian house. The maid smiled as she recognized him. "Mr. Cardwell. How nice to see you again, sir. Please, come right in."

"Hello, Ruth. It is nice to see you, as well. Is the mistress of the manor at home?" Ruth smiled, nodded, and motioned for him to come in the house. She took his hat and put it on the table in the entrance hall. He went into the parlor and sat down. He tried to visit this particular lady whenever he was in New York.

A pretty woman in her early thirties entered the room. He made a mental note that she had not changed since he was in New York several months before. She walked up to him, never taking her eyes off him. With a big smile, she embraced and kissed him. They held the embrace for several moments before either of them said a word. "Where the hell have you been these past months?"

"Abigail Chamberlain, is that any way for a lady to talk? I'll have to take you across my knee and spank that pretty little behind."

"In a pig's eye you will. If you try that, I'll have my butler tie you up and horsewhip you."

"I guess some people never change."

"Yes, and I could say the same about you. You stop in unannounced, stay for a while, and then disappear for months at a time before turning up on my doorstep again. You rogue, I've missed you. Where have you been all this time?"

"I missed you, as well, but you know my business requires me to travel a great deal. I would certainly be here more often, especially to see the most eligible widow in New York."

"Come over here and sit down next to me. Would you like some wine? I'll have Ruth bring us some of that French wine you like so much."

"That would be wonderful."

Abby rang for the maid, and she appeared in a few minutes. Abby asked her for the wine. "You know, Zeb, if you do not start coming around here more often, I may not be able to see you anymore."

This was a scene that had been enacted many times in the past. She loved to tease him. He put his arm around her and whispered in her ear, "If I don't come back again, you will probably send out your small army to find me, tie me up, and dump me on your doorstep."

She laughed. "You are right about that, and don't you forget it."

"How have you been, Abby?"

"Oh, about the same. The biggest excitement these days are the plans everyone is making for the Fourth of July and the fiftieth year of independence. Not much else is happening. Well, there are the usual parties with the same boring and stuffy people. I still play whist one night a week with the ladies, and we attend the theater when something worthwhile is presented. Other than that, nothing changes. The only excitement I have these days is you."

"Why, Abby, there must be hundreds of eligible bachelors in this city chomping at the bit to romance one of the most beautiful women in New York."

"You know better than that. Ever since my husband died in the war, you are the only man I would ever consider marrying, but you never ask."

"I know."

"You really are a bastard, but you're the only one I love."

Ruth served the wine and quickly left the room. "Will you be able to stay for a few days?"

"I will be in New York for a few days, yes, but I won't be able to stay tonight. Tomorrow will be better. In fact, I will arrange it, all right?"

"I have waited all these months; one more day will not kill me." They embraced and kissed again. "Can you at least stay for lunch?"

"Of course."

"Good. I'll tell Ruth to set two places. Excuse me, darling. I'll be back in a few minutes."

After leaving the consulate, Dan decided to have lunch at a nearby tavern before returning. When he came back, the clerk took him to see a Mr. Whitehead, who was introduced as an assistant attaché. The clerk made the introductions and left.

"Good afternoon, Mr. Sherman. I understand you desire some information for a trip to our fair country this summer."

"Yes. I thought it best to ask the natives about their country." They both laughed. "While they are preparing your papers, I would be happy to make some recommendations. You must see London. You will then appreciate the beauty and quiet of the countryside once you leave the city behind. London has its pleasures, but be careful where you go in the city." He went on to recommend the better establishments to patronize and the ones to avoid. He also went on about the various historic buildings and places Dan should visit. Dan tried very hard to look interested. When Whitehead finished and the travel documents were ready, Dan pressed his luck a little.

"I am a stranger here in New York and like a good time. I was wondering if you could direct me to some interesting places of entertainment."

"Let me see. Mr. Melbourne is very fond of a club in Harlem Heights. He speaks of it from time to time. I believe it is owned by a Mrs. Medley."

"Thank you. I think I will make a visit as soon as my schedule permits." Dan shook hands with Whitehead and left the consulate.

CHAPTER 9

ZEB RETURNED TO THE ROOMING house after spending the afternoon with Abby. The lunch was delicious, as usual, and the thought of being with her the next day helped lessen the burden of his responsibilities. They had discussed their relationship, and the conversation covered the same ground, as usual. Abby wanted a more permanent relationship. So did Zeb, but his job kept him away from her much of the time. She told him it did not matter, but Zeb did not want her to experience another loss if something should happen to him.

Her husband had been a naval officer with Perry during the War of 1812 and was from a very influential and wealthy New York family. They had been married shortly before the war in what was then the society wedding of the season. During one of the naval engagements, the area of the deck he was standing on had taken a direct hit. He was killed instantly. Twelve sailors had been struck by shrapnel, and only two survived. He was given a hero's funeral and was buried in New York. Abby had not remarried and remained secluded for several years until her family persuaded her to return to society again. She met Zeb at the theater, where they discovered a mutual interest in drama and literature. Abby had received an exceptional education for a woman due to her father's rather liberal outlook. It was not long before they became more than friends. Zeb's trips to New York always had an extra incentive involved since he had met Abby.

Dan was waiting for him in the empty sitting room on the first floor.

"Well, Dan, how was your day? Did you discover anything interesting?"

"I definitely did."

"Keep going."

"I went to the consulate and managed to get in to see Melbourne."

"You saw Melbourne?" Zeb was impressed.

"Well, I met him briefly. He had little time for me and sent me to see his assistant. I told the assistant that I wanted to travel to England this summer for a vacation. I asked him what places he would recommend for me to visit. He told me about Roman ruins, ancient mounds, Celtic stone circles, and London."

"Is there more?"

"Oh, yes. Melbourne had another visitor while I was there. He was rather large and looked like someone you would not want to get in a fight with unless it was absolutely necessary."

"What did this man look like?"

"He was large, had a dark complexion, blue eyes, and, oh, yes, he had an unusual scar on his face. It looked something like a crescent moon."

"Crescent-shaped?"

"Yes, that's how it looked."

"What did the man say to Melbourne when he was there?"

"Not very much. Melbourne told him to wait until we finished. He obviously did not want me to hear their conversation. Oh, yes, he called him Wollstonecraft or something like that."

"What else did you learn?"

"I stretched my luck a little and asked the assistant if he knew any entertaining places for a gentleman to visit during the evening in New York. He told me that Melbourne had a favorite club in Harlem Heights."

"Dan, let me tell you what I discovered today. That man you saw in Melbourne's office?"

"Yes?"

"He is the same man that was watching Phillips and me at the Lion and Eagle yesterday. The innkeeper told me a blue-eyed man with a crescent-shaped scar on his face had left after we did. He hailed a carriage to take him to the British consulate."

"It certainly sounds like our Mr. Wollstonecraft."

"Yes, and that gives me an idea. Go to that club tomorrow night, and see what you can find out. If you happen to find Melbourne there, buy him a few drinks and very gently pump him for information. Get him to talk about the Masons, and he might let something slip about the plan."

"Yes, but what should I wear? I don't have anything with me for an evening at that club."

"Let me take care of that for you. I have a contact who will be able to help."

"Thanks, Zeb."

"You are welcome. We'll spend some of the money in my contingency fund."

"What about that man with Melbourne?"

"I'll take care of him. If he is looking for me, he knows Phillips on sight, as well. We are fortunate Phillips is on his way to Albany, but that does not mean he is entirely safe. I will send a message to him about our being seen by Wollstonecraft. Take it easy tomorrow during the day. Rest all you can. You will need it for tomorrow night. I'll keep watch on the consulate and follow Wollstonecraft. It will be much better than having him give me a nasty surprise."

Phillips traveled by steamer to Albany. Steamships were rather recent inventions, and he had a close call when the boiler on another ship exploded as they were docking in Albany. The explosion showered pieces of metal and cinders on people, other ships, and the pier. After the close call, he rented a room in one of the inns near the government buildings on Washington Street. His trip, except for the exploding boiler, had been quite pleasant in the spring sunshine.

He had several contacts in the state capital he could visit, but there was one in particular he planned to meet with first. If all went well, he should be able to find the information Zeb needed and return to New York in two or three days.

Melbourne and Wollstonecraft discussed their plans in Melbourne's office later that same evening. Melbourne had decided to spend a quiet night away from Mrs. Medley's and return the following evening. "When you visit Morgan next week, give him the first part of his instructions, and tell him to keep quiet. He must not do anything until the proper time. If the plan is to work efficiently and with minimal mistakes, all of us must perform our duty. While you are meeting with him, have him show you the arms and explosives he has hidden up there in that wilderness. Make sure they are in good condition and well hidden until we need them. Tell Morgan that any deviation from the preparations could jeopardize the entire plan and put him in an early grave."

"Don't worry, I will."

"Good. I want you to leave in two or three days. In the meantime, we will keep alert for Cardwell to make a move. He does not know very much yet, but he knows enough to be a problem for us. When the time is right, we will eliminate him. The next time, you will not fail."

Wollstonecraft ignored the last remark and asked, "Does Morgan know when to expect me?"

"Yes. He will meet you in the usual location. Good Lord, that area up there isn't very far removed from the time those red savages used to live there. Give him his instructions, and don't forget to tell him about the meeting. He must be in New York for that."

CHAPTER 10

THE NEXT MORNING, AFTER A substantial breakfast of ham, eggs, Dutch pastry, and plenty of coffee, Phillips went to one of the state office buildings. The man he planned to see was one of Governor Clinton's aides and loved to gossip about state politics. It would be a good place to start.

Phillips entered the office of Peter Van Dreff. Peter was a veteran of the political system and had supported Governor Clinton in both good and bad political climates. He was dressed in the typical attire of a government bureaucrat—black coat and trousers with a matching waistcoat. He wore old-style Benjamin Franklin glasses low on his nose. Below a receding hairline was a narrow face that gave him the appearance of a ferret searching for prey. "Well, Peter, how is the political business these days? Are you taking good care of the governor?"

Peter peered over his glasses and smiled. "How did a vagabond like you manage to get past my secretary? Don't answer that. You probably became invisible and reappeared in my office. It happens all the time." Peter liked Phillips and enjoyed their infrequent conversations. He was glad to see him, especially since the damned brief he was writing was so dull. "To answer your question, I am as well as can be expected. Politics is the same everywhere. Issues and people are here today and gone tomorrow. Some of us just manage to hang on a bit longer than the rest. As for your inquiry regarding the governor's health, I can assure you he is as healthy and robust as ever."

"I am glad to hear that."

"Yes, I am certain you are. What brings you to Albany this time, my friend?"

"You know damned well I can't stay away from the seat of power and the company of great minds. I have to come here as often as I am able in order to rejuvenate my parched font of knowledge."

Peter smiled. "Horseshit! You are probably here to get someone in trouble. Don't tell me. As long as it isn't me, I don't want to know."

Phillips laughed. "Well, I see these stuffy law books and legal documents haven't managed to entirely kill your sense of humor."

"Phillips, if I couldn't keep my sense of humor in this place, I had better quit."

"Yes, I believe you would." He became serious. "Peter, I need to talk to you. I am interested in the political situation in Albany. What is happening?"

Peter's face brightened. He put down his pen and started to talk. Two hours later, he had given Phillips all the latest gossip, important political events, and his predictions for the coming year. He also recommended other people Phillips should see. By the time Phillips left, he was well on his way to becoming quite familiar with the present Albany situation and obtaining the information needed by Zeb.

While Phillips was talking with Peter, Zeb was waiting across the street from the consulate in a tobacco shop. It was filled with the aromas of expensive mixtures. He looked them over and purchased a few ounces of a particular pipe tobacco he preferred. Zeb pretended to read a newspaper in a comfortable captain's chair by the window. He watched the consulate for nearly an hour and was just about ready to give up when Wollstonecraft walked out. He was a towering man, well over six feet, and big enough to wrestle a bull to the ground. Wollstonecraft started walking at a rapid pace. Zeb quickly left his newspaper on the table, rose from his chair, and walked out of the shop with the now cool pipe still in his mouth.

Wollstonecraft walked to Wall Street and then toward the Hudson River. He passed Federal Hall, where George Washington had been inaugurated, and entered the nearby Masonic lodge. Zeb crossed the street while dodging wagons, carriages, and men on horseback. He took a position under the awning of a printing establishment. He put the pipe in his pocket and waited. He was out of sight of anyone looking out the windows in the Masonic lodge. To the average passerby, he was just a man waiting to meet someone. Zeb did not want to be seen following Wollstonecraft, or he would have taken the chance of going into the building after him. The Masonic lodge was not public enough. It did prove very interesting that Wollstonecraft had gone into that particular building in light of what Phillips had told him.

Wollstonecraft remained in the Masonic lodge about twenty minutes before his large form filled the doorway, and he entered the sunlight shining on the busy street. He began to retrace his route. Zeb followed him, and as they approached the consulate, he contemplated his next move. He weighed the odds of actually entering the building or remaining outside. The group of people entering the consulate helped him reach a decision. He joined them. Once inside, Zeb noticed that no one was at the reception desk. He saw Wollstonecraft go into an office down the hallway to the right. Zeb took a risk and followed. The door to the room just past the office Wollstonecraft entered was unlocked and the inside was empty. Zeb quickly went in. He went to the window and opened it as quietly as he could. With any luck, he might be able to hear the conversation if their window was open, as well. Fortunately, it was a warm day, and their window was open. He crouched down and listened, all the while realizing what a predicament he would be in if discovered. If he were discovered, his best escape would be out the window and into the alley below. A murmur of voices drifted to him from the next room. Zeb was just barely able to distinguish individual words in the conversation.

"Well, Wollstonecraft, how did you fare at the lodge? Is everything proceeding on schedule for the meeting?"

"Yes, it is moving along as planned. They are waiting for more information and instructions."

"Did you inform them that patience is a virtue?"

"I did, but the brothers are having difficulty. They are quite anxious for the plan to move forward."

Melbourne nodded slowly and ran his right index finger over his well-manicured mustache. "Yes, I am certain they are, as are all of us. However, they must continue to exercise patience. It is imperative they continue to go about their business until the day arrives for them to fulfill their destinies. When that day arrives, their patience will be amply rewarded."

Wollstonecraft hesitated before speaking and scratched his earlobe. "Do you really believe we can do this without any errors being made? After all, there is always the possibility that someone will fail us."

Melbourne's reply was like a cold draft of air from a crypt. "If anyone fails in their duty, they will answer to me. A small elite group is dedicated to this task. Failure is unacceptable. The man must be killed and his work destroyed. A lesson must be taught so that others will know how powerful we are. Machiavelli has no contingency for failure. Our enemies must come to realize that we will not be stopped in our efforts to regain what is rightfully ours."

"After he is dead, what will our next target be?"

"I cannot tell you yet, my anxious friend. That may be revealed at the meeting, but his lordship will decide whether or not to inform us."

Zeb's left foot began to fall asleep, and he moved it slightly to get the blood flowing again. The movement threw him off balance, and his boot scraped along the floor. The noise wasn't loud, but it was a noise nonetheless. Wollstonecraft heard the sound and suddenly became uneasy. He made a hand signal to Melbourne to keep talking while he left the room and went next door. He knew he heard something but was not sure what it had been. Wollstonecraft slowly opened the door and saw Zeb crouched by the window. Zeb caught the movement in his peripheral vision. In one swift and smooth motion, he threw open the window as far as it would go and leaped out. The look of recognition on Wollstonecraft's face was unmistakable. Zeb ran quickly down the alley and into the street parallel to the consulate. Wollstonecraft did not dare fire the pistol he carried concealed in his coat. Instead, he followed Zeb out the window and chased him on foot. The two men ran a zigzag course for several blocks. The big man moved quickly for his size, and he gained on Zeb. Zeb turned into a side street and discovered his mistake as soon as he turned the corner. The street was narrow and filled with garbage and other debris except for a serpentine path down the center. He tripped on a small wooden keg and went sprawling in the decaying garbage and trash. The fetid smell of the mixture hit him with the force of an explosion. Wollstonecraft was on him before Zeb could regain his footing. Fists pummeled him, and a hand pulled one of his arms behind his back. A powerful arm wrapped around his chest and squeezed until the pain was intense. Zeb willed his body to act. He managed to free one elbow and jam it into the midsection of the big man. Wollstonecraft let out a surprised gasp and released his grip. Zeb twisted away quickly and regained his footing. He dodged a blow aimed at his jaw and hit the big man on the back of the neck with both fists. Wollstonecraft bent slightly, and Zeb gave him a vicious kick to the left knee and another in his crotch. Wollstonecraft went down in a crouch, and Zeb kicked him again in the temple. Wollstonecraft was stunned, and his large body crashed to the ground. Blood trickled from the wound in his temple. Zeb gasped for breath and thanked all that was holy that he had been lucky enough to fight him off without being killed. This had been too damned close. He got out of there quickly and made his way to Abby's home. Now that he had been seen in the consulate, it was important that he keep out of sight until he could talk to Dan. They would have to leave New York.

When Wollstonecraft awoke, he had an excruciating headache. Only his thick skull prevented him from having a concussion. There was no question now as to Cardwell's fate when they met again. The bastard had been right there in the consulate. Melbourne would be furious. He returned to the consulate and found Melbourne pacing the floor in his office. "Where the devil have you been? Good Lord, you look a frightful mess, and what is that awful smell?" Wollstonecraft explained what had happened, and Melbourne's face turned scarlet. "Cardwell was in the next room listening to us, and you let him escape? You bloody idiot." Wollstonecraft tried to explain in more detail, and Melbourne calmed down a little. "Good Lord, he was right next door. There is no telling how much he heard. How did he get in there?"

"I don't know how he got there, and I don't know how much he heard. Even if he heard every word, all he knows is that we plan to kill someone. He doesn't know when or where. I'll get the men onto him immediately. He's a dead man."

"You bloody well better. I want him dead, and the sooner the better. Cardwell has interfered in our affairs for the last time."

"I'll have the men take care of him while I go to see Morgan."

Melbourne glared at him and held a handkerchief to his nose. "I don't care when or how you do it. Do it, and don't fail me this time."

"I won't."

When Abby saw Zeb standing on the doorstep, her reaction was one of shock followed by concern. "What the devil happened to you, Zeb Cardwell? You look like you've been wallowing with a bunch of pigs and smell like it, too."

Zeb smiled meekly in spite of the recent close call with Wollstonecraft and shrugged apologetically. "You are not far from the truth. I recently had a little misunderstanding with a rather large and persistent gentleman concerning my presence in a certain location. I left him with a headache for his trouble, and he nearly cracked my entire rib cage."

Abby was more than concerned. "Zeb, you damned fool, what really happened? You know better that to try to pass off your escapades as trivial concerns with me."

Zeb did not elaborate. Her fears regarding his recent narrow escape were apparent enough without his adding to them. He tried to steer the conversation away from his close escape. "Just let me in and please give me something strong to drink." He thought he had better give her some version of what happened, so he told her about being on an assignment. A man had chased him from a building and caught him in an alley after he tripped on an old keg. There was a brief scuffle, and he got away. Zeb left out most of the details, especially the consulate. He told Abby he was watching a group of ruffians suspected of smuggling goods into the port of New York in an attempt to avoid the tariff. Abby seemed satisfied, but Zeb could never be sure with her. It was obvious she was still upset, although she tried to hide it without much success.

Abby took Zeb to a room in the rear of the house that was connected to the cooking area. The room served as a storeroom and a catchall for odds and ends. The servants stored most of the cleaning soaps and other materials in this room. She made him take off his clothes and wash the smell from his body. He used rainwater stored in a tub in the corner and a bar of imported soap. He did have quite a pungent odor and was glad to get rid of it. Abby had her servant bring some of her former husband's clothes for him. "Zeb, you have got to stop this. You cannot go around playing boy soldier the rest of your life. You need to grow up."

He tried to lighten the mood in the windowless room. "I don't ever intend to do that—grow up, I mean. Don't you know men never grow up? We are all merely barefoot schoolboys under all our bluster, charm, and sophistication. Of course, some of us are more charming and intelligent than others."

Abby could not resist laughing. She smiled in spite of her anger. "Zeb, you are incorrigible. I don't know if you really mean it or not sometimes. I promise I won't pry anymore, at least not today, but you must stay here and rest. I'll have the cook fix us a nice supper, and then we'll try to think of something to do later this evening."

Zeb smiled and kissed her. "Of course I will. Any little boy would be a damned fool to pass up an evening with you."

Chapter 11

Dan Sherman entered the private club in Harlem Heights slightly after nine. He was dressed in evening attire and cut quite a dashing figure with his freshly groomed mustache and hair. It was a chilly evening in spite of the warmth of the day, and Dan gave the maid at the door his hat and scarf. The white silk of the scarf was a tasteful contrast to his dark hair and youthful face. The club was not only elegantly furnished, but the patrons he encountered as he entered the first room were obviously from the emerging upper strata of New York society. Dan went to the gaming room and slowly walked around the various tables where card games, roulette, and backgammon were played. The players were intent on their efforts to separate themselves from their gold. Like most gamblers, they were oblivious to everything else in the room except the game. Dan accepted a drink from a waiter and walked over to the backgammon tables. Several games were under way, and the crisp sound of the dice being shaken and rolled on the ivory inlaid boards, along with the movement of the pieces, were the only sounds. As was the situation at the other gambling tables, the players concentrated intently on the game. For them, at this moment, the game was the entire universe.

Melbourne was at the second table playing a rather obese man who habitually tugged at his beard before each roll of the dice. His ruddy complexion seemed to change shades with each labored breath. Melbourne gammoned him with a series of high rolls that allowed him to bear off quickly and achieve the win. The doubling cube showed four, so he was doing well. Melbourne was smiling a tight victory grin that came close to a sneer. Then he looked up and saw Dan watching him. "Ah, Mr. Sherman, I see you have found this fair establishment."

"Yes, I couldn't leave New York without visiting this wonderful place."

"I am really glad you did, old boy. A few more games, and if you would permit me, I'll show you around."

Dan had not planned on this seemingly friendly response from Melbourne, but he took advantage of the opportunity. "That is a most generous offer. However, I will look around a bit and then come back for a drink or two."

Melbourne was not that anxious to play the good-natured guide, so he agreed without protest. "All right, Mr. Sherman. I should be finished with this chap momentarily." The heavyset man glared at Melbourne, and Melbourne gave him his best malevolent smile in return. They continued their game.

Several ladies sat at tables around the gaming area. From time to time, they would converse with various gentlemen and accept offers for drinks. He walked past them into the next room. He found a lounge area with plush settees and chairs of red and gold velvet arranged under a magnificent crystal chandelier that reflected light throughout the room. The occupants, mostly couples, were engaged in quiet conversations, with an occasional pair leaving to walk up the winding staircase at the rear of the room. A rather striking girl approached Dan. She spoke softly. "Good evening, sir. Would you care to buy me some champagne?" Dan thought he must have stood out like a sore thumb, in spite of his attempt to fit in. He had better act like he was here for the reason everyone else was.

"Yes, I believe I would."

They went into the gaming room and sat at an empty table near the wall. Dan ordered two glasses of champagne from a waiter who seemed to materialize out of thin air as soon as they sat down. He looked the girl over more carefully now that they were seated at the table. She wore a low-cut green dress that revealed an enticing portion of her breasts. Her honey blonde hair was in long curls, and her eyes were nearly the same color as her dress. She was exquisite, and Dan had to remind himself why he was really there. She continued the conversation. "Have you been here before, sir?"

Dan swallowed to moisten his throat so he could speak. "As a matter of fact, I have not. I am new in New York, just visiting for a time, and have not had the opportunity to visit this, uh, club until tonight." The girl smiled seductively and touched his hand. Those green eyes began to work their sorcery on Dan.

"How did you happen to come here, sir?"

"A man I met recommended this establishment."

"A very good idea."

"Yes. I believe it was an excellent idea. By the way, what is your name?"

She continued to hold his hand. "My name is Lydia, sir. Last names are not allowed. Mrs. Medley forbids it."

"It is very nice to meet you, Lydia." He blushed slightly. "My name is Daniel Sherman."

She looked into his eyes and replied, "It is very nice to meet you, Daniel Sherman."

Dan's ears turned a darker shade of red than his face. They continued to talk for several minutes until they were interrupted by a distraught Mrs. Medley. "Lydia, come right away, my dear. I need you to assist me with a slight problem upstairs. Please excuse us, sir. Lydia will be back momentarily."

Dan quickly replied, the spell broken. "Yes, of course." Lydia excused herself and left with Mrs. Medley. Dan noticed the change from the coy coquette to serious concern. He took a couple of deep breaths to clear his head and glanced toward Melbourne's table. He was still winning as confirmed by his unbridled laughter. Melbourne rose from the table, saw Dan sitting alone, and came over.

"Well, old boy, how are you faring so far this evening? I see you have had company—unless you drink out of two glasses at the same time."

Dan laughed. "Yes. As a matter of fact, a very lovely young lady has been talking to me."

"May I inquire as to her current whereabouts?"

"Of course. Mrs. Medley asked for her assistance upstairs."

Melbourne smiled. "Probably some bloke passed out, or one of the girls has a problem. Don't worry about it; she will be back. From what I have learned here, when one of these girls fancies someone in particular, you are in for quite an evening."

"That is exactly what I am hoping. It would be nice."

"Nice? Hell's bells, that would be heavenly, old boy."

Dan changed the subject. "I take it you know most of the people here."

"Of course. I am probably one of their best clients. I never miss an opportunity to come up here. I can use the diversion, especially tonight."

"Oh?"

Melbourne continued, "Yes. I had a beastly day today. I just cannot get my help to do their jobs properly anymore. If it is not one thing, it is another. The damned dunderheads need to be told what to do all the time."

Dan noticed Melbourne's ring and the symbols on it. An innocent inquiry should not be misinterpreted, he hoped. "I see you have an interesting ring. What is it, if I may ask?"

Melbourne did not seem to mind, although the question seemed to come as a surprise to him. "Of course you may. This is a Masonic ring. It is worn by all members of the brotherhood as a sign of our membership and fraternity so we may recognize one another. It is also a symbol of our pride in being a Mason. You should consider joining us, Mr. Sherman."

"I never really have given it much thought."

"I recommend that you do, old boy. The contacts alone can do wonders for your career. Many fine, upstanding gentlemen are Masons who dedicate themselves to good works and community service. I have been a member for years."

"I have heard from various people that the Masons have a great many secrets, rituals, and ceremonies. Is this true?"

Melbourne became more attentive. "Yes, but they are merely formalities, part of the mystery. They do not really amount to much."

"Then why are they all so secret?"

Melbourne looked at him for a moment, and that sinister smile began to appear. "It is a closed organization with certain goals. We feel not everyone is qualified to belong, and certain things are best left within the brotherhood."

"I have heard the Masons must swear an oath of secrecy and are bound by their lives to keep the secrets of their society. Is there any truth to this?"

"Yes, certain rituals have been handed down for centuries. Some men have tried to reveal our secrets but have met with failure. Only a few of the most elect are trusted with the most important and ancient secrets. They are the only ones deemed worthy of the high honor this entails." The waiter brought their drinks, and Melbourne ordered another. His tone changed. Now he tried to be more relaxed, less serious in his manner. "See here, Sherman, the Masons are a very powerful and influential group for many reasons. If you want to advance yourself in this world, they can help you a great deal."

"Oh? How is that?"

"There are many reasons, such as employment, investments, the right friendships … all of that." Melbourne downed his drink and fixed Sherman with a very intense look. "We have power, old boy, power." Sherman let him continue without interrupting. "In fact, if you knew how much power some of us have, you would be quite amazed."

Dan could not resist the next question. "Oh? In what way?" The effect of this seemingly innocuous question was astonishing. It was as if he had hit a nerve in one of Melbourne's molars. Melbourne stopped talking for several seconds and contemplated his next response. He realized he had said too much already. "Look, old boy, I have talked a great deal. You are here to have a good time. Let's enjoy our drinks and the lovely female companionship. We will be able to talk about the Masons some other time."

Dan knew when it was time to change the subject. "Yes, I agree. I came here tonight to enjoy myself, and it is time to get on with the evening." At that moment, Lydia entered the room and walked over to their table. Sherman took advantage of her return. "Ah, here comes the absent young lady."

Melbourne also needed a reason to end the conversation. He excused himself and returned to the gaming tables for more backgammon. Lydia sat next to Dan.

"Well, Daniel, I see you waited for me."

"Any man who did not should be declared insane and sent to an asylum." She smiled, but not like before. Her smile seemed more genuine, not the coy and flirtatious smile earlier. Something had caused this change. He decided to take a different tack in the conversation. "Tell me, Lydia, where do you come from, and where is your family?" She seemed surprised by the question and paused for a moment before answering.

"I am from Philadelphia and have been at Mrs. Medley's for about six months. My parents died from fever when I was nine, and I was sent to live with my aunt. She was very strict and quite religious. As soon as I was old enough, I left and came to New York. A kind family friend, or so I thought, gave me a letter of introduction to give Mrs. Medley. She took me in and put me to work in my present capacity. I did not realize I would be in this line of work, but the money is good, and Mrs. Medley takes care of us. I am not in a very socially acceptable position and would like to leave as soon as I save enough money."

"What would you like to do?"

"Once I save enough money, I would like to do what any girl my age plans. I want to find a good man, get married, and raise children."

Dan found her to be genuine and unassuming. She was not the least bit arrogant or snobbish. He liked this girl. They seemed to feel comfortable talking with each other. After a few moments, Dan decided to turn the conversation to Melbourne. "Mr. Melbourne is a regular customer here, I am told."

Her demeanor changed immediately. Lydia became guarded and gave him a strange look. "Yes, he is. Why did you ask about him?"

Dan noted the abrupt change. "I am sorry if I offended you."

"Daniel, you seem like an honest and kind young man. Let me give you a little advice. Be very careful of Mr. Melbourne. That is all I can say, and please don't ask me any more questions about that man. In fact, we had better go upstairs before Mrs. Medley finds me here and starts wondering what we are talking about."

Lydia took Dan to one of the rooms on the second floor. It was tastefully decorated, not that Dan was a good judge; he had never been in a bordello before. As soon as they entered the room, there was a knock on the door, which was slightly ajar. A girl came in without waiting for Lydia to answer.

"I'm so sorry, Lydia. I know I am breaking the rules, but I have to talk to you." The girl looked terrible. She had a black eye and a nasty bruise on her left cheek. She was not dressed like the other girls downstairs. She was wearing a dressing gown, and her hair was unkempt.

"Sarah, please get back to your room right now. Remember what I told you earlier this evening?"

"Yes, but I need to talk to you now. I just remembered something and need to tell someone. It may be important. The only one I trust is you."

"Please excuse me, Daniel. I need to take care of Sarah. There is some wine on the table. Make yourself comfortable, and I will return in a few moments."

"Certainly. I'll be here."

Dan thought about leaving after waiting nearly half an hour. But just then the door opened, and Lydia quietly closed it behind her. "I'm sorry I took so long, but Sarah has had a difficult few days. I need to make a difficult decision. I don't know anyone in New York and have no one to talk to except the other girls. Most of them are nice, but they are not my friends. Sarah is the closest I have to a true friend here. I don't know you, Daniel, but I am a very good judge of people. I'm going to take a risk and tell you something."

"Lydia, you don't have to tell me anything you don't feel comfortable revealing."

"No, Daniel, I do. I need to trust someone, and I think your being here tonight is more than just chance. I have very good instincts, and I believe your being here tonight was meant to happen. I don't know why, but I have experienced these moments before when I know something is happening for a very good reason. I trust my instincts about you."

"This must be very important to you, Lydia. It is true—you don't know me. I could be anyone, good or bad."

"Daniel, I know you are not a bad person. Even though I just met you this evening, I feel it in my bones that we were meant to meet each other and that you will able to help."

"I don't know what to say."

"Don't say anything; just listen to what I have to tell you. You may think I am crazy or just a hysterical woman, but hear me out and then decide for yourself."

"Fair enough."

"How well do you know Mr. Melbourne?"

"I only met him briefly at the consulate when I was trying to obtain information for my trip to England."

"Have you had a chance to form an opinion regarding his character?"

"Not really. I only met him for a few moments that day. Then I saw him here tonight and spoke with him for a while."

"I need to tell you some things about Mr. Melbourne. After you hear what I have to say, we can talk about how you might be able to help. Oh, God you had better be the kind of man I think you are."

"Lydia, I will listen, and if I am able to help, I will."

"Mr. Melbourne came here several days ago accompanied by a rather large man who had a funny-looking scar on his face. They were both in a sour mood and soon became quite drunk. They took two of the girls upstairs. The big one was nasty. He beat one of the girls unmercifully. Fortunately, she will be all right when the bruises fade and her broken arm heals. That is where I went with Mrs. Medley earlier. The girl is still in a great deal of pain. I have some training in healing from my aunt, so Mrs. Medley asked me to look in on the girl from time to time. She was having a bad time when Mrs. Medley came to fetch me. Anyway, Mr. Melbourne finally passed out from too much drink that evening. This is the usual routine for him. He is a strange one. Sometimes he meets other women who don't work here and takes them upstairs. Mrs. Medley does not let just any customer do that. He must pay her well."

"What happened?"

"Mr. Melbourne paid everyone off and told them to keep quiet about what had happened. The big baboon left, but before he did, I heard Mr. Melbourne tell him something very strange."

"What did he say?"

"He told the big man to take it easy and not ruin it for them. He told him that pretty soon he would have all the excitement and bloodletting he could handle. All he had to do was be patient."

"Did he say anything else?"

"Only that if someone found out he had caused trouble here, the people they worked for would not like it. I don't know what he meant by that. I'm only telling you this because I hate that man and hope someday he gets paid back along with that ape he brought here. Whatever you do, please do not tell him what I just told you."

"I won't."

"The other girl involved that evening was Sarah. As bad as she looks, the other girl is much worse."

"I need to tell you something, as well. Mr. Melbourne is not one of my favorite people, nor is he of the people I work with."

"What do you mean?"

"I can't tell you for your own good, but I can tell you this—what you just told me about Melbourne and his friend will be very helpful to the people I work with. We are very interested in him for reasons I cannot share with you, but not because I don't trust you. You have been very honest with me, and you deserve to know that much."

Lydia started crying softly, partly from fear and partly from relief. She just placed her trust in a complete stranger, based on her intuition, and she hoped she was not mistaken. "God, look at me. I don't even know you that well and am crying like a baby."

Dan walked over to Lydia and took her in his arms. She continued to cry softly for a moment. He gave her his handkerchief, and she wiped her eyes. "Thank you. Now that I have told you this much, you need to hear more. Wait a moment, and I will be right back."

She was true to her word. Within moments, she was back with Sarah. "I asked Sarah to tell you what happened the other evening. She is reluctant, but I told her to trust you."

"Yes, of course she can trust me."

Sarah looked relieved and began to tell her story. "He was very drunk that night. He talked about something called Machiavelli a great deal. He said powerful men were going to do something. He was rambling and muttering a lot, but he did mention something about Governor Clinton and the canal. He does not like the governor. Also, he said something about explosives. He was pretty drunk, and I could not understand all of it. It was like a dreaming man talking in his sleep. It didn't make much sense to me, but that man is sure a real drinker."

"Thank you, Sarah. You have been very helpful."

"I hope so. That bastard—excuse my language—and his monster friend need to be drawn and quartered as far as I'm concerned."

"I'll take you back to you room now, Sarah."

When Lydia returned, she gave Dan a penetrating look. "Sarah is a good person and does not deserve to be treated like this. Mrs. Medley caters to Mr. Melbourne because he has so much money."

"Yes, and now both of you are in danger if she finds out what you have told me."

"Don't worry, Daniel. We both know how to keep secrets."

"Lydia, I really should be leaving. It is getting late, and I should be going back to the city."

"Don't go yet, Daniel. I want you to stay awhile longer. We don't have to do what most people come up here for. Just keep me company for a while."

Oddly enough, that is exactly what they did.

CHAPTER 12

MATTHEW'S SHIP APPROACHED THE ENTRANCE to Boston Harbor after an uneventful and routine voyage. He had spent a great deal of time during the trip reflecting on the sudden and abrupt nature of his present involvement in the efforts of President Adams and Zeb Cardwell to find Morgan and bring him to Washington. True, he anticipated the trip to Lewiston and York with some degree of eagerness, yet he also felt apprehensive as a result of recent events. The meeting with President Adams, the evening with Zeb, and the concern on Zeb's face when they had parted company outside the Constitutional Tavern that foggy Washington evening all had taken place within a twenty-four-hour period. Still, Zeb had been right. Nothing had gone wrong on the ride to Baltimore or during the voyage that now neared its completion.

Matthew thought about the past few days. The fresh sea air and the motion of the ship as it cut a path through the waves going north all had been like a tonic for him. He loved the sea and the serenity it could provide. The sea was a good place to be alone and indulge in quiet reflection. Matthew knew he must find an excuse for leaving Boston, but that would come. It would give him an opportunity to travel in a part of the nation he had never seen. He had spent the evenings on deck watching the sunset among the mauve and soft pink clouds of the spring sky. It was a good setting for making plans. He would put one of his associates in charge of the business while he was gone. There was no telling how long he would be absent, and the right person's diligence and loyalty should keep everything running smoothly.

The past several years had provided many opportunities to expand the shipping business and earn new profits. The rebels in South America needed supplies of arms, ammunition, clothing, and foodstuffs to keep their revolutions going. This new venture certainly would not be as profitable from a business point of view, but it was very intriguing.

The first thing he would do once ashore would be to check the warehouses, catch up on the latest activities of his fleet of ships, and make all the other arrangements necessary once he had found an excuse for leaving. With any luck, he would be out of Boston and on his way in plenty of time to make his meeting with Zeb in Lewiston.

The dream kept coming back to Matthew. One night during the voyage to Boston, he had fallen asleep after two or three brandies. He thought about it again as the ship made its way through the maritime traffic in the harbor toward his wharf. He had been walking through a small village just before dark—where it was, he had no idea—and heading for no particular destination. The sun had nearly set, but there was still enough light in the early evening sky to clearly see his surroundings. Matthew heard voices from around the next corner. For some unexplained reason, he became cautious and slowed his pace. Instead of continuing his walk, he hesitated and peered around the corner of a building. Several men were gathered near a black carriage with dark shades. It looked like one of the rigs used by undertakers. The men seemed to be waiting for someone. They were nervous and pacing back and forth while speaking in hushed tones. He was too far away to hear what they were saying, but he knew instinctively that he could not let them see him. No one had seen him, nothing threatened him, and there seemed to be no danger to him, yet he was very afraid. He remained out of sight and could not get up the energy to run in the other direction. He kept his compulsive vigil.

The carriage was parked in front of a stone building, but he could not make out the sign over the entrance in the now failing light. Suddenly, three men came out. The two on the outside firmly held the one in the middle. The man they restrained let out a piercing scream, a cry for help if there ever was one. He screamed at the top of his lungs. It was the most terror-stricken plea Matthew had ever heard. It was even worse than the ones he had heard from wounded men during the war. The man struggled to escape from the men. As soon as they were clear of the steps, the men who had been waiting split up. Two men jumped up in the driver's seat of the coach. The rest dragged the captive to the coach. They thrust him in as he kicked and screamed all the way. The screaming soon stopped, the team of horses whipped into action. The black carriage headed in Matthew's direction, and he pressed himself against the side of the building. As the carriage went past, picking up speed all the time, someone pushed aside the curtain and looked directly at him with a terror-stricken look. It was only for a few seconds, but it seemed like an eternity.

Matthew awoke from the dream with the image still clear and vivid in his mind as sweat trickled down his face. His hands trembled, and his heart seemed to beat at twice its normal rate. He had no idea where he was in the dream or where the men were going with the poor unfortunate they had captured. The most vivid memory was that of the screams from the man forced into the coach. Matthew never had many nightmares as a child, and this one left him with an impression of stark, unadulterated fear. He had been in the wrong place at the wrong time, and he had been seen.

He thought about the dream as the ship closed on the wharf, and he hoped it was just that—a bad dream—and that it meant nothing more. Maybe it had been the brandy. Maybe he had just been tired, but the dream still remained in his thoughts as the crew lashed the ship to the wharf.

Phillips had spent his time in Albany wisely. The contacts Peter had provided had proved excellent, as usual, and his own contacts validated the information. It was apparent that there was no direct tie between the governor and Van Rensselaer other than the canal, politics, and the Masons. Melbourne's visits to Albany had been as an intermediary in an attempt to heal the rift between the New York City and upstate Masons. He had been unable to discover any other link. Melbourne also worked to promote better relations between England and the United States. On the surface, his visits had no other purpose. Phillips did discover that a faction of politicians in the state were very envious and jealous of Clinton and wanted him out as governor. Melbourne had also surreptitiously visited some of these people, as well. To what purpose, Phillips did not know, nor could he find out.

One interesting piece of information concerned a trip the governor planned in the late summer. The trip would take him the length of the canal, but this time without the fanfare of the inaugural trip last October. This journey was scheduled to take the governor and Van Rensselaer the entire length of the canal for a quiet, semipublic three or four weeks. The trip would combine politics and private matters. The two politicians wanted, according to the source, to mend some political fences and visit with the memberships of various Masonic lodges in order to bring an end to the divisions that separated the splintered groups. Clinton and the Patroon would be a formidable duo that anyone would find difficult to oppose. They would travel in late August or early September from Albany to Buffalo. Phillips wondered just how much influence Melbourne's visits had in encouraging the trip. He also learned that Clinton was not a well man and had been in ailing health for several months. His doctors opposed the trip, but Clinton was a strong and forceful individual who had overcome an injury to his leg several years before. The governor shrugged off their advice and categorically stated that he would be going, and the physicians were to be damned for all he cared about those charlatans.

When Phillips returned to his room that evening, he found a message from Zeb. The information about Wollstonecraft placed an entirely different perspective on their plans. If he had been seen with Zeb, they were both in danger. He wished the message had arrived sooner, but fortunately for him, nothing had happened while he was in Albany. It was time he returned to New York. Zeb and Dan may need help, and there was no telling what else may have happened since the message had been sent. The trip to Albany had proved to be very informative, but not quite as expected. He would not have been surprised to discover involvement between Melbourne and Clinton or Van Rensselaer, but he was now certain there were not. In fact, Melbourne's visits to Albany must have some hidden purpose, especially since he was meeting with the governor's political opponents. That trip in late summer might prove to be more than mere fence mending.

CHAPTER 13

WHEN ZEB RETURNED TO THE rooming house on South Street, Dan was waiting for him. He looked a little unkempt but quite pleased with himself. Zeb could not resist. "Well, Dan, I see you must have indulged in some of the pleasanter offerings provided by the club you visited last evening."

Dan blushed but did not reply immediately. He waited for a moment and then spoke. "It was certainly a very interesting evening."

"How interesting, Dan?"

Dan told him about the conversation with Melbourne and information he had obtained from Lydia and Sarah concerning Melbourne and Wollstonecraft. Zeb did not interrupt Dan with any questions at this point. He suspected Dan had stayed with the girl Lydia all night, but that was Dan's business. The information he had obtained was important and added to what he had discovered at the consulate the day before. If Melbourne ever connected Dan with Zeb, they would both be marked for execution by Wollstonecraft. Fortunately, Wollstonecraft would be out of the city for a few days, but they still would need to be extremely careful in their movements. It was a good thing that they had the Princeton location for a backup. They needed to get out of New York as soon as possible.

Zeb told Dan what he had discovered, including the incident at the consulate and the fight with Wollstonecraft. It was agreed they would wait two days for Phillips. If he did not return by then, they would travel to Princeton. Zeb would leave a message for Phillips with the lady who ran the rooming house. They should be safe here until then, and it was not likely anyone would find them sooner than that.

They had a leisurely supper at the tavern down the street and went to bed early. Before going to sleep, as a precaution based on experience, Zeb made up his bed so it looked like someone was sleeping. He went down the hall to Dan's room and settled himself on the floor as comfortably as he could. If anyone should visit them during the night, they would be looking for Zeb, not Dan.

Just after three in the morning, in the light of a waning moon, two men approached the rooming house. They led horses whose hooves were covered with cloth to muffle their sound on the cobblestones. They stopped a few yards beyond the rooming house. One of the men, slightly larger and more powerfully built than his companion, approached the rooming house. He carried a bag and a coil of rope. He was dressed in riding boots, breeches, and a light wool coat—all black. He was clean shaven, dark skinned, and had darting black eyes that carefully watched his surroundings as he approached the building. He threw the rope onto the roof, and a metal hook wrapped in cloth bounced twice and caught the ironwork at the edge. He tested its strength and began climbing like a cat up the side of the building. When he approached the window he sought, he quickly kicked it open and swung into the room, his feet crunching on broken glass. He thought it odd that the sleeping figure had not moved yet, but so much the better. He fired two quick shots from a matching pair of pistols into the sleeping man. Then he lit the fuse on a round, heavy object with his flint and steel and tossed it under the bed. He went out the window, climbed quickly down the rope, and ran to his accomplice and their horses.

A thundering explosion shattered the quiet of the peaceful night. Inside Zeb's room, the flames began their fiery dance. The oxygen sucked in through the open window fed the flames, and they spread rapidly. The two men led their horses into an alley where they could watch the building without being seen. They had been instructed to make sure they had succeeded in killing their victim. The light from the flames provided enough illumination for them to see who came out of the building.

The two shots and the explosion that followed woke Zeb and Dan. The force of the blast blew the door from its frame and into the hallway. The fire spread rapidly along the wooden walls and ceilings and soon threatened to engulf the entire second floor. Those who were fortunate ran out of the building into the cool night air. Zeb and Dan grabbed their packed bags and clothes and joined the mad rush out of the building. Panic-stricken people stumbled down the back stairway, trying to escape the flames. They climbed over one another, kicked, shoved, and did everything they could to survive. It was chaos. No laws of chivalry or civilization operated. Zeb and Dan barely managed to reach the fresh air in time before the flames engulfed the entire second floor and spread to the rest of the structure. Angry and frightened, they stood in their underwear as the fire spread. Zeb knew what had happened. If he had not slept in Dan's room, he would be a charred corpse right now. There was no choice any longer.

They quickly dressed in the street amidst the confusion and chaos. People leapt from windows, and screams came from those poor souls still trapped in the fire. It was a nightmare. Zeb and Dan headed for the stable and the waiting horses. They would remain secluded until the first ferry at dawn, cross to the New Jersey side, and make their way to the safe house in Princeton.

The two men who had caused the hellish scene watched Zeb and Dan leave. They nodded to one another after swearing quietly concerning their luck. They had missed their target, but now he was leaving with another man. This time, failure was not an option.

Zeb heard the muffled hoofbeats just in time. He spun around and yelled at Dan to drop to the ground. As Zeb turned back, the first man fired at Dan and hit him in the shoulder. He yelled in pain as the ball hit him, and he fell to the ground. Zeb dodged to his right, and the second shot missed him. The two attackers dismounted and came at Zeb. As they approached him from different directions,

Dan pulled out his pistol with his good arm and leveled it at one of the attackers. They made the mistake of assuming Dan was down for good. Dan squeezed off a shot, and the ball crashed into the larger man's back. Blood pumped from the wound, and he slumped to the cobblestones. Zeb reached for his pistol, but the other man was too close and kicked it out of his hand. He advanced on Zeb with a knife. The blade gleamed in the reflected light from the fire as it slashed toward Zeb. Zeb did not have time to properly dodge the thrust, but the aim was poor, and it only slashed him along the ribs. The cloth split, and blood seeped out from the wound. Zeb sidestepped the next thrust, spun quickly around, and caught the man in the middle of the back with a hard punch. The man grunted and stumbled. Zeb hit him again, but the attacker would not go down. He turned and grabbed Zeb. It took all of Zeb's strength to keep the knife from entering his chest. At the last second, he broke the hold and fell back. Zeb rolled in the street and felt a loose cobblestone. He picked it up and threw it. He was lucky. The stone hit his attacker in the head and staggered him for a moment. Zeb was on him before he could recover. Zeb pulled the knife he kept in his boot and sunk the blade into the man's side as far as he could. He jumped clear of the man as he fell to the ground.

Zeb ran over to Dan and pulled him to his feet. They took the horses, and Zeb helped Dan mount. Zeb climbed on the other horse, and they both managed to stay in their saddles in spite of their wounds. The man with the knife protruding from his side watched them leave just before he lost consciousness.

CHAPTER 14

As PHILLIPS APPROACHED THE ROOMING house the following morning, he could see the smoldering ruins of the building and a group of onlookers still clustered around the area. One partial wall remained, while the rest was completely burned out. A few members of the fire brigade still poked through the ruins, searching for more bodies. He went to one of them and asked what had happened.

"We don't know for certain, sir. There was some kind of explosion, according to the tenants, and the fire spread so quickly that most people were lucky to get out alive."

Phillips asked about the landlady and was told she was in the next house. He found her partially in shock. He tried to get as much information from her as he could about Zeb and Dan. "Did you see Mr. Cardwell or Mr. Sherman get out of the building last night?"

She stared vacantly at him, seeming to look right through him. Then she began to speak, very quietly and slowly. "It was awful. The flames were everywhere. People were screaming and running down the stairs. It was a nightmare."

Phillips pressed her for more information. "Did you see Mr. Cardwell or Mr. Sherman?"

"Yes, I did see them. They were in the last group of people that made it out. They stopped for a few moments and then ran toward the waterfront. I don't know what happened to them after that."

Phillips breathed a sigh of relief. At least they had escaped the fire and gone to Princeton. He thanked her and left.

Melbourne was deciding whether it was worth getting up and trying a little hair of the dog or staying in bed and hoping the hangover would leave his head alone if he did not move. As the dull throb increased in the front of his head, he heard a soft knocking on his bedroom door. He moaned and got up slowly, put on his dressing robe, and went to the door. His servant stood there with a shocked expression on his face. The man appeared quite frightened by something.

Melbourne spoke gruffly to him. "What is it, Moffat? It had better be important to get me out of bed at this unholy hour."

"Please come with me, sir. There is a chap at the back entrance in a terrible state. I think he is going to die, what with the knife in his side and all the blood."

Melbourne was immediately shocked into a fully awakened state. He knew what had happened. Wollstonecraft's men had botched their job. He opened the drawer of a table near the door, took out a small pistol, and put it in the pocket of his dressing robe. Moffat did not see him put the gun in his pocket. He looked at Moffat and said, "Take me to him, Moffat. Let us see what has happened to this poor chap."

When they reached the rear entrance, the man was sitting on the inside of the doorway with his right foot extending out the slightly opened door. Melbourne roughly dragged him inside and closed the door. The wounded man's head sank to his chest. Melbourne fixed one of his malevolent stares on the man and told Moffat to go upstairs for bandages and hot water. When Moffat left to fetch the linen and water, Melbourne spoke to the nearly unconscious man. "What the hell happened?"

The man coughed up clots of crimson that ran down his chin onto his chest. He looked at Melbourne and spoke between labored gasps of breath. "The bastard had a friend. We jumped them after they got away from the burning building, but they managed to shoot Harry and then stabbed me. They took our horses."

Melbourne was insistent. "What did the other one look like?"

The wounded man described Matthew. Melbourne's surprise was unmistakable. Now he knew why the young man who had visited the consulate and Mrs. Medley's was so interested in him. His eyes became hard and dark. "You fool. Can't any of you do anything right?"

The man tried to crawl away as Melbourne aimed the pistol. He pleaded with his eyes, but Melbourne shot him in the heart and watched him slump to the floor. When Moffat returned, he would tell him the man tried to kill him and that he shot him in self-defense. Moffat was not stupid, but he would pretend to believe him for his own good. Melbourne would arrange to have the body dumped in the river within the hour. He stood facing the hallway, waiting for Moffat to return while quietly cursing Wollstonecraft.

Chapter 15

Phillips arrived in Princeton the next day and went directly to the inn as previously agreed. The innkeeper described Zeb and Dan when he inquired as to the location of their room. He could not resist a detailed description of their haggard and exhausted condition when they arrived. He told Phillips that a doctor was with them.

Phillips went to their room and quietly entered. What he saw did not surprise him. He had seen many wounded men before. Zeb and Dan both sat in chairs. Dan's shoulder was bandaged, and he smiled meekly when Phillips entered. The doctor, whose back was toward Phillips, was just finishing bandaging Zeb's side. Zeb signaled Phillips that a reasonable explanation had been given, but nothing more should be said until after the doctor left. The doctor spoke to them after he turned and saw Phillips in the room.

"Well, young fella, I hope you are a good friend to these two ruffians, because they are going to need some friendly help for the next few days."

"Yes, I am, sir. Please tell me about their wounds."

"Of course. This one over here has a nasty knife wound that runs from his sternum to the last rib on his left side. He is lucky the wound was not deeper. He will heal soon, but the scar will be a nasty one. I cleaned it up the best I could, but you will have to keep an eye on it. The other fellow has a bullet hole right through his shoulder and is damned lucky the bullet did not stay in there to cause trouble.

He has lost some blood, but not as much as he could have. He will not be able to use that arm for two or three weeks. Keep them both quiet, and I will check back tomorrow to see how they are doing and to change the bandages."

"Thank you, Doctor."

The doctor put his instruments back into his bag and walked to the door. He paused in the doorway and looked back at the three men. "I don't know what drinking establishments you gentlemen frequent, but I would certainly not return to that one again. I'd better be off. I have an old lady with rheumatism and a sick horse to see before supper. I will see you gentlemen tomorrow. Good day." His eyes twinkled mischievously as he turned and left.

They all laughed at the mention of the horse. Phillips followed the doctor into the hallway and gave him a gold coin. The doctor examined it and bit it before placing the coin in his pocket. He winked at Phillips and said, "Can't be too careful these days."

Phillips went back into the room and stared at both of them. "Tavern fight—hell! I just came from the rooming house in New York. What the devil happened?"

Zeb looked at him, took a deep breath, and then winced in pain from the effort. He told Phillips what happened on the night of the fire, as well as the other information they had managed to gather while in New York. Dan was uncomfortable in the chair, and Phillips helped him move to one of the beds so he could lie down and rest. He was still pretty weak from the blood loss. Phillips asked, "How did the two of you manage to get this far with those wounds? Neither of you were in any condition to travel, especially by horseback."

"We took a coach after we left the ferry and rode down here with passengers gawking at the blood while keeping their distance. We managed to stuff pieces of clothing over the wounds to keep the loss of blood contained. We were in pretty sorry shape when we arrived here. Fortunately, the innkeeper is discreet, especially when he gets two weeks' lodging in advance and more to keep his mouth shut."

"What about the men you left in the gutter, Zeb? Were they dead?"

"I think the one Dan shot is dead, but I'm not sure about the other one. Even if he wasn't when we left him, he couldn't have been able to get very far. We did not want to risk going back to make sure. He may have had help on the way, and we were in no condition to fight off anyone else."

"One thing is certain; Melbourne does not want you alive. And now Dan may be in danger, as well. If that murdering bastard managed to make it back to Melbourne or talked to one of his friends before he died, he could have described Dan. We had better plan our next moves—and soon."

"Of course. We cannot stay here very long. It would not be too difficult to trace us here after that coach ride. When I am fit enough to travel again, we had better head north and rest somewhere safe before going to Lewiston. I think Dan has done enough for now. As soon as he is able to travel comfortably, he goes back to Washington."

Dan protested from his prone position on the bed, but Zeb remained firm. "Dan, you have done enough for now, and Phillips is right. If that fellow we left in the gutter back in New York by some chance did get back to Melbourne and told him what happened, you are in as much danger as the rest of us. No, we will stay here a day or two and then move on. When we are both stronger and in better shape to travel further, we will split up. Phillips, Richards, and I will travel to Lewiston to meet Matthew. Dan will go back to Washington and report to President Adams about the events of the past several days. He will be anxious for news, and a firsthand report will be appreciated."

Phillips filled them in on what he had learned in Albany. The conversation Zeb had overhead in the consulate, combined with the governor's planned trip upstate, gave them something more concrete to work on. The key to the whole affair, Zeb believed, was still missing. Morgan had to be found before they could unravel the rest. This meant traveling to Lewiston and meeting Matthew as scheduled. This had suddenly taken on a greater importance than he had suspected. He hoped he was correct in his assessment of Matthew.

PART 2

CHAPTER 16

THE LONG COACH RIDE HAD left Wollstonecraft cramped and tired after being bumped and jolted on post roads that connected Albany with Buffalo. It was not too many years ago that this particular main branch of the Iroquois network of trails had never seen a coach. The region was lush with spring, and the scent of wildflowers filled the warm air with their fragrances. Trees with their rich and varied hues of green carpeted the landscape when seen from a hill or rise in the road. Melbourne would have been surprised that Wollstonecraft appreciated all this natural beauty.

The coach was continuing to Buffalo, but he got off in Canandaigua and took a room in the tavern as planned. The lake that bore the same name as the village glistened with reflected sunlight down the hill to the south. The deep blue waters were radiant in the spring light and stretched along the bed of their glacial valley until a curve hid the lake behind the surrounding hills.

Wollstonecraft went to his room and unpacked his few items of clothing and personal effects. He changed from traveling clothes to more suitable attire. He pulled on a linen shirt and a pair of wool trousers that were suitable for riding, as well as walking through the forest that still remained untouched in some areas. He did not know where Morgan had hidden the supplies and wanted to be prepared. He pulled on a pair of expensive English boots, his only concession to native craftsmanship. He had no intention of having his feet suffer from some ill-fitting pair of American frontier boots.

Morgan was supposed to meet him that afternoon, so he went downstairs and ordered some ale and a bowl of stew. He took his food to a corner table. He hoped Morgan would show up sober. The last time had not been very pleasant for Morgan. He had arrived with too much gin in him and nearly blabbered all he knew to everyone in the tavern. Wollstonecraft had to sober him up and then physically impress upon him the seriousness of their venture.

If he showed up drunk this time, Wollstonecraft would like nothing better than to kill Morgan. However, Melbourne would certainly not like it if anything happened to Morgan. Wollstonecraft resolved to control his temper. He did not want to spoil his opportunity for the chance to kill some people later this summer. He hoped Morgan would not fail in his part of the affair. He had been told to make sure this did not happen. After all, Morgan was an important component of the plan.

Just at that moment, Morgan entered the tavern. He was of medium height, balding, with graying hair that circled a large head supported by a short neck. His torso was in the advanced stages of producing a potbelly. His walk was steady as he approached the table, and he did not have the crimson complexion that would indicate a recent relationship with gin. Morgan sat down at the table and greeted him with the Masonic handshake. "Greetings, Brother. I hope your journey to our fair part of this country was pleasant?" Wollstonecraft held his temper and managed not to reveal his revulsion for this man. Instead, he returned the greeting and, in a low voice, proceeded to get to the heart of their meeting. "I assume the supplies are well placed away from prying eyes and will be ready when needed?"

"Yes. They are hidden not far from here, but there has been a slight problem with the delivery. Not all the muskets expected were in the shipment."

Wollstonecraft nodded and explained what had happened. "Yes, I know that. We could not obtain the number of muskets we thought would be needed, but there should be enough to do the work."

to obtain passage on a canal packet boat from Albany to Lockport. The distance from Albany to Buffalo was 362 miles with about eighty-three locks along the way. The price of the typical packet boat was four cents per mile and included food and a place to sleep. The packet boats were pulled by three horses that were changed every ten miles or so. A good packet boat captain could make eighty miles in a twenty-four-hour period. At that rate, it would take about five days to reach Buffalo, so he should be in Lockport in less time than that since Buffalo was the western terminus of the canal, and Lockport was where he needed to leave the canal and travel northwest on horseback to Lewiston.

All the arrangements had been made to handle the business while he was absent, and no one was the wiser as to his real reason for making the trip. He told his Boston business associates and friends that he was going to explore the possibility of expanding the business inland to include the shipping of goods along the canal and then westward into the area of new settlements in Ohio and other regions. If it turned out to be a good venture, he would establish an office in Buffalo and become involved in the new inland waterway trade that would soon develop between New York City and Buffalo. He expected the canal to be a conduit for goods traveling both ways between the newly developing areas of the West and New York City.

Matthew was content to watch the passing scenery as the coach swayed and jolted the passengers on their way to Albany. He particularly noticed a different kind of scenery inside the coach. His gaze kept returning to the pretty girl who sat in the corner across from him. Matthew smiled and tipped his hat to the girl, and he was surprised by a smile of acknowledgment in return. This could prove to be a more interesting trip than he had anticipated.

"Yes, I suppose you are right."

"A most unfortunate occurrence in Washington led to the man's death. He was killed while helping us in a particularly important matter." Wollstonecraft did not tell Morgan that Foxworth had been deliberately killed to ensure his silence regarding the arms and the murder of Villineau. Also, suspicion would be pointed in another direction if it appeared that Foxworth had been killed in the line of duty while working for the government.

Morgan was satisfied with the explanation and asked Wollstonecraft if he would like to see the cache of arms. The big man followed Morgan out through the smoke-filled room with slimy tobacco spit and sawdust on the floor. Morgan had two horses tied outside. They mounted and rode south down the sloping main street toward the lake. When they had passed through the main village, they took the trail that wound along the western shore of the lake.

Neither man spoke as they rode leisurely under the towering oaks, maples, and pines that cut off most of the sunlight and cast moving shadows on the trail. The patterns shifted silently in the moderate breeze that blew from the southwest. Tree roots, decaying leaves, and fallen branches from the previous winter's storms were scattered along the narrow trail and among the trees. The horses had to detour around the larger limbs. The men were careful to protect their faces from the branches that slashed and tugged at them as they rode by. The damp smell of the earth and decaying vegetation filled their noses. From time to time, on their left, as the trail wound close to the lake, they saw a shimmering blue between the trees. The air was cool under the canopy of leaves, and Wollstonecraft wished he had put on a heavier shirt to keep off the chill.

Morgan led the way on his chestnut mare for about three more miles until he slowed and turned right up a shallow creek that led away from the lake. Both men had to crouch low in the saddle to avoid the low-hanging branches and grapevines that grew out over the small stream. Eventually they came to a clearing with a narrow trail that led to a small log cabin. Morgan dismounted, and Wollstonecraft followed him. Morgan explained that the cabin had been abandoned several years ago by a settler who gave up on farming the rugged area.

"The cabin is located only a few hundred yards from the road that leads south out of Canandaigua. I took the lake trail to make it seem as if we were taking a leisurely ride along the lake and had no particular destination. The arms were brought in by wagon from Rochester after they were delivered by a canal barge. No one uses this cabin anymore. I didn't want to hide the supplies near Batavia since my role there would make it more difficult. I have an excuse to travel here on business once or twice a month and find the local people are not as curious as some of those in Batavia." Morgan took a brass key from his pocket and walked around to the front of the cabin.

The cabin door had been repaired and reinforced with thick maple boards. The sturdy, well-crafted lock's mechanism yielded quietly to the key. Morgan removed the key from the lock and pushed the door open. The door swung quietly on leather hinges and let in enough light to reveal kegs of gunpowder and crates of muskets stacked in the rear. Foxworth had stolen the muskets from the Harpers Ferry Arsenal over a period of several months. He had managed to steal fifty without being caught. The number would have been higher, but he had been transferred to Washington before he could steal the rest. The guns had been shipped down the Potomac to the Chesapeake and then up the Atlantic to New York. From New York, they went up the Hudson River and then along the canal to Rochester. The boxes had been labeled as agricultural supplies.

Wollstonecraft was impressed. There were ten kegs of powder, fifty rifles, boxes of lead balls, and plenty of wadding and flint. He picked up an iron bar and walked over to the nearest crate. His powerful arms pried open the lid with ease and revealed a dozen gleaming, U.S. government-issued rifles lying in protective cloth and grease. With a little cleaning, they would be ready on a few days' notice and would remain rust free until the time to use them arrived.

"You have done well," he told Morgan. "Make certain this cabin and its contents are not discovered during the summer. The exact

details of the plan will be revealed to you when you come to [New] York for the meeting in a few weeks. Make sure you find a g[ood] excuse for your wife so she won't be suspicious."

"The whole village of Batavia thinks I'm the town drunk, [so] my frequent disappearances and business trips aren't given m[uch] attention. I haven't touched a drop for pleasure since the last t[ime] we met, but I continue to play the drunken fool in every taver[n in] Batavia and LeRoy. I'm the last person anyone in that village wo[uld] suspect of being involved in anything like this."

Wollstonecraft hoped Morgan was right. "If your wife e[ver] became suspicious, it could jeopardize the entire plan."

"Don't worry; I'll take care of her."

Wollstonecraft seemed satisfied that all was in order. "We h[ave] better return to the inn. I need to leave for New York, and y[ou] should return to Batavia."

Morgan locked the door and returned the key to his pock[et.] They returned to Canandaigua by the regular road. Neither of the[m] spoke a word on the return ride, and the late afternoon shado[ws] began to lengthen as they reached the village. Morgan returned th[e] horses to the stable and went back to the inn with Wollstonecraf[t.] After a brief conversation, Morgan left the inn. He would return t[o] Batavia on the next coach. He had some time before it left, so he too[k] a walk to think about the day's events. Morgan knew Wollstonecraf[t] was Melbourne's bully and assassin. He would never forgive him for the beating. Morgan hoped he had convinced him that he held no grudge. It would make it easier to get his revenge when the time came.

Back in his room at the inn, Wollstonecraft lay on his bed for a brief rest. The long trip and the ride to the cabin had tired him. As he drifted off to sleep, he reviewed the options available to kill Melbourne when the opportunity presented itself.

While Wollstonecraft dozed in the inn in Canandaigua, Matthew travelled by coach to Albany on the first part of his trip to Lewiston. The trip was the easy part. It was a pleasant interlude before the real task of carrying out the president's request began. He hoped

CHAPTER 17

THE PEDDLER'S WAGON MOVED SLOWLY along the road pulled by two draft horses purchased in Pennsylvania that had seen better days. The man holding the reins wore a patched cotton shirt, wool trousers, and deerskin boots. Topping off the attire was a battered brown hat with the brim pulled down over his eyes to shelter them from the slowly descending sun directly ahead. A clay pipe jutted from between his teeth, and the strong scent of tobacco smoke left an easily identifiable trail behind the wagon. Pots, pans, and cooking kettles clanged on the side along with other kitchen and household articles. Inside the wagon were bolts of cloth, including gingham, cotton, calico, and silk. The goods also included an assortment of knives, scissors, needles, and thimbles. Patent medicine bottles clinked in their boxes. Mirrors and other glassware were packed securely away in sawdust and paper.

The driver slowed the horses and pulled over to the side of the road. A swarm of mayflies from a nearby stream formed a cloud near the wagon, and the horses flicked their tails and twitched their ears to ward off the winged invaders. The man secured the reins to the brake and climbed down from the seat. A beard covered his face. He stretched and yawned before unbuttoning his trousers and relieving himself in the dust by the side of the road. When he was finished, he looked northward. Lake Ontario lay just over the horizon, past the trees that were becoming shrouded in early evening haze. A few birds circled lazily in the fading light, and the horses looked backward to make sure the man was still there and would take them to a comfortable stable and some oats.

He knocked the bowl of his pipe against his boot and climbed back into the wagon. Lewiston was only ten or fifteen minutes down the road, but Zeb was damned if he'd let his bladder stay full and uncomfortable until they reached the inn. He had been traveling for several days through Pennsylvania and New York and now finally closed in on his goal. The knife wound had healed, but as the doctor in Princeton predicted, it had left a nasty scar. He was still a little stiff, but not as uncomfortable as the first few days of the trip. He released the brake and urged the horses forward onto the road toward Lewiston. The comfort of a soft bed and a good supper would be welcome after another long day of travel. The clanking and clattering of the damned tinware was getting on his nerves, and the sooner he parked the wagon for the night, the better his head would feel.

The orange orb of the setting sun was halfway down to the horizon when he reached the inn. A peddler was always welcome in this part of New York State, and the stable keeper, who worked for the inn, made no exception for Zeb. The horses were unhitched and put in large stalls with plenty of fresh hay and a bucket of oats each for supper. The peddler gave his name as Samuel Trapp out of Hagerstown, Maryland, and sat in the common room to have some ale and a hot supper. The supper crowd was thinning out, and only a few dedicated ale and rum drinkers followed their vocation while paying little attention to the travel-worn peddler.

Zeb made sure he left a card with the innkeeper on the pretext of advertisement purposes. He hoped the slow-witted man could remember his name when Matthew arrived and asked for him. Matthew was due at any time, and Zeb could fill in a few days, if needed, by traveling around the area and selling a few items. It would also give him a chance to go to Youngstown and check out the ferry to Canada and look over Fort Niagara and the lake. Richards and Phillips should also arrive soon.

As far as Zeb could tell, he had not been followed, and Richards would bring word of events in Washington. They would try to locate Morgan before too many weeks of the summer passed. If Matthew could help them accomplish this, another thread in the plot would unravel. If things did not work out as planned, it would not be the first time. The bullets in South America and the knife wound in New York were testimony to that.

Zeb climbed the stairs to his room with his thoughts on a welcomed night's rest and the note he had received at his home. He still needed to find out who sent it. He was unaware of the pair of eyes that followed his ascent. A man with a thick black beard salted with gray and the build of a wrestler scraped his chair back from the table, left half a tankard of ale, and rose to leave. He gave a hand signal to his partner standing by the door and then joined him outside. They spoke softly for a few moments and then left the inn. The sound of horses' hooves faded into the night as the two men rode east toward Lockport.

Matthew was just finishing his supper in Rochester at the Genesee Hotel and looking forward to the coming evening with Sarah Reynolds and her engaging smile. Ever since they had met, they became traveling companions, but only in the most decorous sense of the term. A young lady's reputation was of paramount importance. Matthew behaved as a gentleman at all times. However, his thoughts certainly entertained other ideas regarding the possibilities with Sarah. She was very beautiful and had a good sense of humor. Her chaperone was her aunt. Sarah's dark hair, vivid blue eyes, engaging smile, and laughter had captured his attention during the journey. Sarah was traveling to Lockport with her aunt to visit relatives in the recently developed village that owed its existence to the Erie Canal. Lockport was the sight of the amazing engineering feat of the locks required to lift and lower the barges. The locks had been blasted from solid rock.

They all stayed in Albany while Matthew looked for canal transportation. Sarah and her aunt had agreed with Matthew that a trip on the new canal would be a much more pleasant experience than one by coach. They had found a barge with an honest master and a good crew. The accommodations were more than adequate. They had enjoyed the trip, and even Sarah's sour aunt, with the hat that never seemed to leave her head, smiled once or twice between Albany and Syracuse.

Matthew hoped tonight might be different. Sarah's aunt had come down with a bout of fever and took to her bed in the hotel. The doctor insisted that the aunt be left alone to rest with an occasional visit for food and companionship; she needed rest above all, and a great deal of it. Matthew had suggested, in his most gentlemanly manner, that he could be relied upon to escort Sarah and that her virtue and safety would be well guarded. Sarah had gone to her room to fetch a shawl, and Matthew was finishing a glass of port when she returned to the dining room. They left the hotel and walked through the center of the thriving canal port past newly constructed buildings. The conversation between them until now had been formal and not very personal. Sarah was more relaxed this evening, and Matthew was enjoying their walk.

"I hope your aunt is doing as well as can be expected under the circumstances," he offered as an opening gesture.

"Yes, Matthew, thank you. She is resting comfortably and should be fine until morning."

"I am very glad to hear that."

"I know she seems like a sour old lady, but she is just looking out for me."

"Of course," replied Matthew.

"I believe I may be honest with you, and I feel you will be the same with me."

Matthew was taken by surprise. Sarah was taking an unexpected turn in the conversation, and he was not sure where it was heading. His puzzled look was answer enough for Sarah to continue.

"I like you, Matthew. You are a gentlemen and very kind. When we arrive in Lockport, I will be staying with my uncle for the rest of the summer. If you have the opportunity, I would like you to call on me."

"I would like that very much, Sarah."

Sarah's smile was almost as big as Matthew's. Neither spoke as they returned to the hotel and went to their separate rooms.

CHAPTER 18

RICHARDS AND PHILLIPS RODE TOWARD Lockport in pursuit of the two men. Without Zeb's awareness, they had traveled north sooner than planned. Phillips related the events in New York to Richards, as directed by Zeb, and they had ridden rapidly northward to Lewiston. They had been in Lewiston for only a day when they noticed the two men ride up in the afternoon. Phillips had recognized the taller one as one of Melbourne's men whom he had seen in New York before Mary was murdered. It could not be mere coincidence that the two had arrived in Lewiston at the same time Zeb was expected. Rather than immediately warn Zeb, they decided to watch the two men and see what they did.

Their horses were no match for those ridden by Richards and Phillips, but their intent was not to catch them. They held their mounts back and followed them to the new canal town of Lockport. The village was rugged at best with newly constructed buildings consisting of shipping offices, taverns, a hotel, a post office, and a few houses. One substantial inn had been constructed, and several other buildings were in various stages of construction. The canal was bringing prosperity to Lockport.

The two stopped in front of a tavern, dismounted, and tied their horses to hitching posts. Phillips had to make a quick decision. He might be recognized, but Richards should be unknown to these men. They had to find out why they were watching Zeb and whom they were meeting in the tavern. Apparently, their instructions did not include killing Zeb on sight, or they could have tried that already. Richards and Phillips dismounted and led their horses to another tavern farther down the street. Richards walked back to the first tavern while Phillips waited.

Richards walked into a tavern filled with roughneck bargemen, local whores, and what appeared to be some of the less respectable members of the community. He went to the bar and stood in the beer-soaked sawdust near an overflowing spittoon. The air was rich in smoke and sweat intermingled with the smell of stale beer and gin. He ordered ale and casually began to orient himself to the smoke and noise. Three men occupied a table near the corner—the two men they had followed and a third he did not recognize. The third man was dressed in business garb with a beaver hat resting on the table by his drink. He had a thick mustache and black, greasy hair that hung in lank strips on both sides of his head. The indentation made by the hat was clearly visible as a greasy ring around his skull. They were too busy talking to notice Richards observing them. The greasy-haired man pointed his finger at the bearded man to make a rather emphatic point. Richards had to get closer. Two ladies of questionable reputation occupied the table next to them. He went straight to the table and asked if he could join them.

"Only if we can see the color of your money, dearie," the first one chirped. He pulled out a gold coin and dropped it on the table. A waiter appeared immediately with a bottle and dirty glasses and disappeared as quickly.

Richards poured the women a drink and offered a toast. "To the loveliest ladies in town." His winning smile charmed them. With one ear listening to the conversation at the next table, and the other in use for his repartee with the whores, he endured five toasts of watered whiskey and promises of an exciting and most unusual evening. As the conversation became more interesting at his table, the one at the next took on an ominous tone.

"If that damned bastard gets out of there alive, I'll see that the both of you are sent bound and gagged by boat to New York and taken care of by Melbourne's friend! Do I make myself clear?"

There was no need for a response. Both men knew what they had to do. They had followed orders and reported the movements of the peddler to Simon Wharton. All they had been told was to look for a peddler fitting Zeb's general description and to follow him. Zeb had been discovered in the southern part of York State by one of Melbourne's men, who was part of the network searching for Zeb. The disguise had not proved effective enough, and his identity was confirmed. Orders had been given to follow him, but what Simon Wharton had not anticipated was that Zeb would have help.

Richards left the two ladies to pay a visit to the privy. His apparent drunken gait was of concern to the ladies, who hoped his condition would not affect their plans for later in the evening. As soon as he was outside, he walked quickly up the street to the tavern where Phillips waited. Phillips was at the bar nursing a gin and trying to keep a drunken canal man in a coherent conversation about the advantages of canal travel over land travel. Richards signaled for him to join him outside.

"Look," Richards said, "those two characters met a third man who was giving orders concerning their plans for Zeb. He knows who Zeb is, in spite of the disguise, and has known for several days. He is having him followed and wants him killed now that he's in Lewiston. I don't know why he waited until now, but the order was just given to follow Zeb tomorrow and kill him. What do you think? Should we take care of them now and save Zeb the trouble of being involved, or tell him first and set a trap for them?"

"I don't like traps, but I also don't want Zeb to be left in the dark about what is happening. The only problem is the third man who is giving the orders. He should be silenced or, better yet, captured and interrogated."

"Good idea. He'll probably be waiting here for those two tomorrow to find out if they killed Zeb or not. Let's tell Zeb, set up a trap tomorrow for the two, and then come back and get old Simon and make him tell us what he knows. Jesus, those bastards are everywhere!"

"Not only that, but their intelligence gathering is too damned good. We have one hell of a tough nut to crack in this mission, I'm afraid."

Zeb was awakened by light footsteps outside his room. He quietly pulled the knife from one of his boots next to the bed and rolled out on the side away from the door. He crept behind the door and waited. He held his breath as the door opened, and a hand appeared, followed by a quietly moving figure in the semidarkness. Zeb grabbed the arm, spun the man around, got a choke hold, and pressed the edge of the knife against the man's face.

"Jesus Christ, Zeb. I was trying to get in without waking you," gasped the man. Zeb released him. Relieved, he relaxed his hold on the knife.

"Phillips, you clumsy oaf, I could have snapped your neck with a few more pounds of pressure."

"Yes, you could, Zeb, but the fellow behind you would have finished you if you had tried." Zeb turned to see Richards quietly slipping into the room.

"Well, I'll be damned. Both of you—and sooner than I expected. What the hell is going on that you two have to sneak up on a poor old man and scare him half to death in the middle of the night?"

Richards replied, "Sit down, Zeb. We've got something important that can't wait until morning."

Their conversation was quiet and brief as Richards and Phillips told Zeb about the three men in the tavern and their idea of how to handle them. The professional experience of Zeb and his two assistants was extensive, and they made their plans with cool and calm deliberation. If all went well, they would not only get rid of the threat posed by the two men who had watched Zeb that evening, but they would find out who Simon was and how he might be involved in the scheme they learned about in New York.

CHAPTER 19

THE PEDDLER'S WAGON SLOWLY MADE its way around a curve in the road that ran between Lewiston and Youngstown. Zeb kept a careful watch for the two men they expected to attack him. As predicted, Melbourne's confederates were watching the inn at dawn. Richards and Phillips had hidden themselves in separate locations above and below the inn to be sure they would not miss the two. Richards saw them first as they waited in a narrow alley about fifty yards from the inn.

Zeb collected his wagon from the stable around eight and headed down the street before turning right on the road to Youngstown. The two men followed at a distance on horseback. Richards and Phillips followed them, thus making the hunters the hunted.

As planned, Zeb stopped the wagon on a section of road that ran near the Niagara River. The gorge here was not as steep as it was farther upstream. Still, a fall down to the river even at this point would not be pleasant. Zeb got down on one knee and pretended to inspect the left front wheel, trying to appear concerned about a problem with the hub. He sensed their presence before he could see or hear them. They rode slowly up behind him until they stopped only a few feet from the wagon. Zeb turned and tried to appear as relaxed as possible. "Good day to you, gentlemen," he said in greeting. The two men did not reply. They merely sat on their horses and stared at him. He tried again. "I said good day!"

The one with the beard pulled a pistol from his belt and pointed it at Zeb's chest. "Shut up, mister. Move away from that wagon and start walking toward the river over there." He moved the barrel of the pistol in the general direction of the river and then pointed it back at Zeb.

Zeb obeyed and slowly walked toward the trees by the edge of the road that bordered the incline to the river. Zeb noticed that the second man had dismounted and approached with a length of rope in his hand. Zeb's arms were roughly pulled behind his back, and his hands were tied securely. They pushed him down the bank toward the water below, and he only managed to maintain his balance at the last possible moment to keep from crashing headfirst toward the water and rocks below. The two men followed.

"What the hell is going on? If you want any of the goods in the wagon, help yourself. There is some pretty good stuff in there." The thinner of the two men just laughed and pulled a long, thin-bladed knife from a sheath at his side.

"Mister, we don't want that junk. We just want you dead."

Zeb noticed a brief movement down the riverbank, but he could not be certain what or who it was. It had better be Richards or Phillips. Things were moving too quickly now.

The bearded one spoke through tobacco-stained teeth. "I got a message for you, mister, from New York. Mr. Melbourne says that since there ain't no chance for you this time that you had better tell him—through me, that is—how much you know about him. Seeing as I don't like to see a man die looking at his insides hanging out his belly, I'll be merciful. I'll just have Sam here cut off your nuts and stuff 'em in your mouth." The man roared with laughter. "Funny, huh, Sam?"

His partner smiled but did not laugh. "Yeah, Jake, funny as hell."

"Come on, now. Let's get on with it." Jake approached Zeb with the pistol pointed directly at his head. "Tell us, Cardwell, so I can take a message to New York." The barrel of the pistol rested on the bridge of Zeb's nose. Sam stepped in with the knife and cut Zeb's belt, which resulted in his pants falling down around his knees. Then Sam retreated behind Jake.

Suddenly, a stream of crimson from Sam's slashed throat splashed on Jake's neck. Jake whirled around at the touch of the warm wetness. Sam's head was angled abnormally from his body, and Richards pushed him to the ground. He stood facing Jake with a bloody knife in his hand. Jake quickly aimed the pistol at Richards, but before he could aim carefully enough, there was a loud crunching sound, and Jake's eyes rolled up into his head. The pistol fired harmlessly and hit the trunk of a tree. Jake collapsed like a downed tree. Phillips had knocked him cold with a powerful blow to the back of his head with the blunt end of a Mohawk hatchet he favored for close fighting. His father had acquired it during the Revolution. They untied Zeb and stood aside, watching the big bearded man. His skull was probably fractured, and they all were aware that neither one of the killers should be found here.

Zeb grabbed a length of rope, pulled up his pants, and used the rope for a belt. Richards spoke first. "Zeb, we've got to kill him. He may come around and try to get us later."

Zeb shook his head. "No, I don't think so. He's pretty badly injured. We'd better tie them to a couple of logs here and set them adrift in the river. If they float past the mouth of the river, they won't be found for quite a while. If they are discovered, what can this one tell them? I think we are just as well off putting them in the river. I have some rope in the wagon. Tie those two logs over there together, and then tie each of them to either side."

When the logs were lashed together and the two killers tied to the logs, Phillips and Richards pushed the makeshift raft into the Niagara. Phillips went in the water and made sure it floated out to the main current. Other debris floated in the river along with the logs carrying the two men, and soon they drifted toward Lake Ontario with the deceptively fast current. Phillips came back to shore and rejoined Zeb and Richards.

"You didn't have to wait so long before taking care of those two bastards."

"Sure we did, Zeb," replied Phillips. "We were with you all the way down the bank. You never had a thing to worry about."

Zeb smiled. "That's easy for you to say. You weren't the one they were going to kill. We had better get out of here and finish what we discussed last night. You two go back to Lockport and find Simon. Make him all nice and comfortable, and we'll have a little talk later on. Right now, I'd better continue to the fort as planned and look like a peddler trying to make some money. If those bodies haven't been discovered by the time I reach Fort Niagara, that should give us enough time to finish our business here before we move on."

Zeb was more shaken by the morning's events than either Richards or Phillips knew. He had come very close to being maimed and tortured before being killed. He remembered the stories he had heard about Boyd and Parker during the Revolutionary War—how they had their intestines cut out and were forced to walk around a tree while they unraveled. He shuddered. Melbourne's killers deserved their fate. God only knew how many people they had tortured and killed in the past. Many people must have been avenged today.

It was just past noon when Zeb reached Youngstown. Curious children and mothers stopped him from time to time. He even sold a few items. The fort was just beyond Youngstown. Most of the damage from the war had been repaired, and the stone powder magazine stood on the near side in excellent condition. The main building, constructed by the French during the days of the fur trade, was visible beyond the walls on the side facing the lake. Zeb coaxed the horses as near the gate as he could and stopped. A guard approached him and asked what he wanted. Zeb gave the name of the commander and watched the surprised look appear on the guard's face. He could almost read his thoughts. *What the hell does this old peddler want with Captain Jamison?* Zeb climbed down from the wagon and handed the guard a sealed letter. "Tell your captain that a grubby peddler would be most thankful if he would read this and send a reply."

The guard left and went to the officer's quarters. In ten minutes, he was back. "The captain has given orders for you to be escorted to his quarters. Please follow me, sir." Zeb could tell the young soldier thought it most unusual for a grubby civilian to receive such treatment. Zeb smiled to himself as he followed the young corporal.

Seth Jamison was waiting for Zeb, the letter still held in his hand. "Zeb, it's good to see you, but I must say you are the last person I expected to see around here—and this letter from President Adams! This is a surprise, to say the least."

"It has been a long time, Seth. It is good to see you, as well. How long has it been? Five or six years?"

"I think it has been at least six years, Zeb. I'll never forget those damned swamps in Florida where we were looking for that crazy Spaniard. I still dream about snakes and alligators in the middle of the night."

"That was nothing, Seth. It was just a simple job. You army boys just don't like water."

"Maybe so, Zeb, but this letter is no simple matter. President Adams himself has authorized me to let you have as many men as needed plus our cooperation in making any supplies from the fort available to you that you may need over the next few months. And I am not even supposed to ask what the hell you are up to!"

"No, Seth. You are not supposed to know, but I won't leave you completely in the dark." Zeb gave him a briefing of what had happened thus far, covering only those events he felt Seth should know. "So you see, Seth, your cooperation and strictest confidence are required. I don't know in what way or manner you will be able to help, but I will let you know when the time comes."

"You know you can count on me, Zeb. By the way, we fished two men out of the Niagara this morning. You wouldn't have anything to do with that, would you? Both of them are down in the storeroom, deader than fish."

"Did anyone other than your men see these two?"

"No. Only the three men in the detail I sent to fish them out of the river. They were beached just at the base of the fort near the lake."

"Bury them, Seth, and tell your men not to talk about it. My men and I had to take care of those two this morning."

"All right, Zeb. We will do it, but for God's sake, be careful from now on."

"Don't worry, I will. Just a couple of more things, and then I had better be moving along. I guess you can start helping us sooner than expected."

"Not before we have a drink." He picked up a decanter from a nearby tray. "This is the best damned whiskey I have found around this place in quite a while." He poured both of them a good portion of the amber liquid, and they drank it quickly.

"The first thing I need to know, Seth, is how often the ferry runs to Canada. We are going to have to use it in a day or so. The second item is quite another matter, but the ferry first."

"The ferry doesn't have a regular schedule. You just show up, and if old Jack happens to feel like it, he'll take you across. I know it's not very impressive for the crossing of an international border, but it's all we have. This is the best place to cross. When you come back, just hail him if he's across the river, and he'll bring the ferry over. I'll make sure."

Zeb laughed. "How would you feel about locking up a civilian for a few weeks or months to keep him out of our hair?"

"I ordinarily would not like it at all, but how can I refuse to cooperate with the president's official representative?"

"Well said, and thanks. We may be back later tonight or tomorrow with a delivery for your brig."

Seth refilled both glasses and raised his for a toast. "Good luck and take care. If this is as tough a mission as I suspect, you certainly have your work cut out for you."

"Thanks, Seth. I'd better head back to Lewiston. We'll be back as soon as the man we want can be persuaded—one way or another—that he would like to visit the fort for a while."

Phillips and Richards found Simon in the same tavern at the same table. They sat down with him and ordered a drink. He did not have the slightest idea who they were, but he seemed troubled. He started to sweat, and both Phillips and Richards could feel the aura of fear he gave off. Richards spoke quietly. "Your two men are floating down the Niagara. They botched their job, and the man they tried to kill is still alive. If you want to keep breathing, you will get up with us and leave. If you don't, both my friend and I would like nothing better than to beat the living shit out of you right here and now."

Simon went pale. He rose from his chair without protest and went with them. The shock of the two men's failure to kill Zeb Cardwell had not worn off yet. Richards and Phillips tied his hands to the saddle horn. The three men rode out of Lockport toward Lewiston.

Chapter 20

Simon Wharton lay on his stomach in the last stall of the stable that served the inn. A whale oil lamp illuminated the area. Horses in the neighboring stalls stirred uneasily at the intrusion. The burrs that had been harvested with the hay pressed into the side of Wharton's face, and he tried to turn his head to avoid contact with them. The exposed parts of his body—he was barefoot and stripped to the waist—itched from the hay. His hands and feet were tied. The horse in the closest stall glanced over at the man for a moment and gave off a short, derisive snort before relieving himself. The pungent and warm smell of fresh horse manure filled the air. Zeb, Richards, and Phillips stood at the open end of the stall that contained Wharton.

Zeb spoke first. "I told the stable boy to find something to occupy his time for about an hour. He did not ask any questions when I put the gold coin in his hand." He smiled. "Just like most boys his age—show him a little gold and the cooperation is amazing."

Richards looked at Zeb and then pointed at Wharton. "What about our friend here? Won't his screams be too loud? Someone will probably hear him. He certainly looks like he has a healthy pair of lungs for such a piece of shit."

"We'll gag him for the first few minutes, and if he doesn't suffocate in his own vomit, he'll tell us everything he knows. Isn't that right, you son of a bitch?" Zeb gave Wharton a kick, and the man cowered in the hay, trying to crawl to the far end of the stall.

Phillips winked at the others and said, "Take it easy, Zeb. Don't be too rough on him, or the bastard will croak just like the gentleman that died on us in Maryland. We need him alive, so don't cut him up as much as that dumb idiot we lost the last time."

Wharton made low, whimpering sounds into the straw and started pleading with them not to hurt him.

"Gag him." Phillips rolled Wharton over. He stuffed a rag into his mouth and then tied a longer piece of cloth over the gag and around his head. Wharton's eyes darted from side to side as he watched for their next move. Phillips and Richards pulled Wharton to his feet and shoved him against the boards at the end of the stall. The light from the lamp reflected off his greasy hair.

In moves he had practiced many times before, Richards sent two quick body punches to Wharton's midsection. While Wharton doubled over, Richards struck him in the nose and on the side of the head. Blood spurted from Wharton's nose and ran onto his bare chest. He began to choke. The gag was quickly removed. Wharton collapsed onto the hay and begged for mercy. "I'll tell you anything you want to know. Just don't hit me anymore. I won't even try to do anything to you again. Let me go, and I'll tell you all I know."

Zeb looked at him in disgust. "You weasel. Look at you. Slobbering like a baby and ready to tell us everything. Yesterday you were planning to kill me using those two rats of yours, and now you want mercy. Fuck you, Wharton! You tell me all you know, no deals, and maybe we'll let you live. Now, how did you follow me here, and what is your connection with Melbourne?"

Wharton tried to wipe his bloody nose on his arm but could not quite reach it. He gave up and looked at Zeb. His eyes revealed everything. The sniveling weasel was gone, and the look was calm and calculating. He knew there was no pity to be found with professionals, but he had tried. He would do anything to get away from them and finish his assigned tasks. He spoke slowly and deliberately. "Melbourne sent me here to kill you. All of his men have sketches of you and have been searching for you since the fire in New York. You were seen in southern New York near the Pennsylvania border when you stopped at that village to peddle your worthless trash. You almost made it undiscovered, but the man you sold the cough remedy to recognized you in spite of your disguise. I was ordered to hire some men to track you down and kill you. Following you was easy—the killing obviously was not."

"What do you know about Melbourne?"

"Not very much." Wharton's tongue was loosening enough to give him a chance, he hoped. "Melbourne hired me about a year ago at a Masonic meeting in Rochester and offered a good deal of money. He told me that if I was not too concerned about the legality of the work, things would be fine. I was told to make a detailed study of the canal between Rochester and Lockport and to draw a map including all the villages, bridges, and other features of note. Since I had been a cartographer before becoming a resident of prison for a few years, he knew that I not only could do the cartography but also needed the money. He told me to finish it by next month and that I would be contacted as to the date and location of a meeting where I would give him the map. I was contacted a few days ago with instructions regarding the meeting."

"Who contacted you?"

Wharton hesitated. He was afraid, but he knew that to get out of this alive, he would have to cooperate for the time being. "A big man with a funny scar on his face contacted me with a message to attend a meeting in New York in a few weeks and to kill you."

Zeb looked at Phillips. Wollstonecraft had been in the area. He may even have contacted Morgan. *Damn*, Zeb thought, *if only they knew where Morgan was!* Zeb decided to try a long shot. "Did this man introduce you to anyone else in the area who would be working with you?"

"No. He works alone and doesn't let me know who else is involved in their scheme. I don't even know what they are planning, but it must be something pretty big. I get the impression the big man doesn't want me to get to know any of the others until they want it to happen. He won't even tell me his name."

Zeb decided not to pursue it. He would be using Matt to find Morgan. He changed his line of questioning. "Where is this map of yours?"

Wharton did not answer immediately. The others knew he was weighing the importance of the information against his life. Illogically enough, he refused to tell them. "I won't tell you that. My instructions are to give the map to Melbourne, and under no circumstances is anyone to have access to it. You can kill me if you want, but you won't get that map!"

Zeb seriously considered doing just that but knew it would not help their mission as much as keeping Wharton alive and letting him believe they would eventually kill him. The hour was nearly up, and he needed to get Wharton out of the stable and to the fort. "Richards, gag him again, put him in the wagon, and cover him with something to keep his worthless hide out of sight. We'll take turns guarding him tonight. I'll take him to the fort in the morning for safekeeping with Seth. You two ride to Rochester, find out where he was staying, and try to locate that map. Turn the place inside out if you have to, but find that map."

When Wharton was secured in the wagon, they quietly conferred for a few moments. "That map must be damned important," Zeb said. "Melbourne must not have selected the location for the attack, or he wouldn't need the map. Find it if you can and meet me back here in about a week. If I am not here when you get back, I'll probably be in York with Matt or following Morgan's trail if he is not there. In any event, I'll leave word at the fort. Matt should be here any day now, and we can begin the search for Morgan. While you are in Rochester, see what else you can find out about this Wharton character. Obviously he is not telling us everything, but the Masonic connection is very interesting."

The stable boy whistled to let them know he was returning. When he entered the stable, Zeb was just taking a swig from a bottle of rum and wiped his mouth with his sleeve when he saw the boy. "Good lad. You've certainly earned your wages tonight." The boy looked at Zeb in a somewhat puzzled manner but decided that if anyone was crazy enough to pay him to stay away so he could drink in the stable, the idiot deserved to lose some of his gold.

CHAPTER 21

MATT APPROACHED THE OUTSKIRTS OF Lewiston near midday. A light rain had just begun, and the dust in the road turned a darker shade of brown in random patterns where each individual drop struck. The air was warm, and although the rain was a slight inconvenience for a traveler on horseback, it brought a refreshing smell that only a warm spring rain could create. The rain also served the most useful purpose of masking the clinging odor of dust and horse. His horse grew tired, and Matt slowed him to a more comfortable pace. He was on the ridge road, referred to as "the Ridge" by the locals. According to some, thousands of years ago, the shore of Lake Ontario had extended as far as this area. This would explain the road's higher elevation above the land that stretched to the north as far as the present shore of the lake.

In his ride along the Ridge, Matthew had also noticed a new type of house being constructed in several locations. These houses were made from round stones that were found in abundance as leftovers from the old lakeshore before it receded to its current location. The local people referred to them as cobblestone houses, and they did in fact look very much like the cobblestones that paved some of the streets in Boston and Washington. Some of the patterns were quite intricate, and one that especially appealed to Matthew was a herringbone pattern that presented a most aesthetic appearance.

Lewiston was a short distance ahead. The inn was located at the far end of the main street toward the river. The sturdy stone construction was a contrast to the wooden structures surrounding it even at this point near the village. He was quickly reminded of the reason he was here at this particular time. He suddenly had the feeling that it would be some time before his life returned to normal. The dream he had while aboard his ship between Baltimore and Boston had recurred several times, and he was quite concerned that it might be a premonition regarding the business of finding Morgan. He reached the inn, dismounted, and secured the reins of his horse to an iron ring on a stone post on the east side of the inn.

As Matthew entered the inn and passed through one of the larger rooms, he noted the intricate craftsmanship of the oak paneling, as well as the excellent paintings depicting scenes from the Revolution and several of the new canal. A striking portrait of an Indian wearing a red British officer's jacket hung in the center of the collection of paintings. Matthew thought it was quite excellent. He walked over for a closer inspection and found that the painting was of the famous Seneca chief, Red Jacket.

The innkeeper was busy with the noon meal and asked one of his assistants to take care of Matthew. The assistant led Matthew to a room on the second floor. Matthew immediately inquired about a bath as soon as he placed his bag on the chair at the foot of the bed. He had agreed to travel by horseback, at Sarah's request, rather than continue along the canal from Rochester to Lockport. She had thought it would provide them with a better opportunity to see the countryside. Her aunt had recovered sufficiently to allow her to continue, and a very gentle horse had been obtained for her to ride. They traveled at a leisurely pace and stayed overnight at an inn located in the settlement of Carlton.

They reached Lockport on the second day and found it to be a fast-growing and bustling village. Its location along the canal would soon make it a thriving canal community. Fortunately, one of the more sturdily constructed and pleasantly furnished houses belonged to Sarah's uncle. Her uncle had been one of the engineers who helped build the famous locks that gave the village its name. He decided to stay, and he had ordered the house to be built the previous year. His business ventures were now becoming quite profitable, and he planned to be a permanent resident.

Matthew spent the evening with Sarah and her relatives and promised her he would return for a visit as soon as he had the opportunity. They both laughed that evening, when they had a few moments alone in the parlor, at her chaperone's thoroughly disgruntled demeanor during the last two days of traveling. The poor horse she had been riding had suffered a stream of verbal abuse, but without any profanity. Sarah's aunt was not used to riding and made many comments regarding the lack of comfort involved. Sarah and Matthew had found her plight to be quite humorous, all the while trying to be openly solicitous and concerned. Sarah kept making faces at Matthew behind her aunt's back at every opportunity, much to the amusement of both of them. They were getting along exceptionally well, and Matthew was becoming very fond of Sarah. He made his farewells the following morning and set out for Lewiston and his meeting with Zeb.

The warm bathwater was refreshing after the ride from Lockport. Matthew relaxed and enjoyed the leisure of soaking in warm water. The moment was suddenly interrupted when the door burst open, and a scruffy-looking character walked in.

"Well, now, son, if you aren't the laziest-looking city fella I've ever seen, then I don't know what is! Look at you. Lying there in that nice warm water like you had nothing to do in the whole wide world but be rich and idle."

After a moment, Matthew recognized Zeb in spite of the beard and fake dialect. "Hello, Zeb. You sure look a lot different from the last time I saw you."

Zeb pulled a chair next to the tub and sat down. "Matt, much is different since you left Washington."

"What do you mean?"

Zeb told Matt what had happened since they had last seen each other in Washington. He briefly touched on the major items, such as Villineau's death, the events in New York, the information Phillips learned in Albany, and the recent trouble with Wharton and his henchmen.

"Jesus, Zeb. You mean those crazy fools may try to kill DeWitt Clinton?"

"That's what it looks like, but they aren't fools. Crazy, maybe, but not fools. The major problem we have is that we don't know where or when—only that all the intelligence we have been able to gather points to an event occurring at the end of the summer, when the governor plans to travel upstate to do some fence mending. We think the attack, or whatever they plan, may very well occur along the canal between Rochester and Lockport. I've sent Richards and Phillips to Rochester to try to find Wharton's map."

"That must be who those two riders were that we saw the other day along the road. They were riding east at full gallop and nearly spooked Sarah's aunt from her horse."

"And who, may I ask, is Sarah?"

"I met her on the coach to Albany. She was being chaperoned by her aunt all the way to Lockport. We traveled on the packet boat together. Don't worry, Zeb, she doesn't know the real reason I am here. I told her the same story I gave all the people in Boston—that my trip involved exploring the possibility of expanding my business to include the new canal trade."

"This is not a vacation, Matt!"

"I know that, Zeb. My instructions were to meet you by the end of May. They included nothing about traveling companions."

"Your point is well taken, but my concern, as you may have noticed, is very keen. We are dealing with what has become a very complicated affair. Well, first of all, get out of that damned tub before you soak off all your skin, and get yourself dressed. I hope you brought some good, comfortable traveling clothes. We are leaving for York as soon as you get dressed."

"What about my horse?"

"Don't worry. I've got two fresh ones waiting. Your horse can chew on some hay for a while before they send him back to Rochester."

When they left the inn, a peddler's wagon was parked in front, and the stable boy was holding the horses. Matt was surprised when Zeb told him to climb aboard the wagon.

"What about those fresh horses you just told me about?"

Zeb laughed. "Oh, I forgot to tell you. I have them all right, but not here. We have to pick them up at the fort."

"The fort?"

"Yes, Fort Niagara is just north of here a few miles, and the commander of the garrison has orders from the president himself to cooperate with us to the fullest extent possible."

"You certainly are full of surprises."

"I try. Indeed I do try. But even the brilliant Cardwell makes occasional mistakes." Zeb laughed and urged the horses away from the inn and out into the main street. This time, no one followed him.

As the wagon rolled along the road toward the fort, Matthew tried to get Zeb to speculate further as to what the plot could be.

"I don't know for certain, but as I indicated earlier, Melbourne has devoted a great deal of time and energy preparing for it. From all the information we have been able to gather, it appears that an assassination attempt will be made on the governor when he travels upstate. It may even include something else we are not even aware of, but I'm just not certain. It is only a hunch right now, but I think they are planning something more in addition to killing Clinton. Morgan might be the key. From what we have learned, any plan of Melbourne's would require someone with Morgan's experience. If Morgan is in the area, even in York, this geographic proximity to the location of the plot's main act is too close for it to be mere coincidence. I am certain Morgan is important, and the plan to kill Clinton—if it *is* Clinton—would be a good method of showing how powerful the group really is. With that as a sample of their power, they might proceed to something else that would prove the president's fears all too real."

"How do you think Morgan fits into all of this?"

"I'm not sure, Matthew, but I think he has been sent to this area to act as the local contact and to facilitate the logistics of the planning. What his exact role actually could be, I cannot say beyond speculation. This is where you come in. You need to find out from Morgan, once we locate him, so we can devise a method to stop their scheme. A lot of very unpleasant people are involved, and they seem to have no compunction whatsoever about killing anyone who becomes a threat to them. You will certainly be in danger once we find Morgan, especially if they discover your real purpose in befriending him again. That is why your reason for wanting to find him must be a logical one. We will work that one out once we find where he is."

"I'm certainly getting myself into one hell of a situation, but I will not turn back. Not now. This plot, whatever it entails, must be stopped. I just hope I can fulfill the president's expectations."

"So do I, Matt. So do I."

After the wagon was placed in the safekeeping of personnel at the fort and their horses were checked over for the ride to York, they went to the officer's quarters to speak with Seth Jamison. It was nearly dark, and they could not leave until first light. They had a pleasant meal with Seth and went to bed early.

Zeb and Matt rode down to the ferry at first light. They roused Jack from his cabin and urged the horses onto a large, raftlike structure. The ferry glided slowly across the river. Jack loved nothing better than watching his passengers pull on the oars that powered the ferry while he stood at the tiller and laughed to himself. Where else could you have people pay you to allow them to do the work? His smile was more meaningful than anything he could have said.

CHAPTER 22

THE LAKE BREEZE BLEW WHITECAPS across the water's surface as the late afternoon sun appeared and reappeared among big, white, fluffy clouds. They reached York before dark on the second day after making camp along the lakeshore overnight. As planned, they stopped at the largest inn in order to rest the horses and themselves before beginning their inquiries for Morgan. Zeb would ask the innkeeper, who usually knew everything about his community, and Matt would go down to the docks and ask among the freshwater fishermen. He would use his shipping experience. Once he engaged some of these people in a conversation about ships, it should be easy to ask questions concerning the whereabouts of an old friend.

They ate a quiet dinner while discussing their immediate plans. "We need to find Morgan but not make contact with him until we have decided on a good strategy. I have a few ideas, but we need to find him first. If he isn't here in York, we may need to use a different approach."

"That makes sense, but I cannot just drop in on him and expect him to welcome me with open arms."

"I know that, Matt. But once you do meet him and spend some time, a few hours or even a day or two, you should be able to find out something that will help us. I'm not naive enough to believe he will voluntarily tell you of his involvement, but the fact that we do find him here will confirm, as far as I'm concerned, that he bears watching." After another glass of wine, the two men went to their rooms for some needed rest after the ride from the fort.

The innkeeper hadn't heard of an Andrew Fletcher in York, but he did remember a Morgan who came from Virginia with his wife Lucinda. They lived in York for about two years. Morgan had started a brewery and became moderately successful, but he had left after the brewery burned down and ruined him financially. No, the innkeeper did not know where they were now, but Jock Mackenzie, who lived near the ruins of the brewery, might be able to help. The innkeeper hadn't seen Jock for a few years, but he thought he still lived there.

Zeb found the old log house about a quarter of a mile off the track. There was no evidence of a brewery that he could see, but it could easily have become overgrown by now with weeds and fast-growing bushes. An old bearded man, whose face told the story of a long and hard life, was splitting wood at the side of the house. The sharp crack of the axe on green wood seemed appropriate in this setting. Gnarled apple trees grew among weeds behind the cabin, and bees were busy flying around and landing among the rotting apples that had fallen the previous year. Old Jock eyed Zeb suspiciously as he approached but kept splitting wood with a strength that belied his seventy-odd years. Zeb made the appropriate greeting and managed to get the old man to stop splitting wood for a few moments. He told him he was in shipping with Matthew Prescott of Boston, and they were in York on business. Prescott was a friend of William Morgan and had heard through mutual acquaintances that Mr. Morgan was living in York. Since Mr. Prescott was busy at present and could not come with him, Zeb had come here to try and locate his old friend.

"Yes, sir, Captain Morgan used to live right over there." The old man pointed to a spot about one hundred yards away. It was a clearing only in the sense that no trees were there, but weeds grew among small mounds of what appeared to be rubble. "That's where the brewery was, and Captain Morgan lived on the other side. When the brewery burned down, his house went with it, and he lost everything. Damned fool didn't have no insurance. Folks told him to buy it, but he was too damned stubborn."

"Where is he now, Jock?"

"Don't really know for sure. I heard one fella say he thought the captain had gone to America and some place called Chester, Rochester, or something like that."

"Probably Rochester, Jock."

"Yep, that's it." He scratched his head and then his chest. Two small lice crawled out, and he quickly killed them between his thumb and first finger. "Damned things. Can't seem to get rid of 'em no matter how hard I try."

Zeb needed to confirm the information, so he asked Jock how he knew where Morgan had gone. "Old partner of Morgan's told me a couple of years ago when I met him while getting some supplies at the store. Told me he'd received a letter asking for a loan. I guess he wasn't doing too well. The captain told him he was in Rochester trying to find work as a stonemason."

Zeb thanked Jock and gave him some money for his trouble. If Morgan was in Rochester, they would have to meet Richards and Phillips and then continue the search. He wished he'd had this information before he sent them to Rochester to look for Wharton's map. Zeb went back to the inn hoping he would find Matthew there, but he had not yet returned.

Zeb went to the docks and asked about Matt. He was directed to a waterfront tavern, where he found him in conversation with the owner concerning the trade that would develop along the Great Lakes area now that the canal linked them to the Atlantic. Zeb joined them for a drink, and when an opportunity presented itself, he signaled Matthew to move to a table.

"Find anything about our man?"

"No," replied Matt. "No one knows where he went, but some did know about the brewery and the fire. How about you?"

"I found out where he went a few years ago, but not where he is now. Let's hope he hasn't moved again. He went to Rochester."

"Jesus—Phillips and Richards are there now."

CHAPTER 23

MELBOURNE'S HEAD HURT, AND HIS mouth felt like it was full of cotton. He was doing too much of this, but he couldn't help himself. He enjoyed the pleasures of the evening too much. Gaming and whores were becoming a preoccupation. He went into the adjoining room and splashed cold water on his face. The awakening was not as quick as usual, but the water helped focus his mind.

A meeting where he would finalize his plan was scheduled for that evening. The governor was a disgrace to the Masons. Melbourne would make sure that DeWitt Clinton was taken care of once and for all. The truly loyal Masons would then rally to those who represented the better path to power and glory. Once this was accomplished, Melbourne would be able to fulfill his true destiny.

His valet had placed his clothes in the proper location and helped him get dressed. He had much to do today. The meeting was scheduled to begin at 6:00 PM promptly, and he wanted everything to be ready. He hoped that idiot Wollstonecraft hadn't made a mess of the tasks he had been given. A very select group would be there for the meeting. A sumptuous dinner with plenty of wine and spirits would preface the business portion of the meeting. If all went well, everyone would have their assigned task for their role in the plot. The timing had to be perfect. The governor's barge would pass the selected location on a certain day in August or September. No survivors must be left. The escape routes would be selected for the men to make their way out of the area as quickly as possible. They still needed to select a location for the attack and move the needed weapons and equipment close by. Tonight's meeting was to be the last before the final one in a few weeks.

Approaches would then be made to the appropriate members of the upstate Masons, and they would fall into line. Melbourne smiled as he contemplated his plan. Yes, he had planned well, and the only problem might be Wollstonecraft. He would play a pivotal role, along with Morgan.

One of his immediate worries was the lack of news from Wharton on his orders to find and kill Cardwell. Nothing had been heard from Wharton for a while, and Melbourne grew worried. Wharton was one of his key men in the upstate area. He would send Wollstonecraft to Rochester to find out what happened. After the meeting tonight, everything had to occur on schedule. There could be no failures.

Melbourne left the consulate after breakfast and went to the Masonic lodge to check the room he had reserved and to make certain everything was in order. He was a perfectionist and expected everyone else to be one, as well. It was ironic. Clinton had a meeting of the Grand Lodge scheduled for later in the summer. What a boring affair that would be.

Zeb and Matt rode into Lewiston in the late afternoon. Richards and Phillips were probably not back from Rochester yet. When they entered the common room of the inn, they were surprised to see Phillips sitting alone and drinking ale.

Phillips had returned to wait for Zeb and Matt and then ride with them back to Rochester. Richards was watching the building where Wharton had lived. It was a rooming house across the street from a tavern. They thought it would be better to have all of them together to make the attempt. Two of them might be able to create a diversion, while the other two could enter Wharton's room and search for the map. Zeb told Phillips what they had learned in York.

"Well, I guess our next stop has to be Rochester for two reasons. We need to find Morgan, and we need to get our hands on that map."

"What about the peddler's wagon and the goods?" Phillips asked.

"We can leave that in Lockport," suggested Matthew. "There is a big barn on Sarah's relatives' property. I think they would let us use it if we thought of a good enough reason."

"Not a bad idea, Matt. No one would think to look for it there, and you get another chance to visit with the fair Sarah."

Phillips looked puzzled. Zeb explained about Matthew and Sarah and the journey to Lewiston from Boston. Phillips smiled and nodded his head. "Zeb told me you would be helping us, Matthew. I'm glad to see you have other interests besides shipping and finding Morgan."

Matt did not take offense at the remark. In fact, he had taken an instant liking to the young man.

"I guess there isn't much else to do here at the present time. Let's get some rest tonight and start for Rochester in the morning. We'll stop in Lockport long enough to hide the wagon, and then we'll ride on to Rochester and meet Richards."

Richards sat in a tavern diagonally across the street from the rooming house where Wharton had been staying. People came in and out all day. Rochester was a busy place. There were several carpenters, masons, freight drivers, and assorted tradesmen staying at the boardinghouse. It certainly wasn't a first-class place but seemed to be quite popular. Wharton probably used it just for that reason.

Phillips had left for Lewiston two days before, and Richards was getting bored. They had agreed not to take any chances, but he wanted to find out more about the boardinghouse. He rose from the table, left enough money for his bill, and left the tavern. He crossed the busy street and entered the boardinghouse. The owner had a small counter set up in the main sitting room on the first floor.

"Good day, young man. What can I do for you?"

"Good day to you, madam. I would like to inquire about a room. I plan to be in Rochester on business for a few days, and your establishment was recommended quite highly by a gentleman I met."

"You are quite fortunate. We just had a tenant move out yesterday. I would be glad to show the room to you."

Richards followed her upstairs and made a pretense of inspecting the room. He told her he would take it and paid her in advance. He asked her if she had a tenant named Simon Wharton, and she replied in the affirmative. "Mr. Wharton is a fine gentlemen and away on business at present, but he should be returning any day now." Richards chuckled inwardly. A mental picture of Wharton locked up in the cell at Fort Niagara appeared.

"Mr. Wharton is a business acquaintance and told me he lived in this area."

"He certainly does. He is staying in the room right down the hall." She pointed to the room at the head of the stairs. Richards told her he had to get his luggage. He would stay there tonight and try to get in Wharton's room at the earliest opportunity.

Later that evening, after it was sufficiently dark, Richards took advantage of a lull in traffic within the boardinghouse to enter Wharton's room. He picked the lock cleanly and entered without anyone seeing him. The room was dark except for the ambient light coming in the window from the tavern lights across the street. It was pretty much the same as his room. There was a bed, dresser, dry sink with a pitcher and bowl for washing, and a chamber pot under the bed. There was also a locked trunk at the foot of his bed.

Richards listened for a moment to be sure no one was in the hall and began searching the room. There was just enough light to see. The dresser drawers were full of clothes, a few pamphlets, and some advertisements torn out of the newspaper. There was no map. It must be in the trunk. He worked on the lock for several moments before it gave in to his expert lock picks. The trunk contained Wharton's Masonic clothes, some books, clothing, and a pair of pistols. Tucked into the rear corner was an oilskin pouch tied with some string. He opened the oilskin and found a map. It was quite well done and showed the Erie Canal from Buffalo to Rochester with all the towns, bridges, locks, and other important features included. There was a red mark between Albion and Medina. No notation was made, but Richards felt he had found what they were looking for. He decided to take the map with him and copy it. They could put it back before Wharton's confederates discovered that it was gone.

Just as Richards tucked the map into his inside pocket, he heard a floorboard creak outside the door in the hall. He crawled under the bed. He pulled a knife from his boot. He heard the sound of a key in the lock, followed by the door slowly opening. Richards hoped there wasn't more than one. At least then he'd have a chance. The light from a dim lamp illuminated the room. *My God*, thought Richards, *it's the landlady*. He lay very still and waited. She walked around the room very slowly and stopped in front of the trunk. Fortunately, he had closed and locked it before diving under the bed. She stayed a few more moments and then left. Richards waited about ten minutes before crawling out from under the bed. This would be the first time he had to pick a lock to get out of a room. His next stop was the tavern across the street for a much-needed drink.

CHAPTER 24

MELBOURNE AND WOLLSTONECRAFT WERE ENJOYING a cognac in the consulate after the meeting in the Masonic lodge. It was late, but Melbourne did not feel like going to bed, and he was still in an agitated state. All had gone according to his expectations, and the plan was now entering the final preparation stage. He had sent Morgan back to his hotel and told him to leave on the early steamer to Albany and then take the stage to Batavia. He gave him enough money to cover his expenses back home. His thoughts returned to the meeting.

He had selected twenty men for the task, including Wollstonecraft, Morgan, and Wharton. He had a duplicate of the map prepared by Wharton, and it was good. Melbourne had served with his regiment in both the Napoleonic Wars and against the Americans in what they liked to call the War of 1812. He knew that planning was everything. He also knew from bitter experience that the best plans could fail if those entrusted to carry them out did not do their duty. Consequently, he handpicked all of the men. Some were from England, and the rest were Americans willing to throw in their lot with Melbourne. Some had military experience, while others had experience that came from being poor and forced to break the law to survive. None of them were gentlemen.

He had organized the group into smaller units. One would handle the cannons. Another group would take care of finding a place to stay just before the attack. The man on the scene, Morgan, had helped hide the muskets and powder. Morgan had explained how this was done, and there were comments of approval from the group. They needed to find a barn or stable near the site of the attack and then transport the muskets and powder there from the cabin in Canandaigua. All this would be accomplished, but planning was important, and details were the backbone of the plan. Morgan had assured Melbourne that he was working on the diversion they had discussed. It would certainly gain a lot of attention if Morgan could complete it in time.

The map Wharton prepared was excellent. It showed every village, bridge, lock, and type of terrain the Erie Canal flowed through from Buffalo to Rochester. Wharton had told him this was the only other copy. The men had their instructions and would travel to the area by various means. Some would take the coach routes, some the Hudson River to Albany and then via the canal to Rochester, and the rest would travel by horseback. Melbourne had enough money from his backers to support the operation. If it worked, it would be an excellent investment.

"You realize we have not heard from Wharton? His latest communication should have been in my hands last week. It may be nothing, but I want you to find him and report back to me as to what is going on up there. That filthy Jew, Cardwell, should be dead. If he isn't, we have to find him and finish the job. You must do that for me if he is still in the area while you are there. Also, stop to see Morgan and find out more about his plan for the diversion. I'm curious. His brain appears to work, but I don't think it operates at a suitable level of intelligence."

"I don't trust that bastard Morgan. He's an arrogant son of a bitch. Give me the command, and I'll take care of him as well as Cardwell. By the way, what makes you think Cardwell is a Jew?"

"We have done our research on Mr. Cardwell. His family was among those forced to flee Spain during the early years of the Inquisition. We traced them to Italy, North Africa, and then to New York. He thinks no one knows about his Jew identity, but he is very mistaken. We have highly placed sources in the federal government who are preparing to inform the president about Cardwell. Or should I say, Mr. David Isaacson. Don't become overly anxious; you will have the opportunity soon enough. Even if you don't manage to kill Cardwell, once the president finds out he is a Jew, he is through with his paltry government position. The main plan must be carried out, as well as the plans within the plan."

"What do you mean?"

"All in due time, my friend. All in due time."

"When do you want me to leave?"

"Take this"—he handed Wollstonecraft a purse with gold coins—"and use it for traveling expenses and whatever else you may need. Be prudent with your desires for spirits and women. I want you to leave as soon as you can arrange it. Take the coach to Rochester, and start inquiries as to Wharton's whereabouts. Start with the rooming house. If you don't find him in two weeks, send me a message, and I'll get further instructions to you. Don't do anything until you hear from me. Is that understood?"

"Yes, sir." Wollstonecraft gave Melbourne his best smile while trying to decide how he would kill him when he had the chance.

Melbourne dismissed Wollstonecraft and lingered over his cognac. He had a disquieting sense that something was wrong even though everything seemed to be going so well. Maybe it was just his imagination, but he couldn't help it. It might just be too many late nights, too much wine, and too many women. On the other hand, his gut feelings had rarely been wrong. There was nothing he could do about it except see to it that the plan was carried out and make sure Wollstonecraft did his job. He began to review his plan for the attempt on Clinton as well as the other surprise he had in store for President Adams. If the president thought Cardwell and his cohorts could stop him, he was badly mistaken.

CHAPTER 25

ZEB, MATT, AND PHILLIPS ARRIVED in Rochester during the afternoon. They went to the tavern agreed upon as the meeting place and found Richards seated at a table in the rear. Richards related the events of the previous days and showed them the map. Zeb was impressed. It was drawn to scale and included a great deal of detail. The mark just to the west of Oak Orchard Creek was the piece of information they needed to identify the location of the attack. All they needed now was the date and time, and they still had to locate Morgan as directed by the president. This was going to complicate matters. Zeb would have to split up his team in order to work on both problems.

He spoke softly in order not to be overhead by anyone in the tavern. "Gentlemen, we have to accomplish a great deal in the next few weeks. First, we must try to spoil Melbourne's plan to kill the governor. Second, we need to find Morgan. We need to divide our forces and work on both problems at the same time. Matt and I will continue the search for Morgan. I want Richards and Phillips to go to Albany and see the governor. Tell what we have learned about the plot and try to talk him out of going."

"But, Zeb," Richards said, "what if something happens here and we are gone? You two will be vulnerable if there is another attempt on you. I don't think Wharton was the last one who will try to have you killed. Melbourne has you targeted and won't give up until he knows you are dead."

"That's all right, Richards. I can take care of myself. I don't believe anything is going to happen for a while. We know the governor plans a trip here in late August or early September. The plot cannot take place until then. This gives us time to split our forces. Hopefully we will find out more concerning the plot and locate Morgan."

Phillips spoke this time. "I have a gut feeling that Wharton may have been lying to us. I know he sounded convincing, but think about it. What if the map Richards found was a copy and not the original? We know Melbourne is having a meeting in New York to discuss the plan with his cronies. Why couldn't the map be in New York right now?"

"There is only one way to find out. Richards and Phillips, you return to Fort Niagara and interrogate Wharton again. Be very convincing, but don't kill him. We may still have use for him yet. If he was lying, and Melbourne has the map, then the copy Richards found may be needed by someone up here in the area. We had better copy it and return it to Wharton's room right away before someone comes back and looks for it. Melbourne still doesn't know what happened to Wharton, but he should be worried by now. After you find out, return here and leave a message at the hotel with the usual meeting instructions. While you are gone, Matt and I will make inquiries about Morgan. But before you go, let's get that map copied and back into Wharton's room across the street."

Matt spoke. "Zeb, I'll copy that map. I have some background in mapmaking from the shipping business. I don't see why I should not be able to copy a map with a canal and some bridges."

They all laughed. "All right, Matt. Let's find some paper, ink, and a pen and get you started. I suggest we do it in a place less conspicuous. Let's rent a couple of rooms in that boardinghouse we saw near the river and get to work. After Matt finishes, we'll make our plans for this evening and return the copy Richards borrowed."

The evening was cool for June, and the clouds promised rain by the next day. Richards and Phillips went inside the rooming house where Richards had rented the room from Mrs. Brown. They went into his room and lit a candle so the room would appear to be occupied. They waited until the hallway was empty, slipped out the door, and went down the hall to Wharton's room. Phillips waited in the hallway, and Richards entered the room once again after deftly picking the lock. He went right to the trunk. It was open. He raised the lid and found all the belongings in complete disarray. Someone had been looking for the map. Now what should he do? Should he put the map back or keep it? He quickly decided the best course was to return it. He slid the map into the trunk and positioned it in the corner under the Masonic robes. Maybe the individual would return and find it there and think they had missed it in the initial search. He left the room, locked the door, and signaled to Phillips for them to leave quickly. They returned to the rooming house by the river.

"Zeb, I don't know what is going on, but someone has been searching that room. The trunk was a mess, but nothing seemed to be missing. I didn't even bother to check the dresser, but I bet that has been searched, as well. Someone was looking for that map. Now I'm not sure if Melbourne has a copy or not."

"The only way we are going to find out is to talk to Wharton. I want you and Phillips to leave for Fort Niagara in the morning. I'll give you a letter for Seth giving instructions for you to be left alone to interrogate Wharton. Take whatever you need from our supplies. Matthew and I will start looking for Morgan tomorrow."

As the previous evening had promised, early morning rain fell steadily, and a cool wind blew off the lake. Richards and Phillips followed the path along the river that connected with the road that went all the way to Lewiston. They urged their horses along, and clods of mud flew behind them. They stopped to rest their horses and eat some food at an inn before resuming their ride. They were tired, wet, and eager for a warm fire when they finally arrived at the fort.

Seth read the letter from Zeb and said, "You boys have your work cut out for you. Mr. Wharton is one of the meanest and nastiest cusses I have ever had in confinement. Before you start your work, you had better get warm and let those wet clothes dry out."

They were in complete agreement. A warm fire, some hot food, and dry clothes seemed about the most important things in the world at that moment. Richards told Seth what they would need when they interrogated Wharton. Seth's eyebrows rose in a silent question, but he agreed to provide the items.

They found Wharton lying on his bunk. The lantern threw shadows on the walls of the cell, and the smell of a fire from the empty cell next door filled the air. Wharton rose to a sitting position when they entered. He did not look very happy to see them.

"Well, Simon, how do you like your new accommodations?" Richards asked him.

"You two bastards again. I suppose you are here to release me? No, probably not. What the hell do you want?"

"We need some information, Simon," replied Richards. Phillips moved quickly behind Wharton and slipped a rope around his neck. Richards moved in and helped Phillips tie Wharton's hands behind his back and then tied his feet together. They tied the rope from his hands to the loop around his neck. It was a most uncomfortable position, and any movement of the hands resulted in a tightening of the rope around his neck. Wharton swore several oaths.

Phillips went to the next cell to get the iron bucket with the hot coals and iron rods. The ends had been sitting in the fire for over an hour and were now glowing red from the heat. Wharton's eyes followed Phillips as he entered the cell.

Richards spoke again. "We were thinking, Simon. The last conversation we had in Lewiston was quite interesting, but we are not at all certain you were a good boy and told us the truth. Now, about the map you drew ... how many copies were there?"

"I told you. Only one. It is to be sent to Melbourne in New York for his meeting."

"Now, Simon, a map as important as that—and you had only one copy?"

"Yes, you bastard, only one."

Richards nodded to Phillips. Phillips pulled one of the iron rods from the bucket. It was so hot that they had several layers of leather around the end to protect their hands. "I'm giving you one more chance to tell the truth, Simon, or I will start making your face look much uglier than it does already. What do you say?"

"You are bluffing. You wouldn't dare do this. This is torture, pure and simple. I'm on United States government property."

Richards touched the glowing tip of the iron rod to Wharton's cheek with such a quick and practiced move that Wharton was screaming from the pain before his eyes registered the movement.

"You fucking bastards!" Wharton yelled. Richards moved quickly again, and an identical mark appeared just below the first. Wharton screamed again. "All right, all right! I'll tell you the truth. Don't burn me again. I didn't tell you everything. Yes, the map has been sent to New York with one of Melbourne's men. His name is Wollstonecraft, and he is Melbourne's assistant. Melbourne has the map by now and also is probably quite concerned about why he hasn't heard from me."

"Simon, you have been a bad boy. You lied to us about the map. Is there anything else you want to tell us, or do I have to give you matching marks on your other cheek?"

Wharton looked vanquished. "There is something else. Wollstonecraft has been meeting with a man who lives in the area. I don't know where he lives, but he said he met him in Canandaigua. This man is part of the plan. I don't know what his role is. Melbourne likes to keep us in the dark. All I remember is that Wollstonecraft said the man did some work on the aqueduct in Rochester that carries the Erie Canal over the Genesee River. He is a stonemason and had done work for Melbourne and his associates before. That's all I know, I swear it on my mother's grave."

"Hell, Wharton, you'd swear on anybody's grave if you thought it would save your neck. You had better be telling the truth. If I find out you lied to us, my next visit will include more than iron rods and rope."

Phillips took the iron kettle and rods out of the cell. They untied Wharton and left him on the bunk. They gave instructions to the jailer to have someone put unguent on Wharton's burns. By the time they had a drink with Seth and got to bed, it was past midnight. It would be another long day of travel tomorrow. A warm, sunny day would be most welcome.

Zeb and Matt had started their search for Morgan at some of the local businesses along the canal. They found Rochester to be a booming flour-milling village. The natural power obtained from the falls of the Genesee River turned waterwheels and grinding stones in many mills. The recently completed canal had opened an entirely new method of shipping flour to the settled East and the rapidly growing regions in the West. This was going to make some citizens of Rochester very rich.

Their first luck occurred at the agency that had hired men to work on the canal when it came through Rochester. The greatest engineering accomplishment for the Rochester section was the construction of a stone aqueduct to carry the water of the Erie Canal over the Genesee River. They had a list of individuals whom they had hired for the construction of the aqueduct, and Morgan's name was on the list.

"Do you have an address for Mr. Morgan?" Zeb asked, trying to contain his excitement.

"No, but most of the workers stayed in the rooming houses near the river. They are still pretty much all there. One or two have burned down in the past year. If you inquire at these boardinghouses, you should find someone who knew him."

They questioned the proprietors of six rooming houses and were becoming discouraged. At the seventh, their luck changed. "Yes, we had a Mr. Morgan staying here. His first name was William, and he was a stonemason by trade. He worked on the aqueduct but left right after it was finished." The landlady smiled as she told them.

"Could you describe him to us?" Matt asked.

"Yes. He was of medium height, solidly built, clean shaven, and he liked to dress well. He seemed quite the dapper gent. He even joined the newly formed Masonic lodge. One of his friends, a Mr. Whitney, sponsored him for the Wells Lodge."

"Do you know where Mr. Morgan is now?"

"Can't say as I do. The last I seen him was after the aqueduct was finished. I think he had some sort of argument or misunderstanding with Mr. Whitney; at least that's what I heard. Mr. Morgan left Rochester, and that was the last I seen of him."

"Do you know where we may find Mr. Whitney?"

"Oh, yes. Mr. Whitney worked on the aqueduct with Mr. Morgan. He still lives here but is at work at the moment. If you come back after six, you will find him in the tavern across the street having supper. He is a short man and has spectacles for reading. The tavern owner, Joshua Simmons, will be glad to introduce you."

Zeb and Matt went to the tavern a few minutes after six. They asked for Joshua Simmons and found him in the kitchen checking on the stew that was bubbling in the iron pot hanging over the coals in the large kitchen fireplace. The smell was wonderful and made both of them hungry. Simmons was a friendly fellow with a florid complexion and thinning hair. He pointed out Mr. Whitney to them. Simmons did the introductions and returned to the kitchen to personally see to it that Zeb and Matt received an ample portion of stew and a tankard of ale.

Whitney was dressed in work clothes and was halfway through a bowl of stew. He asked them to please sit down and tell him what they needed to know. Matthew explained that he was a friend of William Morgan and had served with him during the last war. They had not seen each other for some time. Since Matt happened to be in the area on business, he was trying to locate Morgan. He explained that he had traveled the new canal to Lockport and then gone to York in Canada based on his last knowledge of Morgan's place of residence. His inquiries had led him back to Rochester. He explained that Zeb was a business partner, and they had some time during their stay to find Morgan and pay him a visit. Matt mentioned they had been told that Morgan worked on the aqueduct over the Genesee River and that he had worked with Whitney.

"Yes," said Whitney. "I know Mr. Morgan. We did work on the aqueduct together. It was quite a feat of engineering. It is over eight hundred feet in length, has nine Roman arches, and is made from the red freestone found in such plenty near the canal in this part of the state. I imagine a great many structures will be made from this stone. It took two years to build and was finished in 1823. Last June was a big event for us. The Marquis de Lafayette traveled the canal to Rochester on a grand tour. In October, Governor Clinton and his flotilla traveled the canal from Buffalo to celebrate the official opening. The governor traveled on the *Seneca Chief*. That was something to see. The canal is putting Rochester on the map and making a lot of money for the owners of our flour mills. Our population has grown to nearly eight thousand at present. Ten years ago, there were only three hundred some people living here. My apologies, gentlemen. I'm getting off our topic of conversation. Yes, William Morgan was a good stonemason and worked hard on the project with the others. We lived in the same rooming house. Morgan has a wife named Lucinda and two children."

Matt inquired cautiously, "How has he been? Is he happy as a family man?"

"Oh, yes. He is devoted to his family. He even joined the local Masonic lodge with my sponsorship and was working his way through the various degrees until something happened. He became very disgruntled but would not tell me why."

Matt glanced briefly at Zeb and tried to ask the next question as casually as he could. "Do you know where he is now? I would certainly like to visit him and his family if he is still in the area."

"Oh, yes. After he became upset about something with the Masons at the lodge, he moved his family to Batavia. It's not too far from here. The coach route passes right through Batavia on the way to Buffalo. I do not know where he lives, but since the village is small, it should not be too difficult to find him."

The three men were silent for a few moments and concentrated on their stew and tankards of ale. Whitney told them if they had some time, they should visit some of the various sites along the canal, especially the aqueduct and the locks at Lockport. Zeb told him that was a good idea and that they certainly would. Matt thanked Whitney for the information and wished him well. They finished their meal and paid for all three dinners. They stopped back in the kitchen and thanked the smiling Joshua Simmons for the excellent stew and his introduction to Mr. Whitney. On their way out, Joshua told them if they ever needed anything else while in Rochester to see him and he would be most pleased to assist them. They thanked him again and left the tavern.

They returned to the rooming house and found two very tired and dirty characters waiting for them. Zeb looked at Richards and Phillips and said, "Before you tell me anything, take a bath and get that damned stink off you. You both smell like a sweaty horse that has rolled in mud and manure."

"We already did. We can't stand our own smell, either."

When Richards and Phillips returned, clean and presentable, they all sat down to exchange information. Zeb asked Phillips to tell them what they found out from Wharton.

"We were right about Wharton. He did lie to us. Melbourne has the map and is making final plans for the plot against Clinton. At least we know where it is. I think it was the right thing to do to put the map back in Wharton's room. Even though the person looking for it found it missing, they may return and find it there and think they overlooked it."

Richards spoke next. "Zeb, if Melbourne has the map and the final plans are being made for the attack on Clinton, we might not be in time."

"I don't think so. The information we have is that Clinton plans to come upstate on the canal in late August or early September to make some political speeches and check on his baby, the canal. This should give us enough time to prepare countermoves once we find out the date and time. Even if we don't find the exact date, we can take measures to protect Clinton and watch for an attack. What we need to do now is continue with our intent to split up and travel to Albany as planned. Take the next available coach from here and visit our friend Peter—have him arrange a meeting with the governor. Peter has more influence than he lets on. Tell Clinton what we know and ask him to consider canceling or delaying his trip. If he does not agree to that, convince him that we should have some of our men travel with him for his own protection. While you are in Albany, Matt and I will go to Batavia and visit Morgan."

Chapter 26

Richards and Phillips left for Albany on the early-morning coach. At breakfast before they left, Zeb instructed them to return to Rochester and not to come to Batavia. They were to leave a message at the Rochester House Hotel, and Zeb would check periodically until he learned they were back.

After the two men left, Zeb wrote a brief report in code for President Adams. He had been sending him reports through a prearranged intermediary to keep the president informed as to his progress. If the president needed to contact him, Zeb had given instructions for the message to be left at the post office in Rochester. He had paid a visit to the post office the previous day and rented a private mailbox. He would need to check that at least once a week.

The coach traveled at a moderate but bumpy pace along the post road to Albany. Richards and Phillips were not enjoying the trip; they preferred their horses, but the coach was direct and made pretty good time. When they were about halfway between Canandaigua and Geneva, another coach passed them in the opposite direction, and Phillips happened to glance over. His face went pale; Wollstonecraft was traveling in the other coach. Melbourne must have sent him to check on Wharton. He nudged Richards awake when they stopped in Canandaigua.

"I just saw that bastard Wollstonecraft in a coach headed in the other direction a few miles back. I hope to hell he doesn't run into Zeb and Matthew. If he sees Zeb, they are in for trouble. I only hope Wollstonecraft is in the area to check on Wharton. Melbourne must be worried and sent his attack hound to sniff out Wharton. We should go back and warn Zeb."

"We can't do that. Zeb told us not to worry about him and Matthew. We have to take him at his word. We need to warn Governor Clinton about the plot on his life, and I think we should continue."

"I don't like it, Richards. You don't know how strong that son of a bitch is. He almost killed Zeb in New York."

"Zeb can take care of himself and has done pretty well considering all the close calls he has had over the years."

"I guess we have to trust him to take care of himself. Anyway, there is no certainty Wollstonecraft will even run into them."

When they arrived in Albany, they went directly to Peter's office. Peter was out for a few minutes but would be right back. When he returned, he was surprised to see them. "Well, look who is here. I haven't seen you, Phillips, in several weeks. What brings you here this time?"

"Remember what we talked about the last time, Peter?"

"Yes, you are always pumping me about the political situation in Albany, and I always talk too much."

"That's what we like about you, Peter. You are a good friend and not stingy with information. This time, it isn't information we are after, but something else. Can you get us in to see the governor?"

"And why would the likes of you two want to see the governor? Come to think of it, why would the governor even consent to see you?"

"This is serious, Peter. Clinton plans to travel upstate later in the summer, doesn't he?"

"How the hell do you know that?"

"Never mind. It's true, isn't it?"

"Yes. He plans to go late in August or sometime around then, depending on his schedule."

"Peter, we have reason to believe there will be an attempt on his life. We know the location, but not the exact timing. We want to warn him and ask him to consider changing his plan. Will you set up a meeting for us?"

Peter was shocked. He looked like he had seen a ghost. Who would want to kill Clinton after what he had done for the state and the country? The canal would open the West to settlement and trade. The governor was a hero. "Who plans on doing this?"

"We only know about a few individuals who are involved but have no definite proof. We have overheard conversations and interrogated some individuals. We are still gathering more information but know enough to recognize it as a real threat. We want to convince him to cancel the trip or at least offer him some protection."

"You know I will help in whatever manner I am able." The color started to return to Peter's face, but he was still shaken. "Let me see what I can arrange for later in the day. The governor is in Albany for the next few days before he goes to his country home for part of the summer. Come back at four thirty, and I'll try to have the meeting arranged by then."

"Thank you, Peter."

Matt and Zeb traveled by coach. They didn't feel they would need horses in Batavia since Rochester was only a brief coach ride away. They agreed on what Matt's story would be when he found Morgan. If fact, they had used it already. Matt was traveling on business along the canal, and he was considering expanding his shipping business to include the Great Lakes. The opening of the canal had tremendous possibilities, and he wanted to take advantage of them. He wanted to see his old friend again and had managed to find him in Batavia. They also agreed that Zeb would not go with him to see Morgan but would stay at one of the stops to the east of Batavia. Matthew would continue alone. Morgan knew Matt from the war and should have no reason to suspect his story as anything other than the truth. Matt would stay as long as required. If he found anything of importance, he would send a message to Zeb or tell him in person.

Matt had intended to tell Zeb about the information his father had found regarding Morgan. If it were true, Morgan was Matt's uncle. Matt's father and Morgan had been separated when they were young; Morgan was sent to live with a family in England, and Matt's father was sent to live with a family in Boston. The family would have been Matt's grandparents. He could not understand why his father did not tell him this until just before he died, but he was glad he did. Matt's problem now was that not only must he finally tell Zeb, but he needed to figure out how to use this to their advantage in convincing Morgan to return to Washington with them.

"Before I go on to Batavia, I need to tell you something."

"This must be serious from the look you are giving me."

"I need to apologize for not telling you this sooner, but it never seemed to be the right moment."

"Just tell me, Matt."

"All right. Just before my father died, he told me that my grandparents had adopted him when he was young. He came from a family in Virginia. Apparently, the mother was a widow and could not care for her two sons. She sent one to England and the other to Boston. The one who went to Boston was my father. The other son was sent to England. My father said his name was William Morgan."

"Matt, do you realize what you are saying?"

"Yes, of course. Morgan is my uncle."

"How good was the information your father had regarding this matter?"

"He said he was pretty certain it was true."

"If Morgan is your uncle, this could complicate our business here."

"He does not know it, and when we were in the war together, I did not know it, either."

"True, but you have a blood relationship with him. Will you still be able to carry out your part of this, even if it means Morgan is convicted of spying and spends the rest of his life in a federal prison?"

"I can live with that, Zeb. I can't forgive him for being a British spy. President Adams said he did not plan to ask for the death penalty. This makes it a little easier for me. I don't think I could help capture him and be responsible for his execution."

"At least you are being honest about it. I wish you would have told me sooner, but now that you have, we need to figure out how to use this. In fact, I think this might turn out to be an advantage. If necessary, you can tell him what your father discovered, and this may encourage him to be more open with you and possibly let something slip about the plot. I don't think we should count on it, but it could happen."

"Do you still want me to go to Batavia alone to find Morgan?"

"Of course. We will stay with our current plan. You use your judgment whether or not to tell Morgan about the family connection."

The coach made a stop in Caledonia, and Zeb decided to get off there and stay at the local inn. It was a small village, and he would have to find some way to spend the time waiting for Matt. If Matt did not return in a few days, he would need to travel to Rochester and check the mailbox. Hopefully he would find something to do to fill the time that was more interesting than walking around a small village or staring at the four walls of his room.

Matt arrived in Batavia after a brief stop in LeRoy. It was a small village, so it should not be too difficult to find Morgan. He found a room at the Eagle Tavern. After settling in, he went to the common room and asked for Morgan. Everyone knew Morgan. He could be found at the local newspaper, the *Republican Advocate*, or one of the local taverns, including the Old Snake Den. He lived with his wife and two children in a small house on the southern edge of the village. Matt thanked them and walked to the newspaper office.

As he entered, his arrival was announced by the loud jingling of a bell attached to the top of the door. A man appeared in a doorway that led to the area where the printing press was located. His hands were black with printer's ink, and he wore Ben Franklin glasses and an ink-stained cap. "May I help you, sir?"

Matt told him he was an old friend of William Morgan and happened to be in the area on business and wanted to pay him a visit.

"My name is David Miller. William Morgan and I are business partners. William decided to try the newspaper business and bought in as a partner. I do most of the work, and he helps out occasionally. I guess his family left him some money, so he is able to get along, but it cannot be too much since he doesn't live very extravagantly. He isn't here right now, but you should find him at home. He lives in the last house on South Street across the creek. His place will be the last one."

Matt thanked David Miller and told him he hoped to see him again before his visit was over. He left the newspaper office and headed back to Main Street. It was a pleasant day, and he decided to take a walk around the village before finding Morgan's house. There was quite a bit of activity, and the local stores and shops appeared busy. He passed an interesting building along the creek the locals called the Tonawanda. It was a solid stone structure with a sign in front indicating it to be the Holland Land Company Office. He would have to ask Morgan about that. Across the street was a beautiful mansion that a passerby told him belonged to Joseph Ellicott, the famous agent for the Holland Land Company. He noticed other mansions during his walk and discovered that they were the Fisher Mansion on Main Street, the Trumbull Cary Mansion to the east, and one that had a great deal of land. This was the Mix House.

He went back down Main Street, crossed the creek, and followed South Street to the last house. He knocked on the door, and it opened slightly. He could hear a baby crying, and a small child played with some wooden blocks a few feet inside the doorway. A young woman answered the door. Matthew thought he must have the wrong house.

"How may I help you, sir?" She looked tired, and the baby fussed in her arms. From the smell of the child, he needed to be changed.

Matt introduced himself and briefly explained why he was in Batavia. She opened the door and let him in. "I am certain William will be very pleased to see you, Mr. Prescott. My name is Lucinda Morgan, and these are my children. This little one is Benjamin, and the toddler over there on the floor is Daniel. As you may have noticed, they keep me pretty busy. Are you married, Mr. Prescott?"

"No, I am not, Mrs. Morgan. Please, call me Matt. Is your husband at home?"

"He was here a short time ago but went to visit with some of his friends at Ganson's Tavern in LeRoy. He should be back home for supper. Why don't you join us for supper?"

"Thank you, Mrs. Morgan. I would be most delighted to have supper with you and William. I need to finish settling in at the inn, and then I'll come back. Would six be all right?"

"That would be fine. We'll look forward to seeing you then."

Matt left Morgan's house and returned to the inn. He decided to take nap for a couple of hours and catch up on some needed rest.

CHAPTER 27

PETER WAS WAITING IN HIS office when Richards and Phillips returned in the afternoon. He had good news for them. Governor Clinton had agreed to see them within the hour. They were to go with Peter to the governor's office for the meeting.

"I told you he would probably not believe you, and he certainly gave me that impression when I told him. However, he is a reasonable man and wants to talk to you face-to-face."

"Thank you, Peter. We certainly appreciate your help," replied Richards.

They followed Peter to the governor's office and waited while Peter went in to announce their arrival. His head appeared in the doorway in a few moments, and he motioned them to come in. The office was not at all ostentatious as they had expected. Governor Clinton was seated behind a simple walnut desk in a comfortable chair. There was little furniture in the room. He had two bookcases and a writing table. There were several paintings and sketches of the recently completed canal on his walls. "Welcome to Albany, gentlemen. Please have a seat. Peter, see if you can find some refreshment for our guests."

Peter scurried from the room and came back with a tray, four glasses, and a bottle of brandy. He poured drinks for everyone, sat down, and waited for Governor Clinton to continue.

"Peter has told me a very disturbing story. You believe there is a plot to kill me on my supposedly secret trip on the canal later this summer. I must be frank with you, gentlemen. I find this difficult to believe, but I am willing to hear what you have to say. I have a great deal of respect for President Adams, as well as Zeb Cardwell and his agents."

Richards acted as the spokesman. "Governor, we have discovered a plan to kill you at a point on the canal west of the Oak Orchard River, which is about halfway between Rochester and Lockport. We have reason to believe the attempt will be made for political reasons, but that is still speculation on our part at this point."

"Who plans to do this, young man?"

"This is the strange part. A man who works in the British consulate in New York is the leader of the plot. His name is Melbourne."

"My God, that cannot be! Melbourne is a respected member of the diplomatic community and a fellow Mason. We have spoken on several occasions. This is preposterous. Your information must be wrong."

"I know this is difficult for you to believe, Governor Clinton, but our information is pretty reliable. In fact, people have been killed in an attempt to hide the plot from us. Mr. Melbourne is more than he appears to be among political and diplomatic circles. We are seeking other individuals in order to obtain more information, and we do not want him to know how much we have found out."

"I have people who can protect me on this trip. Out of respect for you and President Adams, I will not mention this to anyone, of course."

"We would urge you most fervently, Governor Clinton, to allow us to provide a discreet presence during your trip in order to offer additional protection."

"That will not be necessary. I have my people, and they will be sufficient. I really think this is all preposterous, but being a practical man, I will take your advice under consideration and keep an eye on Mr. Melbourne."

"Thank you, Governor. We appreciate your taking time from your busy schedule to meet with us."

The governor nodded and rose from his chair, a signal for everyone to leave. He shook hands with Phillips and Richards. Peter led them from the building and back to his smaller office.

Richards was the first to speak. "Thank you for arranging the meeting with Governor Clinton. I know this whole thing must seem hard to believe from his point of view, but he has not gone through the events of the past several weeks we have experienced. This plot is real, and Melbourne intends to kill the governor. We intend to prevent this from taking place."

"If it is any satisfaction for you, I believe you. I will try to speak to the governor again and remind him of this meeting and your warning. He is a strong-willed man and does not like people telling him what to do, but he will listen to reason if the facts are presented to him in a logical manner."

"Well, we don't have all the facts and details yet, Peter, but we know this is going to happen. We have to get back to Rochester, so we will say good-bye and get a good night's sleep before we subject our backs to the discomfort of the coach ride again." They left Peter and returned to the hotel to get some sleep before their coach left early the next morning.

PART 3

CHAPTER 28

MATTHEW RETURNED TO MORGAN'S HOME that evening as previously agreed. This time, his knock on the door was answered by Morgan himself. He appeared very glad to see Matthew, and his smile seemed quite genuine. Matthew noticed that Morgan had gained some weight and lost some hair since the war.

"Well, I'll be damned. If it isn't Matthew Prescott in the flesh. How long has it been? I don't think we have seen each other since about 1814. You don't look a day older. Come in, come in." Matthew knew this was not true since twelve years had passed, and they both looked older. He didn't argue with Morgan.

"William, it is good to see you, as well, especially since we lost touch with each other, and the chances were pretty good our paths would never cross again." Morgan's face turned serious for only a split second, but enough for Matthew to notice. Matthew wondered if he suspected anything. Given his involvement in the plot to kill Governor Clinton, he should be suspicious. "It is merely by luck that I found you. I am traveling up your famous canal to check out the business possibilities for my shipping company in Boston. We think the trade with the interior will increase rapidly and result in the flow of raw materials and agricultural products eastward on the canal to Albany and then down the Hudson to New York City. It will also allow goods to be shipped westward to your part of the state and further west of Buffalo into Ohio. The other new settlements are certain to follow. We are considering opening an office in Buffalo. When I was in Rochester, I was talking with a fellow—I can't remember his name—who worked on the construction of the aqueduct. We were talking about the Battle of New Orleans, and I mentioned the names of some of the men I served with, including yours. He told me you had worked on the aqueduct with him and then moved to Batavia. So I decided to take a side trip and visit you."

"What did the man say about me?"

"He told me that you were a good mason and worked hard on the aqueduct in spite of some of the poor foremen you had to work under."

Morgan seemed to accept Matthew's story and invited him to sit down. "Matthew, this house is pretty basic, but we call it home."

"It is very nice, William. I realize this is not Boston or New York. In fact, someone told me earlier today that this village has only been in existence since around the turn of the century."

"Yes. Batavia is located at the junction of two major Indian trails. The Albany to Buffalo trail is our main street, and the other trail came from the south and goes northward to Lake Ontario. The Indians used to call Batavia 'Big Bend' after the sharp turn the Tonawanda makes from a northward flow to a more westward one."

"I noticed a stone building with a sign called the Holland Land Company when I took a walk earlier today. What is that all about?"

"That is the main office for the company that has been selling the land in this part of the state. The land agent was Mr. Joseph Ellicott, and his associate was Mr. Paulo Busti. They must have been two pretty busy fellows. I have heard that Mr. Ellicott is in New York City for a rest. This is indeed a very interesting community. May I give you a quick summary of our little village?"

"Of course, I'd like to hear more about Batavia."

"I have only been here for three years but find their recent history quite fascinating. Joseph Ellicott, as agent for the Holland Land Company, could not sell off the lands until the Indian claim was settled. This was done in 1797 at the Big Tree Treaty. Chief Red Jacket represented the Indians at that meeting. Once the claim was relinquished by the Indians, Joseph Ellicott was free to start selling parcels of land in the purchase. He named the little settlement Batavia around 1801, and it began to attract new settlers. Mr. James Brisbane was the first merchant to open a store, and others followed. Most of the early log structures have been replaced by homes built from lumber cut in our mill. We have a post office and became an incorporated village in 1823. Our village is growing and should prove to be an important one in this part of the state."

"I imagine the canal will help you grow."

"We certainly hope so, but we would have been more pleased if the canal had been routed closer to us."

Matthew decided to take a chance and change the subject before they had dinner. "Tell me, William, how have you been these past years since the war? If I remember, you told me you were from Virginia. How did you happen to end up in Batavia?"

Now it was Morgan's turn to make up a story. "After the war, I wanted to be a mason again and found work back in Virginia. I met my wife there and then lost my job and had no prospects. We decided to try our luck in Canada, but that did not work out, so we went to Buffalo and then Rochester. We inherited some money from my wife's family and heard about this village. We decided it would be a nice place to raise a family. The area has good prospects, and the people are friendly."

Just at that moment, Lucinda announced that the evening meal was ready. Matthew was hungry. They ate a meal of pork and beans, cornbread with molasses, and dandelion greens that Lucinda had cooked from a recipe given to her by a neighbor. The meal was filling and quite good. The room was warm from the coals left from the cooking fire, and the chimney was not drawing very well, so the air was smoky. William and Lucinda did not seem to notice. Fortunately, a window was open to let in some fresh air. Matthew could have done without the mosquitoes, but a price had to be paid for the fresh air.

Lucinda watched the children while she cleared the table. She sent the men to the front room that had four simple wooden chairs, and she lit some candles since it was starting to get dark. Morgan lit a pipe, and the two men talked about old times. Matthew found it difficult to believe Morgan could act so casual and at ease when he was involved in the Machiavelli plot. Morgan was certain that no one, especially Matthew, knew anything about the weapons and powder cached in the cabin in Canandaigua that he was keeping for Wollstonecraft. Matthew needed to get Morgan to talk about something, so he decided to talk about the Masons. Zeb had filled him in on what they knew about the Masonic connection and Melbourne.

Matthew steered the conversation to the Masons by telling Morgan that he had been approached in Boston to join the Masons but had not made up his mind as yet. Morgan became more attentive. "Yes, Matthew, the Masons are quite an interesting organization. I have been a member for several years and am currently a member of the local lodge. They are a fine bunch of fellows and are trying to help me find work."

Of course, Matthew thought to himself, *they certainly have already found work for you.* He asked, "What do you do with your time now that you are not gainfully employed?"

Morgan gave him a suspicious look that disappeared as quickly as it appeared. "I meet with friends who are helping me find work. I also have been helping David Miller, the owner of the local newspaper. I do odd jobs for him, and he pays me what he can afford. This helps some. We are working on a special project. We want to wait until the right moment to let everyone know what we are doing."

"Well, I hope it helps you find a position or brings you some financial reward."

"Maybe it will, if I am lucky."

It was getting late, and Matthew wanted to let Lucinda and William get to bed. Matthew said he would be staying a day or two longer and would return if it was all right with them. Lucinda told him that of course it would be fine. They would like to see Matthew again before he left for Buffalo. Matthew thanked Lucinda for the wonderful meal and told them he would stop in tomorrow evening to say good-bye. He left the house and went back to the inn. He needed to find out more about Morgan, but without raising too much suspicion. This was a small village, and it would be hard to ask people about Morgan without someone relaying the information back to him. He needed to come up with a way to do this tomorrow before he headed back to Caledonia and brought Zeb up to date on what was going on with Morgan.

CHAPTER 29

WHILE MATTHEW WAS HAVING BREAKFAST the next morning, a message was delivered to him at his table by a young boy about ten or eleven years old. The boy asked if he was Mr. Prescott. Matthew told him he was, and the boy gave him the note and ran out the door. He almost slipped on a pool of tobacco juice in the doorway because he was in such a hurry. Matthew unfolded the note and quickly read its contents. Lucinda Morgan wanted to see him, but not at her house. She asked him to meet her around noon at a friend's house in Elba. The little village was about six miles north of Batavia. The note said it was urgent that she see him and that William had gone to Canandaigua to look for work. There was a stable that rented horses, and the ride should not take him very long. Her friend would take her in a carriage since she had to come to Batavia to pick up some flour and other staples that day. Matthew wondered what this was all about. Maybe she had found out about Morgan's involvement with Melbourne and Wollstonecraft, but Matthew did not think this was possible. Morgan was too smart to talk about the plan. If he did and it was discovered, they would both be dead.

Matthew went to the stable and made arrangements for a horse. It was a pleasant enough June day with plenty of sunshine, a few fluffy clouds in the blue sky, and a light breeze blowing from the southwest. The horse wasn't anything to write home about, but it got him to the house in Elba, located on the west side of the main street of the little village. When he reached the house indicated on the small map included with the note, a boy was waiting for him. He took his horse to a barn behind the house.

The house was owned by Mr. Jonas Maltby. His wife, Charlotte, was a close friend of Lucinda's. Lucinda made the introductions, and Charlotte asked Matthew to please sit down. The house was constructed in the federal style and was quite large by local standards. Jonas Maltby was a silversmith and earned a very good living for his family. The family had moved to Elba from New England after Jonas's brother, a local farmer, had convinced them to move west. His business was going quite well, and they were not sorry about the move. Jonas excused himself after meeting Matthew and went to his workshop to work on a piece that needed to be finished by the next day.

"You must be wondering why I asked you to come all the way out here when we could have talked in Batavia. Charlotte is a very dear friend, and I am able to confide in her. We had planned to have lunch together today, and I wanted to speak with you about something William is involved in. I did not want anyone in Batavia to know we were meeting, and this seemed like a good location."

This does not sound good, Matt thought. "If I may be of any assistance to you, I will certainly do my best."

"Thank you, Mr. Prescott. I know you and William knew each other during the war, and your visit has been quite a surprise to both of us. William wasn't completely honest with you last evening. He has been a member of the Masons for some time but has fallen out of favor with them. He is a stubborn man and is working with David Miller on a book about the secrets of the Masons. I'm afraid if this book is published, it will anger a lot of people, including some who may wish to harm William. I don't know who to talk to or what to do about this situation. I wanted to tell you about this since you are not from here and may be able to talk to William and convince him to stop this nonsense."

"I don't know how successful I can be in convincing him, but I will try to speak to him before I leave. How close are they to completing this book?"

"From what William has said, it probably won't be finished until late summer or early autumn."

"What are his reasons for publishing the book?"

"William has experienced difficulties with some of the Masons. For some reason, they don't seem to like him very much. He wants to make them pay for their treatment of him. I am not really certain how important these secrets are or if they really mean anything. I always thought of these secret societies as a group of men playing at being boys again with special rituals, handshakes, and all of that nonsense. I know William hoped that being a Mason would help him find a position. If he publishes this book, I am afraid they will never have anything to do with him again, and then where will our family be? Most of the influential men in this area are Masons."

Charlotte looked at Matthew. "Mr. Prescott, I probably know a bit more about the Masons than Lucinda. Many of our friends are Masons, and they have been hearing rumors about this book William is supposedly working on. I encouraged Lucinda to ask you to visit today because I think William needs someone to speak plainly to him and tell him that this endeavor could be very dangerous. I don't believe he would listen to any of the local people. There has been talk of this book, but no one has seen any part of it yet. Mr. Miller is keeping quiet about the contents, and so is William. Knowing William as we do, we suspect the book includes many of the secrets of Masonry that all Masons swear an oath not to reveal. My husband will not have anything to do with William. He is a Mason, and his friends are Masons. They don't like the idea of this book being published."

"I am not a Mason and don't really understand all of this, but I will talk to him. When will he return to Batavia?"

"He told me he plans to be back in two or three days."

"I have some business appointments that will take the better part of a week or so. I'll come back after they are completed and speak with William. I'll send you and William a letter as to my arrival date."

"Thank you, Mr. Prescott. You don't know how much this means to me. I have two small children, and I don't know what I would do if anything happened to William. I am probably being overly worried, but I just don't know what will happen if that book is published."

Matthew was invited for lunch, and he gladly accepted. After the meal, he took his leave and returned to Batavia. He left the horse at the stable and paid the fee. He went to the inn and packed his bag. He paid the innkeeper and took the next coach to Caledonia.

Chapter 30

While Matt was looking for Zeb in Caledonia, Wollstonecraft was in Rochester looking for Wharton. When he arrived in Rochester, he had gone to the rooming house. The landlady told him she had no idea where Mr. Wharton could be and that she had not seen him for quite some time. All of his belongings were still in his room, and the rent was paid for three more months. He told her he was a very good friend and had come to Rochester to pick up some papers that Mr. Wharton had been working on for him. She told him to feel free to look around and left the room. He immediately went to the trunk and looked for the map. After searching the contents of the trunk, he finally found the map. If the map was missing, it would be trouble for all of them. Melbourne would explode with rage. He took the map, rolled it up, and put it in the inside pocket of his coat. He thanked the landlady for her time and went across the street to have a drink before going to Lockport to look for Wharton. She breathed a sigh of relief when he left. There was something ominous about that man, and she wanted nothing more to do with him.

Matt found Zeb walking along the little stream that flowed through the village and emptied into a larger stream to the north. The locals called the small stream Spring Brook, and the larger one Oatka Creek. Zeb told him there was an old Indian trail that followed the Oatka back upstream to the west and connected to another trail that went into LeRoy. Zeb got right to the point. "Did you find Morgan?"

"Yes, I found him." He told Zeb about the conversation they had, as well as the visit to Elba and Lucinda's concerns about the book Morgan was writing with David Miller. Zeb wasn't sure about the fallout from the book. Maybe Morgan's wife and Mrs. Maltby were overly concerned about the possible danger. "Do you really think the Masons would actually harm him if he published the book?"

"I am not sure, but we cannot take any chances. We will have to keep our eye on him and get him out of here if this book causes him any problems. I promised President Adams we would find him and bring him back to Washington. I received word from Phillips that while he and Richards were traveling to Albany, they saw a coach headed west with a very familiar face looking out the window."

"Who was it?"

"Wollstonecraft. My guess is he is looking for Wharton. Melbourne has not heard from him lately and is getting worried. He sent Wollstonecraft to look for him and make sure the plan has not been compromised. We need to check into this, keep an eye on Morgan, and get our plans ready to stop the attack on Governor Clinton."

"You mean he still plans to make the trip even though he was warned by Richards and Phillips?"

"Yes. He doesn't really see any danger involved. In fact, he knows Melbourne and didn't seem to believe that he could be the one who wants him dead."

"Let me try to sort this out. Clinton is still traveling up the canal at the end of this summer. Morgan is supposedly writing a book that reveals the secrets of Freemasonry. Wharton is in prison at Fort Niagara, and Wollstonecraft is in the area looking for him because he has gone missing. Morgan is somehow involved in this plot. We know the location of the attack, but not the method. Do I have most of it?"

"Well, Matt, you do, but not all of it. We are going to need more of our people to protect the governor. I don't have enough available, so we need to find some people to help us in addition to the men Seth Jamison can provide from the fort. It would be better if they were in this area. A friend of mine who used to work for me lives near Batavia. He is a Seneca Indian and helped me with some difficult assignments in South America and Europe. I think he is currently living on the local reservation that our government has so graciously allotted to their Indian allies after taking all their land. I can write you a letter of introduction, and you can visit him to ask for his help."

"Why can't you go with me?"

"I have another message from President Adams, and he wants me to return to Washington to brief him on what has happened so far. I haven't talked to him since April, and he likes to see me from time to time. Based on what you have told me, and the other events that have taken place, we need to split up for the time being. Phillips and Richards will stay in the area to watch your back. Wollstonecraft may recognize them, but he doesn't know you. First, go to Lockport on the pretext of visiting Sarah, and keep an eye out for Wollstonecraft. Phillips and Richards are good at disguises, so they won't be recognized. They will watch out for you and make contact, if necessary. We have made arrangements at key post offices you may use to contact each other. I'll fill you in later. After you find out what Wollstonecraft is up to, get word to Phillips and Richards, and they will pass the information to me. Then go back to Batavia and talk to Morgan as you promised his wife. While you are there, go see my friend and give him a letter I will write. His name is Joseph Parker. If he is willing to help, get in contact with me. I'll try to come up with a plan that will protect Governor Clinton when he comes up the canal later this summer."

What Zeb did not tell Matt was the other reason he was returning to Washington. President Adams had received a letter informing him that his top agent was a Jew. Of course, the letter was not signed, but the intent was obvious. Someone was trying to get rid of him, and Zeb now had a pretty good idea who it could be. He knew President Adams was a fair man and certainly did not hold any anti-Jewish beliefs. This was all he needed now. It was bad enough that Spain had expelled the Jews in 1492, and his ancestors were forced to flee to North Africa and Turkey before coming to Charleston in the last century. Unfortunately, there were others in Washington who thought the Jews received only what they deserved during the Inquisition and would love nothing better than to see Zeb lose his position and be destroyed in the process, if necessary.

CHAPTER 31

ZEB AVOIDED THE MAIN TRAVEL routes and made his way to Washington on horseback and coach. His backside was sore, and he almost broke an arm when a coach overturned in a deep rut in Pennsylvania. Two of the inns he stayed in had so many bugs in the bedding that he slept in the stable on some straw next to the horse stalls. It took him two weeks, but he finally was in Washington and waiting for his meeting with President Adams. The president's secretary came into the room where Zeb waited. "The president will see you now, Mr. Cardwell."

Zeb entered the office and waited while President Adams finished signing some papers. He looked up and told Zeb to have a seat. "I'm sorry to call you away from your duties, but I needed to see you in person. I want to speak with you regarding the letter I received about you being Jewish. Is this true?"

"Yes, Mr. President, it is."

"How would they know? Apparently, you have kept this a carefully guarded secret for a long time."

"I didn't tell you since I thought it was something no one would ever discover. I apologize for not telling you. I am not ashamed of my heritage, but there are some people in the government who would make this information public if they found out and try to force me out of my position. However, I have a suspicion that the note did not come from one of these people."

176

"Zeb, no apology is needed. Who do you think sent the note?"

"I think it came from Mr. Melbourne or one of his conspirators. If they can discredit me and have me removed from my position, they may believe it will help them accomplish their goals. I'm sure they will try other avenues to discredit me."

"Zeb, you know I don't really care if you are Jewish or Hindu or, God forbid, an atheist. I burned the note, and as far as I'm concerned, it was never received. We will keep this between us and hope the matter does not reach the light of day again."

"Thank you, Mr. President."

"Hopefully, you will be able to return to the North as soon as you take a few days' rest. That is a direct order, Zeb. You look worn out."

"I do admit I am a little tired, but I am fine. I will take a couple of days to attend to some personal business in Washington and then return to western New York."

"Please tell me what has been happening. I have your dispatches, but I need to hear it directly from you."

"Of course, Mr. President." Zeb told President Adams everything that had happened since the night he had dinner with Matthew Prescott. The president listened intently and interrupted Zeb from time to time to ask questions. When Zeb was finished, the president sighed and looked troubled.

"Zeb, I have some information that may be of help to you and your men. The official in charge of the armory at Harpers Ferry has reported that a number of muskets are missing from their inventory. He believes they were taken sometime last autumn while a man fitting the description of one of the slain prison guards was working there under an assumed identity. He cannot prove this, but it seems to be more than coincidence. The man left without giving notice and was never seen again at the armory. There were several kegs of gunpowder missing, as well. As you know, it is quite difficult to steal these items from a federal armory, but it apparently was done."

Zeb thought for a moment before he spoke. "It would be good if we could tie this to the business Melbourne and Morgan are trying to accomplish. If the muskets and gunpowder went missing last autumn, they could have been shipped to another location, possibly in the area where the attack on Governor Clinton is planned. Maybe this has something to do with Morgan's involvement. It would make sense that part of his role is to hide and keep watch on the muskets and gunpowder until they are ready to be used. This means he would have to keep them somewhere dry and out of the way. If we can trace his movements the past few months, we might be able to find out where they are. Of course, this is all based on the assumption that Melbourne is responsible for the theft of the muskets and gunpowder, and they are now in western New York where Morgan is keeping them until needed."

"At least this is something you may investigate when you return. Let me see. It is now late June, and the governor's trip up the Erie Canal is scheduled to take place in late summer. There is not much time left."

"No, time is getting short. Two or three months seem like a lot, but in this case, they are not. Mr. President, I need a favor. I need more men to help counter this plot against Governor Clinton. I have an idea but need your approval and a letter of permission. It could be very sensitive if it is not handled properly, and that is my responsibility." Zeb explained his idea of using some local Seneca Indians as part of their group. They would make an appearance in a very remote area and would not be seen by anyone except Melbourne's henchmen and the people on Governor Clinton's packet boat.

The president pondered this before he replied. "You know this could create a great deal of fear and concern on the part of the people in that region if this became common knowledge. Some still remember what it was like before the Indians were on their reservations. It is my understanding that the Iroquois were ferocious fighters, especially the Mohawk and the Seneca."

"As I said, Mr. President, I will take full responsibility for this. My friend is well respected by the members of his tribe, and if we use the right approach, he should be able to recruit enough men to give us the extra help we need."

"I don't really like this, Zeb, but I trust your judgment. I will give you a letter that allows these men to bear arms again but leave it up to you as to how they are used. Please destroy the letter after it has served its purpose. Congress will have apoplexy if they find out what we are doing. Of course, it wouldn't be the first time and undoubtedly will not be the last. I will have my secretary draw up the document for you, and I will sign it so you may take it with you today."

"Thank you, Mr. President."

"By the way, how is our Mr. Prescott doing?"

"You were right, Mr. President. He has turned out to be quite an asset. We need him now that we have located Morgan but have placed him in a dangerous position. If any of Melbourne's people find out Matthew is working with us, he is a dead man. I have Phillips and Richards watching him while I am gone."

"Good. I'm glad we made the right choice. Well, I don't want to hold you up any longer. I know you have business to attend to and want to head back up north. Please continue to keep me informed. Godspeed to you and your men, Zeb."

"Thank you, Mr. President."

Zeb left the office and waited until the document he had requested was ready. He left the White House and headed for his home in Georgetown so he could get fresh clothes and rest for a few hours before he went to Harpers Ferry. After that, he would travel back to western New York. If it took him two weeks, it would be the middle of July by the time he arrived.

While Zeb was traveling back to Washington, Matt returned to Lockport on horseback. He had found a good mount at the stable in Caledonia and left the owner a substantial deposit. It was now early July, and the whole village was preparing for the fiftieth anniversary of the Declaration of Independence. Flags and patriotic decorations were displayed by most of the homes and businesses. He discovered a parade was scheduled for the Fourth of July, and there was a village picnic planned that would include speeches by politicians and prominent businessmen. Matt could do without the speeches. He left his horse in the barn and reminded himself to rub him down as soon as he could and give him some oats. As he walked out of the barn, Sarah walked from the house to the barn.

"Matthew, what a surprise! I wasn't sure when I would see you again."

"Well, I have managed to conduct some business and decided to take a few days off and visit you. By the way, how is your aunt these days?"

Sarah laughed. "I think she is fine, but I'm not sure. She has returned home to her family in Connecticut, and I plan to stay here for the rest of the summer. My uncle insisted that I stay, and he sent a letter to my parents telling them it would be a good change for me."

Matthew smiled. "Yes, I agree. Your uncle is a pretty intelligent man."

"Matthew, I have an idea. Let's take a walk so I can show you the village. I'll go tell my uncle. He likes you and should give his permission."

"Sounds like a good idea. While you speak to your uncle, I'll go rub down my horse and give him something to eat."

When Sarah returned, she was with her uncle. "Have a nice walk, you two, and, Matthew, be sure to put some cotton in your ears. This girl can talk up a storm when she has a mind to." Matthew laughed, and Sarah blushed.

They walked in silence for a few minutes, enjoying each other's company. Matt felt a little guilty since he welcomed the walk with Sarah for two reasons. First, of course, he was glad to be with her again. Second, he could keep an eye out for Wollstonecraft while they were walking around Lockport; the description Zeb gave him was pretty clear. Matt wondered where Phillips and Richards were but realized they would keep out of sight unless he needed them.

"Matthew, I've been thinking a lot about us since we met. Please don't think me too bold for speaking like this, but I can't help it. I want to tell you about a decision I have made. Girls my age are supposed to be ladylike and proper. I realize we have not known each other very long, but I wish to say something while I have the courage, so I will come right out with it. Matthew Prescott, I like you. I would like us to be friends but realize you have a business to manage, and this is the last thing you probably need to deal with right now. Please don't say anything until I am finished." Matthew knew when to keep quiet. "I am not usually like this. I am usually quite reserved and keep my thoughts to myself, but after I met you, I have changed. I would like you to visit me this summer when you have the opportunity. Oh God, I hope I am not making a fool of myself."

"Sarah, I would be delighted to visit you this summer, but I need to tell you something. I've been doing a lot of thinking about you. Something has happened that I cannot explain. You have been in my thoughts, as well, and I have a confession to make. They weren't the kind of thoughts I can tell your uncle about." Sarah blushed again but remained quiet. By this time, they were walking down a lane with trees on both sides and out of sight of any houses. The path led to the main street, which was about one hundred yards away. Sarah took his hand, and they walked slowly without speaking until they were near the village.

CHAPTER 32

WHILE MATTHEW AND SARAH WERE on their walk, Wollstonecraft was in the tavern previously used by Wharton and his men. Wollstonecraft knew this was the tavern based on his previous contact with Wharton. The tavern was filled with cigar and pipe smoke, and tobacco juice soaked into the sawdust on the floor. The wet sawdust and tobacco juice stuck to his boots, and he made a mental note to clean them after he left. He ordered gin and started a conversation with the tavern keeper. He talked about the weather and the canal for a few moments to loosen him up and then asked about Wharton. The tavern keeper knew who Wharton was and mentioned that his friends usually came in later in the afternoon. He told Wollstonecraft that he had not seen Wharton for some time. In fact, two men he did not know had been here with Wharton a few weeks back, and they left together. That was the last time he had seen of him. A few of his friends still came in, hoping that Wharton would show up one of these days. Wollstonecraft finished his gin and told the tavern keeper that he would be back later. He left the tavern and decided to pass the time by looking around the growing village, especially the locks that were one of the wonders of the Erie Canal. Melbourne would have been surprised to know that Wollstonecraft was capable of admiring anything.

As Wollstonecraft was taking his walk, Matt and Sarah came out of the path and into the main street of the village. Matt spotted Wollstonecraft right away. Even from the rear, he knew it must be him. He was a large, beefy man, and Matt was glad the man did not know him. Matt knew he must be very careful. From what Zeb had told him, Wollstonecraft was a bear—and a killer bear at that. Matt and Sarah were walking in the same general direction as Wollstonecraft, toward the Erie Canal locks. He made Sarah change direction. He did not want Wollstonecraft to see him with Sarah. It was dangerous enough that he might be found out, and he did not want to endanger Sarah. If he could find some way to shorten their walk and then come back on his own, it would be much better.

Matt suggested they return to her uncle's house. He told her he needed to send a letter to a business contact in Buffalo and would be back as soon as he could. Sarah was suspicious but did not say anything. His mood seemed to have changed. Well, she would let it go for now and approach the subject later. When they returned to the house, Matt wrote a letter that would not be mailed to anyone, but it gave him an excuse to return to the village alone.

He found Wollstonecraft still lingering by the locks. Eventually, Wollstonecraft walked back to the village and entered a tavern. It looked like a pretty disreputable place, but Matt knew he had to go inside if he was going to discover anything that would help Zeb and the others. He wasn't known around here yet and would not be recognized. He went in, ordered ale, and sat at a table in the corner where he could barely make out Wollstonecraft through the haze of smoke that filled the tavern. *When in Rome*, he thought to himself, and he lit a cigar he had purchased in Rochester. Matt sipped his ale and pretended to be lost in thought. Eventually, two men came in and looked startled when they saw Wollstonecraft. They immediately went over to his table and sat down. He could just barely make out their conversation.

Wollstonecraft fixed his most malevolent gaze on the two men and said, "Where the hell is Wharton?"

The short, stout one replied, "We don't know where he is. We have been coming here nearly every day for the past few weeks to see him, but he has not shown up. Another strange thing has happened too. Jake and Sam seem to have gone missing, as well."

Wollstonecraft wanted to strangle the two of them right then and there, but he had to keep his temper. These two were just pawns and reported to Wharton. They did not know who to contact if anything went wrong. It seemed that Melbourne's plans had a crack in them. "All right. Here is what I want you to do. Go to taverns in the surrounding villages and ask around. See if anyone saw Wharton with two men, and see if anyone knows where they might have gone. I'll be here tomorrow afternoon waiting for you. As soon as you find something out, come here and report to me."

They both nodded their heads and hurried out of the tavern without even having a drink. Wollstonecraft finished his drink and left. He walked to a nearby inn and went inside. Matt knew he had to get a message to Phillips and Richards, so he went to the post office and left a coded note for them as instructed by Zeb.

Wollstonecraft tried to figure out what had happened to Wharton, Jake, and Sam. It had to be more than coincidence that all three of them were missing. The only thing that kept him from panic was the map. He had the map, and no one else could possibly know the location of the attack. There were several possibilities, and he had to find out which one would be chosen. He had to return to New York soon to report to Melbourne and attend a meeting. The final meeting had been postponed until this month. Some of the brothers had been called away on business, and the meeting date had been changed. Melbourne was not happy, but there was nothing he could do about it. He had superiors, and they must be obeyed.

The bad feeling he had about Wharton was reinforced by the information about Jake and Sam. They were two of his best men, and if they were missing, something bad had happened to them. They would need to be replaced, but he needed to find out what had happened to all three of them to make sure the plan was not jeopardized. This was completely unexpected. Cardwell was supposed to be dead by now. They knew he was heading this way, and Wharton had orders to eliminate him. If Wharton had failed, and

Cardwell knew anything more about the plan, it could jeopardize everything. Wollstonecraft decided to do a little investigating of his own tomorrow.

CHAPTER 33

JULY 3, 1826, DAWNED AS a clear, blue-sky day in Lockport. The whole village was preparing for the big celebration the next day, as were most of the other villages in western New York. After all, this was the fiftieth anniversary of the Declaration of Independence, which made this a very special Fourth of July. The local politicians and leading citizens of the village would participate in the parade. Orators reviewed their speeches, and ladies all over the village prepared food for the picnic to be held after the parade. Matthew and Sarah planned to watch the parade and then go to the picnic.

Wollstonecraft rose early and headed to Lewiston. This was the last location they knew Cardwell had been based on the information received from Wharton. He might be able to find out more than the two idiots he had talked to yesterday. He took the morning coach and arrived early enough to visit a few taverns. He knew he had to be careful not to seem too concerned about the men. All the taverns were open and doing a good business. He talked to the tavern keepers, but none of them had seen Wharton or any of the others. He decided to have lunch at the inn and then return to Lockport to meet the two idiots at the tavern in the afternoon.

Phillips retrieved the message from Matt at the post office. They decided it would be best to meet face-to-face with Matt, and they waited for an opportunity. They were both wearing old, dirty clothes and had stopped shaving; their beards had been growing for a few days. They certainly looked the part. No one would give them a second look. They loitered around the village until they saw Matt walking alone, heading down a narrow lane toward the village. They caught up to him in the tree-shaded lane, and he was startled when he saw them. Matthew did not recognize them at first and thought they might be Wollstonecraft's men. He knew that was far-fetched, and then he realized it was Phillips and Richards. Phillips spoke first. "Well, boy, you seem to be having a pretty good time while the rest of us are out working our asses off trying to discover how much that bear Wollstonecraft finds out about some of our recent activities in these parts."

Matt laughed. "Yes, I guess you could say that. Zeb thought it would be a good idea for me to come here with the chance that I might find out what Wollstonecraft is up to. Now we know he is trying to find out what happened to Wharton and the other two. I'm trying to find an excuse to leave Sarah this afternoon and go back to the tavern. Any ideas?"

"Yes," replied Richards. "You stay with Sarah and her uncle's family, and we'll take care of listening to what Wollstonecraft and his friends have to say at the tavern this afternoon. At least we won't stand out like a sore thumb in that tavern the way we look. God, you took a chance yesterday. It is a wonder Wollstonecraft didn't notice you and wonder what someone dressed like you was doing in that tavern. Apparently, he was too preoccupied with finding Wharton and didn't pay you any mind. Meet us here after supper tonight, and we'll make plans for our next moves. Enjoy the rest of your day with your lady friend." Phillips and Richards laughed as they disappeared into the trees. Matthew smiled to himself as he returned to the house.

Later that afternoon, two disreputable-looking men with manure on their boots entered the tavern in Lockport and ordered gin. They took their drinks to a table near the door and seemed to be lost in conversation when Wollstonecraft walked in. In a few more minutes, the other two men showed up and sat with Wollstonecraft. Phillips and Richards pretended to be talking while they listened intently to the conversation three tables away.

"What have you been able to find out?"

The spokesman for the two answered. "All we were able to discover was that Wharton was seen on horseback leaving here with two other men. He didn't seem too happy to be going with them. In fact, the man noticed that Wharton's hands seemed to be tied."

"What did the two men look like?"

"He couldn't tell. They were riding pretty quickly past him, and their hats were pulled down, so he couldn't see their faces very well."

"Is there anything else you can tell me? Has anyone seen Jake or Sam?"

"Not that we were able to find out."

"Don't bother coming here anymore. In fact, go to Rochester and stay in the rooms we have for you until you are contacted."

The men nodded their understanding and left. Wollstonecraft got up, looked around the room, and did not seem to notice Phillips and Richards sitting at one of the tables. He left and went back to the inn.

Wollstonecraft was angry. How could Wharton and two of his best men just disappear? It was obvious someone had taken Wharton, and he had a pretty good idea who it was. They had to find Cardwell and get rid of him once and for all, but he had to return to New York to face Melbourne and attend the meeting. Melbourne was going to be very unhappy with the news. He needed to return to New York on the first stage leaving Lockport. On second thought, he decided to take the canal to Albany. This would give him a chance to see the location they had selected for the attack again and avoid the jolting and bumping of a long coach ride.

Matthew and Sarah were returning from the picnic and walking in the tree-lined lane. "Matthew, will you be kind enough to send me a note or letter while you are gone?"

"Of course. You took me completely by surprise, and you know how men are about their freedom and bachelorhood. You know I care for you. My business has kept me so busy that I have not had much time for friendship with other women. When I met you on the trip to Lockport, I was able to spend some time with you, even with your chaperone as company. My life is very complicated right now, but I hope it will be less so in a few months. I will come to visit you and your family when I am able, and I will write to you between visits."

"Matthew, I do believe you are the one blushing right now." They both laughed, and she squeezed his hand. "Matthew, that will be fine with me. I can wait, but it will not be easy."

CHAPTER 34

ZEB WANTED TO INVESTIGATE THE type of muskets that had been stolen from Harpers Ferry so that he could prepare his men for what they might face later that summer if Governor Clinton still insisted on making the trip on the Erie Canal. He decided to visit the arsenal at Harpers Ferry and talk to Colonel Martin, who was in charge. It was very warm for early July. He had sent a message to Colonel Martin that he would be there in the afternoon. The colonel was an expert in arms and munitions and would be able to give Zeb a great deal of information on what was stolen.

Zeb found Colonel Martin in his office. "Zeb, you old son of a gun, how have you been?"

"Very well, Colonel, except for a recent encounter with a man and a knife."

"Why am I not surprised? You have more battle scars than anyone I know, including myself."

"Well, not that many, Colonel, but I have a few."

"How may I be of service, Zeb?"

"I understand some of your rifles and other items seem to be missing."

"Yes. I can't for the life of me figure out how the bastards did it. This place is pretty closely guarded. We are the only armory for the U.S. Army other than Springfield, Massachusetts. Between the two armories, we produce all the weapons for the army. We are pretty sure we know who it was."

"Well, I hope you find him." Zeb could not tell even Colonel Martin that the thief was the guard at the prison in Washington who was killed by Melbourne's men or that he was working for Zeb as a double agent. "I am involved in an investigation that may be related to the theft of the rifles and other munitions. I would like to know what type of rifle was stolen."

"Sure, Zeb. They were Hall rifles. They were designed by Captain John Hall. The army started using them in 1819. It is now the main rifle currently in use by the army."

Zeb knew a little about the Hall rifle, but he wanted the colonel to tell him the details. "What do I need to know about the Hall, Colonel?"

"Well, Zeb, let me see. The Hall is a breech-loading rifle that was patented in 1811, and as I said, the army started to use them in 1819. It is a very nice piece. It uses what Captain Hall calls a falling breech and can be fired using either a flintlock or percussion firing system. In fact, Captain Hall works here at Harpers Ferry now and has designed quite a bit of the machinery used to manufacture the rifles."

"Is Captain Hall here today?"

"No, he is not, Zeb. There was a death in the family, and he had to travel to New England."

"What else can you tell me about the Hall, Colonel?"

"The Hall is different from the usual muskets. The back part of the barrel—the chamber, if you will—is a separate piece that pivots upward for reloading. You still must load the ball and charge from front to back, but in a much shorter section of the rifle. It is a lot like loading a cylinder of the cap and ball revolver. The concept is the same, except that the bullet travels through the rest of the barrel and is thus more accurate and obviously travels a lot farther."

"So the rifles stolen were Hall rifles?"

"Yes, they were. Every single one of the twenty-five they took was a Hall. They also took percussion caps, powder, wadding, and a lot of rifle balls. I'll tell you, Zeb, after this theft, we have increased our security, and it is going to be harder for someone to get any weapons out of here than before. Would you like to see a Hall rifle?"

To be polite, Zeb said yes. He knew what the Hall looked like and was not happy that these were the rifles Melbourne would use to arm his men for the attack on Governor Clinton. The colonel and Zeb walked over to the manufacturing building. Colonel Martin showed him the assembly process and several finished rifles. It was Zeb's business to know about weapons, and he was impressed. He thanked the colonel for his time and left for Washington to prepare for the trip north.

Zeb went to his house in Georgetown and had a late supper. His servants had everything ready for the trip. This time, he had decided not to travel by land. He would sail to New York, travel up the Hudson, and take the canal back to western New York. He had already contacted Phillips as to where they would meet and what needed to be done next. He did not think he would be spotted in New York as he switched from a sailing ship to a steamer for the trip up the Hudson River to Albany. He could pretty much stay out of sight on the canal packet boat until he was in Rochester.

Matt was leaving for the post office in Lockport to check for messages when he met with Phillips. He looked like one of the canal men who took the packet boats up and down the canal. "I have some information for you from Zeb. Let's keep walking and try to look like we accidentally ran into each other and are just having a quick conversation."

"What is the information?"

"Zeb wants you to go back to Batavia right away and talk to Morgan. Then he wants you to see his Indian friend on the reservation. Try to find out more about that book Morgan is supposed to be writing, and make an effort to talk him out of it like his wife asked you. Also, see if you can find out where he has been going. Richards and I will be doing the same, but separately from you. We'll contact you when we think we have something useful, and you do the same. You know the procedure."

"All right, I'll leave as soon as I can. Now that the big celebration is over with, I can tell Sarah I have to leave on business again."

"One more thing. Be careful. We don't know who else is working for Wharton or where they are. The other two have gone to Rochester, and Wollstonecraft is heading to New York for some meeting. We will have some of our people check on that. I think your friend Morgan is supposed to be there, as well, so you may have to talk to the Indians before you see him again. It doesn't really matter which you do first. I have to get out of here; we've talked long enough. Don't worry—Richards and I will be in the area."

Chapter 35

Matt went back to Batavia. Sarah thought he was going back to Buffalo to talk to some people about his new shipping venture. He found Morgan in one of the taverns. He was sitting with David Miller, and they were deep in conversation. Matt approached their table and waited until they realized someone was there. Morgan's face brightened, and he nodded to David Miller. "This is my old friend Matthew Prescott. We served together in the last war at the Battle of New Orleans. He came to visit me a few weeks ago, and it appears he wants to see me again. Hello, Matthew. What can I do for you?"

"Mr. Miller and I have already met. He told me where you lived when I first came to Batavia. If you would be so kind as to excuse us, Mr. Miller, I would like to talk to William for a few minutes."

"Certainly. I have to get back to the paper and make sure the press is still working properly. We just fixed it, but it keeps acting up every so often."

Matt sat down and waited for Miller to leave. "Look, William, I am concerned about some rumors going around Batavia about you and Miller. It seems that the two of you are involved in writing a book about the Masons. No one is very happy about it, especially the Masons. They are quite angry about the prospect of their secrets being exposed to the general public. Is this true?"

"Yes. Since it seems to be general knowledge, I guess it wouldn't hurt to talk about it. Mind you, even though you are a good friend, I won't tell you exactly what is in it. The book should be ready in a few weeks, and we can't wait to get it printed."

"Why are you doing this, William?"

"As one friend to another, I must say the Masons take themselves far too seriously. I find a good many of them to be arrogant men who look down their noses at me and many others who are not as well off financially as they. The book should help take them down a peg or two."

Matt realized that Lucinda was right. Morgan was trying to embarrass the Masons for the way he had been treated. It was like a youngster trying to get even with the local bully. He needed to try to dissuade him from writing the book as he had promised Lucinda and as Zeb had directed. "Isn't this a dangerous venture? What about your safety and that of your family? Don't you think it would be better just to drop all of this and concentrate on earning a living for you and your family?"

"I think I can do both. I'll be honest with you. I am no longer a Mason. They threw me out of the lodge. If I publish the book, I will become known. It will probably help me."

"Even so, as your friend, I think you need to seriously consider what you are doing and the effect if could have on your family."

"I'm not worried about my family. I still want to do this, but I will consider what you have said. I have some business in New York and will be gone for several days. We can discuss the book when I return."

Matt decided he needed to tell Morgan about the family connection. "William, I need to tell you something that you will find very hard to believe. My father found out that he had a brother whom he was separated from when very young." He told Morgan the story.

Morgan looked shocked. How could anyone have found out he was in England? This could blow his cover and ruin the plot to kill Governor Clinton. He needed to find out if Matt's visit was more than just an old friend coming to see him. Of course, just because he had been in England proved nothing. He needed to find out more. "Did your father find out anything else?"

Matt knew where this was going and needed to deflect as quickly as possible. "No, he only knew that he was your brother and wanted me to know before he died. He didn't tell me to try to find you. I am only here as a friend who knew you during the war. Now that I know you are my uncle, my visit has two purposes."

"Two purposes?"

"Of course. To visit an old friend and to see my uncle."

Morgan was not completely convinced, but he wanted to believe Matt. He would decide whether to tell Melbourne at the meeting in New York. "What a coincidence. All this time, I thought of you as a friend from the war, and now I find out you are my nephew. This calls for a drink."

"Please reconsider the book. I think it will only cause hardship and suffering for you and your family."

"I don't think so. I'll be doing the country a favor by publishing their secrets."

Matthew realized he wasn't getting anywhere and decided to talk to Lucinda, but not while Morgan was around. "When are you going on your trip, William?"

"I leave tomorrow and should be gone for about two weeks. Why don't you stay here in Batavia until I return?"

"I think I will. I'd like to look around a little before I go back to Boston. I have some other things to do this afternoon and will visit you and Lucinda after you return from your trip."

Matt also decided he would talk to David Miller, but he would wait until Morgan was gone on his trip. He needed to get word to Phillips and Richards that Morgan was leaving. That would put him in New York in just a few days. This confirmed that Morgan would be at Melbourne's meeting.

He left the tavern after wishing his uncle a safe trip. He walked down the street to check out the post office. The post office was not in a separate building, but instead occupied part of the local dry goods store. Matt went back to his room, wrote out his coded message, and sealed it with the wax he had just purchased. He took the message to the post office and paid for it to be delivered to Albion, where Phillips or Richards would find it in a couple of days and forward the information to Zeb's men in New York. He hoped it would get there in time.

It was early evening by the time he was done. Matt returned to the inn to have some supper and then took a walk before going to bed. He decided to go to the reservation the next day and find Joseph Parker. He didn't know what to expect. His best bet was that Parker liked Zeb and would agree to help. If not, Zeb planned to see Parker and talk to him. Matt fell asleep that night trying to figure out the best approach.

Matt got up early the next day, had a quick breakfast at the inn, and went to the stable to rent a horse. He took some water and cornbread with him, along with his pistol. He didn't know who else might be in the area that might be connected to Morgan and the plot, but he wanted to have some protection with him. He was not certain it would do him any good, but he felt better having it with him. He followed the road northwest to Plain Brook and stopped at the only store in the small settlement. The proprietor was a florid-faced man with a bald head and a sour disposition. He asked Matt, in a very unpleasant tone of voice, why he wanted to know where Parker lived. Matt told him it was none of his business. The proprietor became angry and left to wait on another customer. Matt left in disgust. As he walked to his horse, a man approached him. "Are you looking for Joseph Parker?"

"Yes, I am. That storekeeper in there is one miserable bastard."

The man laughed, and Matt realized he was Indian. "I'm going to the reservation, and I will be glad to take you to Joseph. My English name is Francis Smith, and I am Joseph's cousin. That storekeeper treats us worse than he did you. He thinks Indians are dirt and only sells his goods to us because he likes money more than anything else."

They rode out of Plain Brook and headed west toward the reservation. There was little conversation, and Matt was glad he wore a hat because the day had come on sunny and hot. They stopped to water their horses at a friendly farmer's well, and Matt shared his cornbread with Francis. Francis told Matt that everyone was not like the storekeeper. The farmer was a good man and treated the Indians fairly. He told Matt his cousin Joseph liked to have visitors. Joseph had lived among the white men for a number of years and was able to move easily between the two cultures. Unfortunately, many whites looked down on the Indians and preferred to have as little contact with them as possible.

They reached the reservation and followed a narrow road and several side trails until they came to a clearing with a well-kept log cabin and a small barn. A stream, which Matt later learned was the same creek that ran through Batavia, was just beyond the cabin.

Francis called out to see if anyone was home. In a few minutes, a man came out who was dressed like any other person Matt had seen in Batavia, but he wore moccasins instead of boots. He looked at them curiously before speaking. "Well, Francis, I see you have managed to lure another white man here for us to scalp and mutilate. I hope you fed him well before bringing him here." His laugh was so infectious that Francis and Matthew soon joined him.

"Joseph, you know we only do that to every other white man I bring here. This one is lucky. He was asking for you at the store, and he discovered that Mr. Winters is a crotchety old fart who refused to tell him where he could find you. I introduced myself and brought him here to see you. He looks harmless enough, but I think he has a pistol in his jacket pocket."

Matt was surprised. He thought the pistol was pretty well hidden. "Yes, I have a pistol, but only for self-defense. I don't plan to use it here."

"Well, that is good to know. I can't scalp you if you shoot me." Then he laughed again. "Seriously, who are you, and why do you want to see me?"

"My name is Matthew Prescott, and I am a friend of Zeb Cardwell. I have a message from him."

"My God, why didn't you say so before? Come in, come in. Francis will take care of the horses and join us in a few minutes. I think I have something to help clear the dust from your throat."

The inside of the cabin was as neat as the outside. Joseph had never married but had many relatives who helped him maintain the cabin and property. He told Matthew this while he found some cups and a bottle of homemade wine. They sat at a beautiful cherry table, and Matthew gave the letter to Joseph.

Joseph read the letter and then looked up at Matt. "He thinks a lot of you to send you to me asking for this favor. Zeb and I go back a few years, and he wouldn't ask me for help unless he had a real need. Here, take a look at this." Joseph handed the letter to Matt. Zeb outlined the basic problem they faced and told Joseph that he could trust Matt completely. He didn't mention the attack on the governor, but Matt was to fill Joseph in when he saw him in person. Francis entered the room and sat down with them. Joseph poured him some wine.

"Joseph, I need to tell you a little more about what is going on, and then I'll explain the favor Zeb wants from you. Is it all right to speak with Francis here?"

"Of course. Francis will keep all of this to himself. He would dishonor me if he did not." Francis nodded.

Matthew told Joseph about the suspected attack on Governor Clinton later in the summer and where it would be. He also explained that Zeb needed more help to counter the attack by Melbourne's henchmen.

"Matthew, you may not realize it, but we Indians cannot bear arms. The white community would be incensed, and a bunch of them would probably come out to the reservation to kill us."

"Zeb told me he will ask special permission from President Adams and to assume that he will give it. You may go ahead and make your plans to help us if you agree. We will meet next month to update you on what we know at that time and then make plans on how we will try to stop the attack on Governor Clinton. I'll tell you how we will stay in contact during the next few weeks so you can send messages to us and vice versa."

"My people have suffered a great deal. They have tried very hard to maintain their dignity and self-respect. All we want is to be left alone and keep our culture and language so we can pass them on to the next generations. On the other hand, I owe a lot to Zeb Cardwell. He has treated me fairly and is a good man. Let me think about this. Come back here in two days. I'll have Francis meet you in Plain Brook and bring you out here again. I hope I will see Zeb, as well. See if you can get him to come out here to visit me before our plans are set."

"I think he plans to do that, Joseph. Zeb values your friendship a great deal."

"Now, while you are here, have some more wine. You have a hot and dusty ride back to Batavia."

CHAPTER 36

It was hot in New York. The interior of the Masonic lodge was warm, and the men were sweating. The lodge meeting had been shortened so the few that needed to could attend the important meeting of the Craft after the others left. There were ten men sitting around a table. Two men were standing outside the entrance to ensure their privacy. They could have been at a tavern, except there were no tankards or cups in front of them. The group included Melbourne, Wollstonecraft, Morgan, and Sir Geoffrey Bournewith from England. Sir Geoffrey was one of the leading architects of the plan. He had been sent by his fellow conspirators in England to attend this meeting. The others included Eldridge Weatherbee from Hartford, Jeremiah Fulsome and Harry Cunningham from New York, John Worth from Washington, Philip DeBeers from Albany, and Thomas Van Wyck from Philadelphia. All of these men were high-ranking Masons except Morgan and Wollstonecraft. They were all wealthy and had contributed generously to the group. Their businesses included shipping, munitions, banking, and agriculture. Sir Geoffrey was the leader of the group and spoke first.

"You all know why you are here. We have been planning this venture for some time. This will be the last time we meet until Machiavelli is successfully completed. Governor Clinton and Stephen Van Rensselaer will be deceased and the first phase of our plan completed. All of you have been instrumental in completing important tasks associated with this first phase, and some of you will be directly involved in the operation being discussed this evening. Mr. Melbourne, Mr. Wollstonecraft, and Mr. Morgan will lead the operation, and it is in their hands we are placing our trust. The rest of you have been most gracious in providing funds and other needed items. I thank you for this." He looked directly at each man in turn sitting at the table. "The rest of you will provide logistical support, such as locations for our men to find a safe haven after the attack is completed. They will need to stay out of sight for quite some time. We may even need to move some of them out of the country. Mr. Van Wyck will make those arrangements, if needed." Van Wyck nodded his agreement. "Now I will ask Mr. Melbourne to go over the plan with you for your final approval."

Melbourne rose and went to the map on the wall near their table. The map was similar to the one copied by Zeb's men. "This is the area for the operation. Governor Clinton will travel up the canal during the first week of September. As Sir Geoffrey told you, he will be accompanied by Steven Van Rensselaer and several other men. Some are government officials, and others are businessmen who support him. With any luck, we will be able to eliminate all of them. When they reach this location, we will be waiting for them. It is distant enough from any villages and quite secluded."

The location chosen for the attack had been changed. The map showed it to be closer to Albion. When Wollstonecraft reported to Melbourne and told him that Wharton was missing, Melbourne was suspicious. He did not like unknowns entering into the equation of his meticulously planned effort. He decided to change the location in case the map had been seen by someone else and reported to Cardwell. This was now a game of chess, and he was going to checkmate Cardwell.

"There are forests on both sides of the canal at this point, but the canal passes through a natural clearing. There is about twenty yards of open land on both banks of the canal. Our men will have cannons positioned on the north side, well camouflaged and positioned so they cover as wide an area as possible. We will use grapeshot to rake the boat. The surprise this will cause will then allow my men to close in and kill the rest with the rifles we have obtained from the armory. We will leave the cannons behind. It will be difficult enough to transport them secretly and place them in the proper position; we don't need to take them with us when we escape. After the attack, the men will disperse in twos and threes and travel by canal and coach from Rochester and other points east. We have a change of clothing near the attack site for everyone. When they reach their assigned destinations, they will remain until it is safe for them to leave. Does anyone have any comments or questions at this point?" No one did. "Good. Let me go over some of the pre-attack details. Mr. Morgan has secluded the rifles in a cabin near Canandaigua. They will be transported by wagon to Albion, where they will be hidden until needed. Once the attack is finished, the rifles will be buried by Mr. Morgan and Mr. Wollstonecraft at a remote location of their choosing. The cannons are being supplied by Mr. Fulsome from one of his factories. They have no markings and cannot be traced. Oh, yes, we have some explosive devices that will be used to burn the canal boat to the waterline and the people on it. We want to make our point."

Melbourne looked at the men around the table. They were giving him their undivided attention. "Let me give a quick planning summary. The men involved in the attack will travel to the area in pairs. They will stay in Albion and Medina and then meet at the designated staging area before going to the canal and taking their positions for the attack. Since we don't know the exact time the Seneca chief with Clinton and his entourage will pass by, scouts will be posted east of the location. Yes, Clinton is using the same boat he traveled on for the opening of the canal. The cannons will be shipped disassembled in crates labeled as agricultural goods up the Hudson and then along the canal to Albion. They will then be taken to the location of the attack, assembled, and camouflaged. Our men will be dressed as western frontiersmen to further confuse them in case anyone happens to survive. In fact, come to think of it, it might be good to leave one person to tell what happened." The men in the room nodded in agreement, including Sir Geoffrey. "I am finished with the outline of the plan. Does anyone have any questions?"

Eldridge Weatherbee cleared his throat. "Yes, I have a question. What will we do if anyone makes a mistake and this plan goes wrong? Do we have any contingencies for this?"

Melbourne scowled for a split second and then smiled. "I have checked and double-checked these plans, and so have the men working with me. I realize there is always a chance that something may go wrong, but I am very confident that this plan is foolproof and will succeed." Mr. Weatherbee seemed satisfied with the answer. "Sir Geoffrey has some additional remarks for us. Sir Geoffrey?"

"Thank you, Mr. Melbourne. As you all know, this is just the first phase of our plan to return our former colonies to us. After this phase is finished, we will meet again to discuss what I have in mind for the Americans. Your continued support is crucial to this, and your loyalty to the Masons is even more important. My supporters in England are grateful for all of your efforts in helping us achieve our goal. Let us hope that, in the not-too-distant future, our colonies will be returned to us and ruled as they should be by England. Now, let us vote on this. You all have paper and quill. A yes or no will be sufficient." The men voted, and Melbourne collected the ballots. Every one was a yes. Sir Geoffrey announced the results. "Thank you for coming, and good evening."

Everyone left except Melbourne and Sir Geoffrey. "Melbourne, I wanted a few words with you before I leave. I am counting on you to continue your good work and make this a successful venture. If everything works out the way we have planned, England will have to bring these colonies back into the empire. There are some things I wanted to discuss with you, but not in front of the others. As much as these men have helped us, we cannot trust any of them. Make sure you keep an eye on them. If any of them do something stupid like talk to their friends, business associates, or fellow Masons, I want them eliminated. In fact, I want them eliminated if you even suspect they might compromise this venture. Do I make myself clear?"

"Yes, Sir Geoffrey, very clear."

"Good. There has been a slight change in plans. I want you to remain in New York, as will I, during the attack on Clinton. There is no discussion of this. It has been decided that you are too valuable to our cause. We need you for the next phase. Inform Mr. Wollstonecraft that you desire him and Mr. Morgan to lead the attack. After all, they are both expendable. Now, what have you been able to do about Mr. Cardwell and his little band of American patriots?"

"We still have not been able to eliminate him. He is smarter than I thought and has as many lives as a cat."

"Keep after him. You have your men watching the ports and the coach lines?"

"Yes. If he is seen, we will have him."

"One other item. I don't like Morgan. I think he is the weakest link in this chain. Once he has done his work with the rifles and participated in the attack, find some way to get rid of him. There is one very important part of this phase that no one knows except the high council. Let me tell you all about it, old boy." Sir Geoffrey told Melbourne about the real purpose of the first phase and the part Melbourne was to play.

When Melbourne was able to speak, he thanked Sir Geoffrey for his trust and told him that Morgan would be taken care of after the attack on Clinton.

"Excellent. As I just informed you, I will be staying in New York until the attack is finished. Then I will return to England and wait for the start of the next phase of the plan. I will contact you when we are ready."

"As you request, Sir Geoffrey."

CHAPTER 37

ZEB ARRIVED IN NEW YORK with Dan Sherman, who was now fully recovered from his wounds. They were booking passage on a steamer to Albany. As he was paying, he noticed a man watching them. When Zeb turned in his direction, the man looked away and started walking out of the terminal. Zeb told Dan to stay close, and they followed him. Zeb did not want to go very far from the docks since the steamer was leaving in less than thirty minutes. On the other hand, he could not allow Melbourne to find out he was in New York. The man continued on foot, which was good for Zeb and Dan. If one of them could get ahead of the man, they could hold him and try to find out what he knew. Dan ran down an alley and doubled back a block ahead of the man. As Zeb closed in from behind, Dan reached out and pulled the man into an alley. Zeb arrived at the same moment, and they dragged him deeper into the alley and out of sight of street traffic.

The man was shocked. He recognized both of them as the ones described to him who had escaped from the rooming house fire. "What the hell is going on here? What do you two want with me?"

Zeb saw the fear in his eyes and knew that he must work for Wollstonecraft. "If you want to live to walk out of this alley, you had better start telling us why you were watching us, and do it right now."

The man spit in Zeb's face. That was all they needed to encourage him to talk. A few well-connected punches and a bloody nose gave the man second thoughts.

"All right. You don't have to get so rough with me. I know you two got away from the fire, and I know you have a big price on your heads. There are people paying good money to make sure you two get very dead."

One of the buildings in the alley was made of brick, and Zeb shoved the man headfirst into the wall. He collapsed like a dead fish. Dan checked him, and the man was still breathing; he was just knocked out. They did not want to kill him, so they dragged him farther into the alley and tied his hands and feet with some old rags they found. They made their way back to the terminal and the steamer to Albany.

"Zeb, how did they know we would be coming through New York to Albany?"

"I don't think they knew our exact route. Melbourne has many people in his hire and must have placed them in various locations that we might use. That poor bastard was probably going to the terminal for the past few weeks and got the surprise of his life when he actually saw us. I blame myself for being too confident. I knew they would be looking for us, but I didn't think they would spot us making a quick change from a ship to the steamer. This means we need to be very careful for the rest of the trip. We need to get back to the western part of the state and talk to Matt. If the governor still intends to make his trip, we need a good plan to counter what Melbourne has in mind. I thought Morgan was the key to this plot, but now I think he is just one link in a bigger chain. Let's get on that steamer before it leaves without us."

Matt was back in Batavia and wanted to speak with Lucinda Morgan. He stopped by the house and found her there with the children. "Matthew, do come in. William has not returned from his trip, and I don't think he will be back for at least another week."

"I need to speak with you about William. I managed to talk to him before he left and asked him about the book he is writing. He doesn't seem to believe he is in any danger if the book is published. I wasn't able to convince him to change his mind and told him I would speak to him again after he returns from his trip. By the way, where did he go on his trip?"

Lucinda looked puzzled by the question. She wondered why Matt would ask that, but she told him because she trusted him. "He told me he had to travel to New York to meet with some people who might be able to find a better position for him. He did not give me any details, and I did not pry any further. They are paying his travel costs and providing his room and board while he is in New York."

"I'll talk to him when he returns, Lucinda, but I don't know if I will be any more persuasive than before."

"That's all right, Matthew. You have been a good friend to William, and at least you tried."

"Thank you, Lucinda. I would feel much better if I had been successful. Let me know when William returns from New York, and I will speak with him again."

"I will, Matthew. I'll send a note to the inn when he returns."

Matthew left Lucinda and walked to the newspaper to talk to David Miller. He wanted to find out more about the book and why Miller was helping him.

While he walked to the newspaper office, Matt thought about the second visit he had made to see Joseph Parker. Francis had met him in Plain Brook again and taken him to the reservation. Joseph had thought about Zeb's request and agreed to help. He had some ideas on how his people could help and wanted to speak with Zeb. Matt told him he would leave a message at the tavern in Plain Brook for Francis when Zeb returned to the area. Matt would bring Zeb to his cabin to discuss the planned attack on Governor Clinton and how they could protect the governor and his party.

David Miller was at the newspaper. He said he would be more than happy to speak to Matt about Morgan and the book, but not in public. They went into his small office in the back and closed the door. "I'd like to know more about the book Morgan is writing. I understand you are helping him and will print the copies when it is ready."

"It certainly is public knowledge that we are up to something. Word gets around fast these days. You can't even spit in the street without the whole village finding out about it before the sun sets."

"Why is Morgan so obsessed with this book? He seems to be willing to go ahead with the publication even though he knows the Masons will not be pleased. He does not seem very worried. Should he be?"

"I'm not sure. Yes, some of them have made threats about the book, but I don't think they would actually do any physical harm to Morgan. He will certainly be on their short list of unpopular folks, and he may have to leave Batavia for a while. The book is an obsession with him. He was left off the list of members of the new lodge and has held a grudge ever since. He thinks that by publishing their secrets, he will get even. I have often wondered how he knows so much. He never rose very high in the series of Masonic degrees but seems to have a lot of information."

"Why are you helping him?"

"He has offered me a good sum of money to publish the book. In fact, he has given me an advance already, and I don't even have any galley proofs ready yet. If I didn't know better, I would think somebody is backing him. He certainly doesn't have that kind of money for this venture."

"When do you plan to print the book?"

"I would like to have it ready by the first part of September."

"You seem like a decent man, David. Why would you involve yourself in something like this?"

"I guess it's the old story of boredom. Nothing much has happened around here lately except the opening of the Erie Canal, and that missed Batavia because Joseph Ellicott was not successful in convincing the governor and the politicians in Albany to have the route go through our little village. I believe we would have been much bigger in a few years if that had happened. The canal has been an economic boon to this region. Buffalo is growing fast and will expand even more as the amount of goods shipped both ways increases. This country is growing, and the canal will be a big part of that growth. You mark my words."

"You are probably right. I'm here to see how my shipping business can benefit from the canal, especially from Buffalo westward. Anyway, I wanted to ask you to reconsider the publication of this book on the Masons and try to talk Morgan out of it. I promised Lucinda I would intercede on her behalf since I have known Morgan for a number of years. We served in the last war together, and I would like to see him make something of himself and have enough money to support his family."

"I can't argue with that, but I have a contract with William Morgan, and I don't intend to break it. I'm a businessman, Mr. Prescott. You must understand that."

"I understand business, all right, but this is personal. At least consider what I have requested and give it some thought."

"Fair enough. I'd better get back to work and make sure those men out there don't foul up another edition of this newspaper."

CHAPTER 38

ZEB AND DAN WERE STAYING in Albany until their packet boat left the next morning. They were hungry. Zeb decided it was safe to eat in public as long as they did not stay in the tavern or inn too long. They found an inn with a rear exit that catered to politicians and bureaucrats, and they sat in the back of the dining area. They had just placed their orders when they saw two men enter the room. Zeb and Dan did not know who they were, but the men were very interested in them. They sat at a table near the door and kept an eye on Zeb and Dan.

"Son of a bitch, those two are up to no good as sure as Johnny Appleseed loves apples. I think we have a problem and had better take care of it before any more of them show up." Zeb quickly outlined a plan. They both got up from the table and moved quickly to the rear door. It opened onto a dirty, garbage-strewn alley that ran from the street to about thirty feet beyond the door, where it curved around between buildings. Zeb waited by the door and sent Dan into the curved section of the alley. The door opened just as Dan made it around the corner, and two men came running out. Zeb tripped the first one, who managed to fall against his companion. Zeb started running toward the street, and they both followed. Instead of continuing to run, Zeb stopped and faced his attackers, who by now were both holding very sharp knives. Zeb dodged them both and grabbed the first one around the neck. He had the knife against the man's throat in seconds.

"Kill the bastard, John!" shouted the first man. John made a move toward Zeb but then stopped with a strange look in his eyes. His eyes rolled up into his head, and he fell to the ground with Dan's knife in his back. His companion began kicking and screaming, and Zeb slit his throat. He pushed him away before any more of his blood could splash on his clothes.

"Jesus, this is all we need. Let's get these two out of sight and get back to the hotel. We need to get the hell out of here." They dragged the two men past the back entrance and out of sight around the curve in the alley. They covered them with garbage. Hopefully they would not be found until Zeb and Matthew were far from Albany.

They didn't know how lucky they were. Two days later, Wollstonecraft went looking for his men when they failed to report. He visited all of the places they had been assigned. At the last one, the inn where Zeb and Dan had ordered supper, he found them. One of the people cleaning up the dining area told Wollstonecraft that he had seen two men that fit their description, but they had left in a big hurry out the back door. Wollstonecraft went out in the alley and started to look around. He walked toward the street but hesitated for a few seconds. He turned around, sniffed the air like a beagle after rabbits, and walked to the back of the alley. As he walked into the curve, he saw several rats scamper out of his way. The smell was very strong, and he knew from experience what it was. The flies had been busy, as well. He kicked at the garbage and exposed a maggot-covered leg.

As Wollstonecraft was finding the decomposing bodies of his two men, Zeb and Dan urged their horses along the coach roads to the western part of the state. If they traveled quickly, changed to fresh horses often, and stayed away from inns and other places frequented by travelers, they could be there in a few days. Zeb knew the men they had killed would be found, but he hoped they would have a day or two before that happened. The bigger the lead they had, the better off they would be. They would have to find a place to stay out of sight of Wollstonecraft and his gang of killers, who should soon be after them. Now that they knew Wharton was missing, and Zeb and Dan had been seen in New York, the hunt for them would be more intense. Wollstonecraft was not stupid. He would figure out where they were headed and have his men pursuing them as quickly as possible. Zeb knew just the place they needed to be for a few weeks until Melbourne got tired of Wollstonecraft and his men not finding them.

CHAPTER 39

MATT WAS IN HIS ROOM at the inn in Batavia when there was a knock on the door. It was John Parker with a message from his cousin Joseph. Matthew read the message and told John he would be outside in a few moments. He had an extra horse ready, and they headed out of Batavia to the reservation. When they arrived at Joseph's cabin, they found Joseph, Francis, Zeb, and Dan sitting around the table. Zeb introduced everyone.

"Things are moving pretty quickly now, Matt. Dan and I were seen in New York and Albany on our way back here." He recounted the events in New York and Albany and their long ride from Albany to the reservation. "I thought this would be the best place to stay while Wollstonecraft and his men are looking for me. Melbourne doesn't know about Joseph, and we want to keep it that way. Dan and I need to stay out of sight for a while and let things play out until we are ready to stop the attack on the governor. We need to do some planning and figure out our next steps. Let's go over everything we know so far."

Zeb reviewed the events of the past few months. Matt told about his conversations with Morgan, Lucinda, and David Miller. Zeb was very interested in the book Morgan was writing. "From what you have told us, Matt, it sounds like Morgan is not writing this book on his own."

"I agree, Zeb. I think he has some backers who want this book published to embarrass the Masons. Maybe they have promised him some sort of protection, and that is why he doesn't seem too concerned about his safety. It may even be Melbourne and his group who are trying to discredit the upstate Masons through Morgan. This could even be tied to the plot against Governor Clinton. However, for the life of me, I cannot see how killing the governor will help them embarrass the country or get their former colonies returned to England."

Joseph seemed lost in thought. He nodded to himself and then spoke. "I have been thinking about this whole plot since Matt first asked me for help. We are missing a piece or two of this puzzle, and now I think we have found one of them. The connection with the Masons is definitely a key to this. They seem to be using Morgan for more than a conspirator. Here is what I believe is going on with these people. They have a group where the leadership is English and wants to regain their former colonies. As far-fetched as this may seem to us, I think it is real. Killing the governor will be a story carried by all the newspapers in this country, not just in New York State. The governor is a national figure and a prominent Mason. So is Van Rensselaer. In order to send a message that they are a force to be reckoned with, they kill some prominent people and use the publishing of Morgan's book to throw more fuel on the fire. The Masons will react to protect their members. Morgan's life will be useless, and they can sacrifice him to further their ends."

"Yes, Joseph, that may be true," said Zeb. "But how does this help accomplish their plans?"

"I don't think they are finished. They must have something else planned. I think their plan is like a three-legged stool. They have two of the legs but are in need of a third. I think they want to kill another person of political stature."

"If they do, who would it be?" Dan asked.

Matt was the next to speak. "Oh, my God, I know who it is. I think they want to kill the president."

"The hell you say," said Dan. "Why would they want to kill President Adams?"

"It all is starting to make sense now," said Zeb. "Think about it. How do you change our foreign policy? If you get rid of the men at the top and replace them with your sympathizers, you can accomplish nearly anything. Hell, anything could happen given those events. Joseph, I think you are on to something. But why kill just the president? Why not get rid of the vice president, the secretary of state, and a few other key people? They might even be planning to get rid of Andrew Jackson, as well as a few other potential future presidents."

The enormity of the idea took a few minutes to process. Matt was the next one to speak. "How do we know this is what they plan to accomplish? All we know about is the plot on the governor. We have no hard evidence that they plan to do anything else."

"Think about it. The name of the plot is Machiavelli, and anyone who has read *The Prince* knows this is just the kind of scenario Machiavelli himself would have loved. It's entirely evil, but brilliant. Bear with me for a few moments. We know about the plot against DeWitt Clinton and that Morgan is planning to publish a book that reveals the secrets of Masonry. Both of these events together are bad enough and have been taking up our time and efforts these past few months. What if this is just what they want? They keep us occupied up here in western New York while another part of the plan takes place in Washington and other locations. A good number of our people will be here, while the main event unfolds elsewhere. If they can kill someone like Villineau inside a heavily guarded prison, it might be quite easy for them to assassinate a president and some key government officials. I wouldn't be surprised if they have plans to run their own candidate for president, as well as fill other key offices. Once these men are in place, they can change our foreign policy and bring our country back into the British Empire."

"Zeb, this is all speculation at this point. We need some evidence to confirm your theory."

"You are absolutely right, Matthew. We do need some hard evidence, and I know just the person we need to get it from."

"Jesus, Zeb, that could only be Melbourne himself."

"Exactly. Let's come up with a plan to capture Melbourne, interrogate him, and find out what the hell they are really up to. Joseph, you could be the key to this, and I'll tell you why."

The men discussed several options over the next two hours and finally agreed on a plan. They would try to capture and interrogate Melbourne, protect the governor and his retinue, and protect any other prominent figures targeted for death. Matthew was given the task of continuing to speak to Morgan to try to find out more about his involvement. Zeb needed to get messages to some of his other men in Washington, and they needed to be on watch for Wollstonecraft, who was probably in the area at that very moment. This certainly would change Zeb's plan to stay on the reservation for a while. He would have to travel and take his chances with Wollstonecraft.

CHAPTER 40

MRS. MEDLEY'S WAS BUSY, AS usual, and Melbourne was gambling and drinking his favorite French wine. Several of the young ladies were new, and Melbourne was looking them over as the night progressed. One especially striking girl had been watching him all evening, and Melbourne decided to make her his choice. He went over to her and introduced himself. Samantha smiled her sexiest smile and went upstairs with him. When they reached the room, she made him undress first and then promised to be right back. There was wine on the table by the bed, and Melbourne went to it like a fly to honey. He poured himself a glass, drank it down without stopping, and poured another. As soon as he finished the second glass, he began to feel drowsy and sat on the edge of the bed. He soon forgot about the reason he was in the room and lay back on the bed. Samantha returned and checked on him. He looked at her, but he was unable to move or understand what had happened to him. A feeling of euphoria overcame him, and he felt strangely at peace, unlike his usual demeanor and personality. In the recesses of his brain, there were warning signals, but they didn't reach the right destinations. The door opened, and Zeb and Dan entered the room.

What Melbourne did not know was that Joseph Parker was familiar with an herbal compound the Seneca had used for special ceremonies that induced a drowsy state in a person and made them feel peaceful and secure. It was made from burdock root, bloodroot leaves, corn tassels, and some other secret ingredients. The resulting compound had the additional property of making the person under its influence truthfully answer any questions they were asked. Even better for Zeb's purpose, the person under the influence of the drug would not remember anything. Joseph had told him that everyone who took the drug thought they had been sleeping soundly and had no memory of anyone speaking to them or of events that transpired while they were under the influence of the drug. Consequently, the drug became know as "the truth maker." No whites knew of the drug and its properties, and Joseph told Zeb only because the nature of the problem they were facing was so serious. They decided to use the compound on Melbourne but didn't know how they could manage to give it to him. Dan had suggested Mrs. Medley's as the best place, and Zeb readily agreed. Zeb and Dan had traveled to New York in disguise and stayed at Abby's home. Dan had contacted Lydia through Abby's servant and arranged for the wine to be drugged with the extracts of the plants. Zeb knew a discreet chemist, and the chemist made a liquid extract from the ingredients for him. Apparently, it was doing its magic on Melbourne.

Zeb started to question Melbourne. "How are you feeling?"

Melbourne's pupils began to dilate, and he felt very relaxed. "I feel like I could fly away and drift over the ocean."

Matthew and Zeb both smiled. The drug was having the desired effect. Zeb started with some basic questions before moving on to more serious ones. By the time he was finished, both Zeb and Dan were shocked at the audacity of the entire plot. Melbourne's brain kept telling him that something wasn't quite right, but he could not figure it out. He answered every question, and the results confirmed Zeb's suspicions. However, the actual plan was far beyond their speculations. Dan and Zeb helped Samantha get Melbourne under the covers before they left. She removed her clothing and climbed into bed with him. She would tell him he fell asleep after making love, and hopefully he would remember nothing that happened.

They returned to Abby's and went over what they had learned from Melbourne. Joseph had been right in his theory that the plot was more far ranging than just the assassination of Governor Clinton. The Craft had quite a list of high officials they planned to kill. The list of people to be eliminated included President Adams, Vice President John C. Calhoun, Secretary of State Henry Clay, Daniel Webster, and Andrew Jackson. They had assassins assigned to each person. They were all to be killed on the same day as the attack on Governor Clinton. They were all potential candidates for president. The Craft had handpicked people to be placed in higher office who would do their bidding. Eventually, the United States would become part of the British Empire again. At least, this is what Melbourne and his cohorts thought would happen.

Zeb and Dan needed to leave New York. It was not safe for them, and they had much to accomplish. They needed to go to Washington and make arrangements to safeguard the men on the list. They could easily have taken Melbourne and gone after Wollstonecraft, but Melbourne had told Zeb there were others waiting to replace anyone who failed in their duty or was killed. Eliminating Melbourne only meant someone else would take his place. Melbourne did give them Sir Geoffrey's name, but that was all. Zeb thought he was probably back in England by now. He decided to provide protection for the officials Melbourne named and then work on a plan to stop the attack on Clinton. If they started arresting or killing any of the conspirators, it would alert the others that the plan had been compromised.

This time, Zeb and Dan made it out of New York without being seen. However, there were two ladies who were very unhappy to see them leave. Abby never knew when she would see Zeb again, and Lydia was very fond of Dan and made him promise to return when his business was completed. When they were back in Washington, Zeb sent messages to Matt in Batavia, Andrew Jackson in Tennessee, Henry Clay in Kentucky, Daniel Webster in New England, and John C. Calhoun in Charleston, South Carolina. Zeb used a special code that only these men knew so that they would know the message was bona fide. Zeb assigned agents to protect each of them.

It was now the end of July, and word had spread around the country that two of its Founding Fathers had died on the Fourth of July. Both Thomas Jefferson and John Adams had died on the fiftieth anniversary of the Declaration of Independence. Jefferson was eighty-three years of age, while Adams was ninety. The more superstitious thought it was no coincidence and that it was God's way of reminding everyone how important these two men had been. On the other hand, the more practical-minded citizens saw it as an interesting coincidence, but nothing more than that. The newspapers all carried headlines about the deaths and included long articles about the significance of their lives.

Matt had read the stories in the *Republican Advocate* published by David Miller. He was worried about Andrew Jackson and hoped Zeb could protect him from the assassins that were supposed to kill him. Zeb had devised a counterplan, and if all went well, no one would ever know about Machiavelli except those directly involved.

Matt talked to Morgan again in the same tavern. Morgan was very nervous and kept looking toward the door. Soon he knew why. A huge man came in with a crescent-shaped scar on his face. Matt knew his life depended on how he handled the next few moments. Wollstonecraft sat at their table, and Morgan introduced Matt as his friend from the last war. Wollstonecraft gave Matt a look like a predator just before attacking its prey. He must have decided Matt was harmless and asked Morgan to leave with him. Morgan excused himself and told Matt he would be right back. Matt was more than happy to wait in the tavern.

"Morgan, let's take a walk. I need to talk to you." They walked down Main Street for about a quarter of a mile and then returned. Morgan was shaken and had two quick drinks when he came back to the tavern.

"Are you all right, William?"

"Yes. It's just that man. I owe him some money, and he scares the hell out of me. It's really nothing. I'll be all right after some business is taken care of."

Matt decided to press the issue. "What business could that be if you are afraid of him?"

"It is not just him. The people he is associated with are very dangerous. I wish I could tell you more, but everything is not always as it seems."

"Is there anything I can do to help?"

"Not right now, but if I need your help, I will certainly let you know."

Now that Matt knew more about the plot, as related in the coded message from Zeb, he decided not to press the issue of the book on Masonic secrets. They believed it was part of Machiavelli and should be left to take its own course.

"I need to go to Canandaigua in a few days to meet someone about a possible job offer. I'll talk to you after I return."

"Fine, I'll see you then."

Matthew made another trip to the reservation and asked Joseph if he could have Morgan followed. Joseph thought about it for a few moments and came up with just the right person for the task. One member of his tribe was of mixed parentage, white and Indian. He found it easier to mingle with whites and to travel around outside the reservation without too much hostility. He was a skilled hunter and tracker and would be a good choice.

"When will Morgan be leaving for Canandaigua?"

"He told me he has to meet someone on Friday, so he will be leaving Thursday and staying over at the local inn."

"All right. I will ask my friend to travel to Canandaigua and then follow Morgan to see what his business really turns out to be. I'll contact you after he returns, and then we'll speak with him to find out what he has learned."

Matthew returned to Batavia to wait until he heard from Joseph.

CHAPTER 41

WOLLSTONECRAFT WAS BEING REPRIMANDED BY Melbourne. Melbourne looked tired, and Wollstonecraft took some pleasure in this. "How could you not find them? You have men all over the area. He couldn't have disappeared into thin air. My God, man, can't you do anything right?"

Wollstonecraft tried to change the subject. "We managed to track them to Rochester but then lost them. They must have slipped out of Rochester and gone into hiding somewhere. By the way, you don't look very well."

"Keep looking for them. I want both of them dead—and the sooner the better. Your concern for my health is quite touching. I had a very busy time at Mrs. Medley's the other evening and met a new girl who was wonderful. The thing is, I fell asleep for a while and woke up with the strangest feeling. It was as if something of great import had happened, but I could not remember what it was. I still have the feeling but cannot figure out what it was. Anyway, keep looking for them until you find them and put them away for good."

"Yes, sir." Wollstonecraft was thinking that his ploy had worked. It was usually a good ploy to get him to talk about women or wine—or both. He actually thought Melbourne must be going a little crazy. This was the weakest reprimand he had received yet. He had better keep an eye on this new turn in his personality. Maybe he could find a weakness and take advantage of it. He left the consulate and headed back upstate.

Zeb was making arrangements to protect President Adams and the others marked for assassination. Even though he knew the plot against these important men was the most crucial part of Machiavelli, he realized they must still protect DeWitt Clinton. If Matt was able to find out Morgan's role in that part of the plot, they would be able to make better plans to deal with it. It was now August, and the end game rapidly approached. Once he heard from Matt, he could make final plans to handle the protection of the governor. It was also important to keep track of Morgan's efforts to publish his book on the Masons. They might be able to use this to their advantage depending on how events took place.

Morgan was in Canandaigua again to check the cabin to be sure nothing had been disturbed. He stayed at the inn and rode out to the cabin on the usual trail. The only thing different about this trip was the man who followed him. He followed on foot because it was quieter, and he was able to travel long distances without tiring. Morgan rode his horse into the clearing and dismounted. He unlocked the door and went inside to make sure the crates were still there. He checked to be certain they had not been tampered with or had suffered some other type of damage. While Morgan was inside the cabin, his follower watched from the edge of the clearing. He would have liked to have gotten into the cabin while the door was unlocked, but he knew there would be time to find another way after Morgan left. He waited until Morgan was gone and approached the cabin. The door was locked quite securely, and he did not want to break down the door. He needed to find some other way in that would not leave any evidence that someone had been there. There was only one window in the cabin, and it was covered with wood planks, so he could not see anything inside. On closer examination, he found the frame of the window to be loose. He used his knife to pry the frame away from the cabin wall and was rewarded with the entire frame falling into his arms. *Sometimes these white men are pretty dumb*, he thought. He set the window and its frame against the cabin wall and climbed through the opening. The light from the open window illuminated the crates stacked inside. He opened the crates and found the rifles and other materials. He put everything back, climbed out, replaced the window, and left.

Wollstonecraft was on his way to make the final arrangements for the attack on Governor Clinton. He would make sure all the men were in place, the munitions were moved from the cabin to Albion, and the cannons were stored for use as soon as they had a confirmation date on the governor's travel plans. He would also intensify the search for Cardwell and his partner. He had a feeling they would cross paths before too long. He would like to kill them personally and decided to tell his men to keep both of them alive for him if they were captured. He would enjoy this. It gave him something to look forward to.

Joseph sent Matt a message about the discovery of the cabin. When Matt arrived, he found Joseph sitting on a bench in front of his cabin and carving a bird. He waved to him and motioned for him to come over and sit down. Joseph told Matt about the cabin and what his friend had found. Matt knew about the Hall rifle and how effective it could be. The casks of gunpowder could indicate that they planned to make explosives or use cannons. He needed to contact Zeb right away. In the meantime, they decided to have the cabin watched in case the contents were moved.

A few days later, Zeb received word from Phillips that Governor Clinton planned his trip along the canal for early September. His schedule was to be in Rochester on the fifth and travel to Lockport on the sixth. This meant the attack would probably be on September 6 at the alternate location Melbourne thought he was so clever in changing. Now he needed to get his plans in motion. It was now August 9. Zeb had only one month to get ready. He had to return to the reservation and organize the men and weapons needed for the counterattack on Melbourne's men. He didn't want to leave Washington. Zeb would have preferred to stay and make sure the protection for the president, vice president, and other key officials was as good as he could make it.

PART 4

CHAPTER 42

ZEB'S MEN AND THE SENECA Joseph picked were all gathered at Joseph's cabin. Zeb had picked Phillips, Richards, and Dan to take part in the counterattack. He did not want Matthew to be part of it, but he relented when Matthew insisted he be included. After all, he had been in it this far and wanted to finish it one way or the other. Joseph had ten Seneca, including Francis and the tracker, whose name was John Barr. Seth had given Zeb fifteen of his best soldiers, who would be dressed like Indians.

Everyone was there except John Barr and two other men who had been watching the cabin in Canandaigua. They had been gone for over two weeks, and Joseph was getting worried. Much to his relief, they came into the clearing that very moment and joined the rest. They had some very interesting information for the group.

The men had been watching the cabin in Canandaigua for several days. One morning, a wagon appeared on the road just west of the cabin. The muleskinner steered the wagon into the clearing and stopped his mules and wagon near the door. Four men jumped down from the wagon. From their descriptions, two of them were Morgan and Wollstonecraft. They loaded the crates and other materials into the wagon and covered the contents with several furs. After everything was loaded and secured, they headed back toward Canandaigua and took the main road to Batavia. It took them four days to make the trip. Francis and his partner wanted to follow them all the way to wherever they were going, so they did not come to the reservation right away. The final destination turned out to be Albion. When they got to Albion, they unloaded the rifles and other items and stored them in a building by the canal. By this time, Francis had managed to walk near the men and heard what they said. He learned that two wagons would be used to transport two cannons to a location just a few miles west of Albion. This was the site for the planned attack.

Zeb asked Francis to show him the location on their map. It was not the same as the one on the map they had taken and copied from Wharton's room in Rochester. "All right. Let's give them credit for being cautious," Zeb said.

Francis continued his narrative. They decided to stay in Albion for a few days to see where the cannons were taken. Sure enough, two days later the wagons appeared, and the cannons were loaded after dark and taken to the attack site. They were placed so they could cover the canal from two different angles. It would be perfect for raking a packet boat with grapeshot and causing the greatest number of casualties. Now all they had to do was figure out how to take out the two cannons and the men using them. Zeb questioned Francis for more details before deciding the course of action they would take in protecting the governor and his party on the packet boat. He then explained in detail the plan he wanted them to follow. Everyone received a specific assignment. He told them to set up a model of the site and to practice the actions that needed to be made for success. They would need to move very precisely and quickly in order to surprise Melbourne's men and keep them from harming anyone on the packet boat. In fact, the best outcome would be if the governor and his party did not even know an attack had been prevented.

Morgan was back in Batavia working furiously with David Miller to finish his book and get it printed. They both had received death threats. They were quite clear. Print the book and you will be dead men. They ignored the threats and kept at their work. Lucinda became very worried and tried to find Matthew, but he was not at the inn. In fact, he had not been there for several days. The innkeeper had no idea where he was. She was very disappointed and returned home.

Morgan worked hard to get the book ready so that it would be printed at the same time as the attack on the governor. He had no idea the plot he was involved in was much larger. He could be a dead man for printing the book or helping with the rifles and other munitions that would be used in the attack. He could be a blacklisted Mason marked for death or hanged as a spy for helping with the attack. Of course, Wollstonecraft had told him that Melbourne wanted the book published to cause a controversy that might become newsworthy and help the Craft with their efforts. Morgan did not really care about any consequences that might occur from the printing of the book or the assassination of the governor. He thought he was continuing to do his duty for England and was well paid for his efforts. He hadn't thought that Melbourne considered him expendable. If he lived, he had to keep his mouth shut. If he died, it did not matter. Morgan and Miller used material they had from their experience as former Masons. In addition, Morgan was using material provided by Melbourne. By the end of August, the book was nearly finished.

While Morgan and Miller were finishing the book, and Zeb and his men were practicing to stop the attack on the governor, Melbourne's men were making their way to Albion and Medina. Once there, they would all meet and receive their final instructions for the attack. They would be given a rifle, lead balls, powder, and knives. Hopefully, these would only be needed to dispatch those left alive after the cannons finished their work. After everyone was dead, they would bury the rifles and leave the cannons. They would then leave the area and go into hiding as planned. Of course, Melbourne was not one of them. He was staying in New York City and letting Wollstonecraft handle the attack. Sir Geoffrey gave him specific instructions to stay in New York and be ready for the next phase of the plan after Clinton, Adams, Clay, and the others had been eliminated. Sir Geoffrey especially liked the publishing of the book on Masonry. He did not like some of their secrets being revealed, but he thought it would create quite an uproar when it was published. The truly important secrets were known to only a select few, and none of these would be given to Morgan.

Peter was with the governor going over the guest list and itinerary for the trip up the canal. "Now, Peter, you have contacted all the people and made sure they are coming?"

"Yes, Governor. They all agreed to accompany you on this trip."

"Have you checked the itinerary to be sure everything has been arranged?"

"Yes. Everything should be on schedule as planned. Governor, if I may, I would like to say something that you probably won't like."

"Go ahead, Peter. This has never stopped you before."

"Governor, I can't help thinking about the warning Zeb Cardwell's men gave us several weeks ago. I wish you would cancel this trip and wait until next year."

"Peter, you are a worrywart. Hell, the people I had to deal with in Washington when I was in the Senate were probably more dangerous than the ones that may want to kill me. If you haven't noticed, I'm getting old. I'll probably be dead in a couple of years, anyway. No, Peter. I'm going on this trip, and the devil be damned."

Some of the most unbearable summer heat and humidity occurred at the end of August in South Carolina. John C. Calhoun was at his home in Charleston. He was in his study while the guards Zeb had assigned were placed in strategic locations inside and outside the house. The vice president thought it was all a bunch of foolishness, but he knew Zeb well enough to understand that he must have some pretty good information to take these measures. If there was an attempt on his life, he was glad it was Zeb's men protecting him.

He decided to take a walk down to the end of the peninsula and see if there was a breeze coming off the sea to help provide some relief. It was early evening and a good time for a walk. Three of the guards went with him, garnering strange looks from the citizens of Charleston who were out on the street at that hour. Most respectable citizens of Charleston were home having dinner. John C. Calhoun was Charleston's most famous citizen and could pretty much do as he pleased. He was a serious man who loved the South and his beautiful city. He nodded to several people he knew. When he reached the low stone wall that bordered the end of the peninsula where Charleston had been built, he paused for several moments and thought about what was happening in his beloved South today and what might happen in the future. He was a firm and constant supporter of slavery, but he realized that the growing industry in the North would serve as a counterpoint to the "peculiar institution" that was the economic basis for the labor-intensive process of growing cotton and other agricultural products in the South. The next decades would prove to be a challenge for the South, and he needed to be there to help protect and defend her. He loved politics and the challenges it provided, but he loved the South more than anything. If Zeb Cardwell kept him alive to continue his work, that was worth a great deal.

Chapter 43

When the president returned to the White House from his early-morning swim in the Potomac, there was a message from Zeb on his desk. The message was an update for him on events in western New York. In addition, Zeb expressed his condolences on the recent death of his father, John Adams. The president was concerned about the book Morgan was writing. He was a Mason and knew how his fellow Masons might react. He hoped cooler heads would prevail and the book would never be seen by the public. He knew Zeb and the band of men he had collected to protect Governor Clinton would be risking their lives. He prayed that they would emerge whole and unscathed but knew this was wishful thinking. He knew enough about war and battles and the terrible damage bullets and grapeshot could inflict on the human body. He hoped Zeb would be able to capture Morgan and bring him back to Washington for trial and punishment.

The governor's trip up the canal was supposed to be unannounced and private. However, a man as important and famous as DeWitt Clinton could not go anywhere without being recognized. His activities were newsworthy events. He was recognized on the packet boat by many people along the canal, and the word got out that he was making the trip. People turned out at every bridge, town, and village along the canal to wave at and cheer for him. Clinton was a veteran politician and campaigner and took it all in stride. He made several impromptu speeches in addition to meeting with various politicians along the way.

As the boat passed through a quiet stretch near Rochester, Clinton relaxed with his friends and talked about politics and his great optimism for the growth of the country. He knew the canal would open trade with the West. It was already expanding, and people were moving into new territory west of Buffalo. His dream was becoming a reality. He wondered what the country would be like in fifty years—even one hundred. *Too much change for an old campaigner like me*, he thought. The governor and his party would stay in Rochester for two days and then travel to Buffalo. The weather had cooperated. It was warm and sunny, a fine stretch of good weather for late summer. The rest of the trip should prove to be quite as peaceful and uneventful.

Wollstonecraft was very unhappy. He had looked all over for Cardwell. He even went to see Morgan in Batavia again and asked him to be on the lookout for Cardwell. Morgan didn't give a damn about finding Cardwell. All he wanted to do was get the book published, help with the attack, and get the hell out of Batavia. He knew he had to leave after the attack. The death threats were getting more numerous, and he began to take them seriously. After the attack was finished, he would come back to Batavia and get the book printed and distributed to the public. Then he would take Lucinda and the children away. He had enough money from Melbourne. In fact, Melbourne had told him in New York to stay around long enough to publish the book and then leave Batavia and go back to Virginia and wait to be contacted for his next assignment. Morgan was pleased that they still needed him for the cause. He just wasn't sure he wanted to go back to Virginia. He could sort that out once he found a safe place for himself and his family.

Zeb met with his men on September 4. They would leave today and tomorrow and travel alone or in pairs to a prearranged meeting location near the attack site. He went over the plan with them for the last time, and they all knew their roles. "All right, let's start leaving, and I will see you tomorrow evening." Joseph would travel with Zeb, Richards with Phillips, and Matthew with Dan. The others would leave in well-spaced intervals so that the group would not be noticed on the roads. The first group had some tasks to accomplish to prepare for the counterattack.

Chapter 44

September 6, 1826, was a warm, overcast day without rain. Some of the passengers on the packet boat sat on the open top deck enjoying the fresh air. As they approached Albion, they all ducked as the boat passed under a bridge. Several miles west of Albion, an explosion shattered the calmness.

"Peter, what the hell was that?" shouted the governor.

"I don't know, but we had better keep going." Peter realized the governor should have listened to the warnings from Phillips and Richards. War whoops and agonizing screams filled the air. Just inside the woods, men were fighting in close quarters. There were Indians and frontiersman in a life-and-death struggle. Pieces of metal pelted the packet boat. Four of the passengers were bleeding from various cuts and wounds. Suddenly, a Seneca Indian in full battle dress ran toward the packet boat. "Don't be alarmed. I'll get you past this as soon as I can." He leaped on the back of the lead mule and urged the animal to move faster along with the other mules. After about half a mile, he leaped from the mule. "You should be safe now. Keep moving, and don't come back." He ran back toward the fighting.

"Peter, go back this minute and find out what is going on."

"I know what is going on, Governor, and I think you do, as well. We had better keep going and get away from the fighting. I think

Zeb Cardwell just saved your life." The governor looked at Peter, had second thoughts, and nodded in agreement

The first group of Zeb's men to rendezvous near the attack site had found the hidden cannons the previous night. They spiked them so that they would be useless in the attack. It was surprising that Wollstonecraft did not post guards during the night. They watched from their hiding places as the attackers arrived by canal at dawn and took up their positions. The loud noise those on the packet boat heard was the first cannon exploding when Wollstonecraft gave the order for the attack to begin. This was just the beginning of their nightmare. The cannon exploded, instantly killing the five closest men. The man attempting to discharge the second cannon was dispatched from behind with a tomahawk. The Indians let out the old war cries their fathers and grandfathers had used in the Revolutionary and French and Indian wars. Woolstonecraft's men became demoralized and ran. Wollstonecraft shot two of them before he was wounded in the arm. The tide of battle turned quickly. Joseph, Francis, the other Seneca, and the soldiers from Fort Niagara cut down Wollstonecraft's men and killed them without mercy. After all that effort to steal the Hall rifles and ship them to the site, the only one fired during the fight was by Wollstonecraft, killing two of his own men. When Wollstonecraft realized what was happening, he ran east along the towpath.

"Richards and Phillips, go after Wollstonecraft, and don't let him get away."

Wollstonecraft breathed heavily as he ran toward his horse that was tied to a tree to the east. He ran as fast as he could, with Phillips and Richards gaining on him. Richards and Phillips were not fast runners, but they did the best they could.

"Move over and let me get him." Francis flew by them and leaped on Wollstonecraft's back. His tomahawk flashed in the sun as the flat side crashed into Wollstonecraft's head. He stumbled and fell with Francis still clinging to his back. "Tie this monster up before he comes to and breaks me in half." They tied and gagged him and left him to be picked up later. That proved to be a mistake.

By the time they arrived at the scene of the attack, it was pretty much over. Zeb had a lot of blood on him, but none of it proved to be his.

"Two of them are still alive. Three of the Seneca and five of the soldiers are wounded, but they should be all right if we get them some medical care." Zeb was proud of his group, especially the Seneca. The plan had worked because of their help. He sent Phillips and Richards to catch up with the governor's packet boat and check for casualties. Morgan was nowhere to be seen.

"We need to get this place cleaned up. I don't want any evidence of what happened here left for anyone to find. Sure as hell someone may show up just to find out what the noise was all about. Everyone needs to change fast so they aren't seen wandering around and scaring the hell out of the local population." Joseph and the rest of the Seneca laughed. "We'll load the rifles and anything else you find in the wagon and take it out of here. Bury all the bodies back in the woods deep enough so animals don't find them. Roll the cannons back into the woods as far as you can and cover them with branches and anything else that will hide them. They are too big to bury or take with us. Someone will eventually find them, and the locals will have a real mystery to solve."

The dead were buried in a common grave. After the dirt was packed down, they covered the area with leaves and dead branches. The survivors were given water, and their wounds were cared for. Zeb had made arrangements for any survivors from Melbourne's group to be taken to Fort Niagara and placed into custody. He didn't take any pleasure in killing Melbourne's men, but it was better than the murder of Governor Clinton and the rest of the people on the packet boat.

Phillips and Richards returned. "What did you tell the governor?"

"It was funny, Zeb," said Richards. "I don't mean laughing funny, but strange funny. The governor agreed to talk to us since he knew who we were. Our friend Peter was on the packet boat. The governor seemed to accept our version of what happened, but he looked shaken. I think Peter and the governor both really know what almost happened."

"And just what is our version?"

"I told them we were practicing for a drama that would reenact one of the Revolutionary War battles that happened here in New York. I said it was part of the local celebration of the fiftieth anniversary of the signing of the Declaration of Independence. I told them the cannon was old and exploded because some idiot put too much gunpowder in it."

"They actually believed that outrageous story?"

"No, I don't think they did, but they didn't question it, either. They were happy to continue on their way to Buffalo."

Zeb laughed. "I can't believe you told that story to the governor and got away with it." Some of the men started laughing, and soon the rest joined them. It helped relieve the stress from the recent fight. "I want everyone to get out of here. We have a wagon to load, and some of us need to get to Fort Niagara. Go get Wollstonecraft and bring him back here. Let's get these wounded men and the rest of the material in the wagon."

When Richards and Phillips returned a few minutes later, they were running and out of breath. "You won't believe this. He's gone, and there's not a trace of him anywhere."

CHAPTER 45

MELBOURNE HAD HANDPICKED A TEAM of assassins to kill the president, the vice president, Andrew Jackson, and the other officials. One assassin was tasked to kill each. They were supposed to complete their assignments as close as possible to the attempt on Governor Clinton. None of the assassins knew the attack on Clinton had been a failure. By the same token, none of Zeb's men providing protection for the other high-ranking officials knew the outcome of the attack on Governor Clinton.

The same evening as the attack on Governor Clinton, three assassins were preparing to carry out their assignments. John Grosvenor prepared to assassinate the president. He had been watching the White House for several weeks and the routine President Adams followed. The president was consistent in one thing. Now that the weather was warm, he went for a swim in the Potomac every morning. Grosvenor had almost decided to kill Adams between the White House and the river, but he came up with a better plan. He would use the cover of darkness to kill the president. He smiled to himself from his place of concealment. The plan had been too simple, but that did not matter. What mattered was killing John Quincy Adams.

Hiram Middleman was in Charleston, South Carolina, to kill John C. Calhoun. He waited to gain entrance to the house after dispensing with the guards. He was ready to make his first move as soon as darkness blanketed the city.

Peter Wexler was in Tennessee. He had the toughest assignment. The Hermitage was a difficult house to get into, but he had found a way. His disguise as an itinerant preacher had enabled him to gain access to the house and grounds. This gave him a very good reason to be in the house. Now it was nearly time for the prayer service he had arranged for Andrew Jackson and his family.

It was nearly suffocating in the closet where Grosvenor was hiding. He had walked right into the White House during the day in the guise of a carpenter who had been hired to work on one of the unfinished rooms. He had worked most of the day with no one paying him any particular attention except the guards who were looking for him at that very moment. The closet was in an unused room down the hall from the president's bedroom. The guards were still searching when he opened the door and went to the president's study. The door was unlocked. President Adams sat at a desk reviewing some papers. He looked up over his reading glasses into the barrel of a very nasty-looking pistol. He did the first thing he could think of. President Adams threw his inkwell at the intruder as Grosvenor fired a shot. In a spectacular collision, the bullet smashed the inkwell and sprayed ink all over the bedroom. The bullet missed Adams by inches. Two guards burst into the room and saw the assassin advancing on the president with a knife. They shot him on the spot, and Grosvenor dropped to the floor. His wounds were not fatal, but the hangman's rope would be. A shaken Adams spoke to his rescuers. "I want to thank you, gentlemen, from the bottom of my heart for saving my life. You will both be amply rewarded for this."

One of the men replied, "Mr. President, we were only doing our duty. We are just glad we managed to stop him." The president realized now how serious the plot was that Zeb had discovered. He hoped the others who were in danger would be as fortunate as he had been this evening. The would-be assassin was taken from the White

House to prison, and President Adam's staff was left to clean up the mess. Between the ink and the blood, it was quite a task.

The itinerant preacher led the family in prayer. He made sure he was close to the nearest door. The only people in the room besides himself were Andrew Jackson, Jackson's wife, and two of their servants. The guards were outside. After the first prayer, the preacher pulled a pistol from his Bible and shot Andrew Jackson. The small-caliber bullet hit Jackson in the shoulder, and he fell back on the couch. His wife and servants started screaming when the blood soaked his shirt. The preacher ran from the house with one of the servants right behind him. "Stop that man! He just shot Mr. Jackson!" The guards knocked him to the ground, but Wexler came right back to his feet again with a knife he had pulled from his boot. "Don't get near him. We'll handle this," one of the guards told the servant. "Drop the knife, or we'll shoot you dead right here, right now." Wexler lunged at the guard on his left, and as he did, the other guard shot him in the side. Wexler grunted and fell. He dropped to the ground and lay very still. "The bastard cut me," the other guard snarled.

"Don't worry. You will live. It's only a scratch." Two more guards came running. "Go into the house and see how Mr. Jackson is doing. He's been shot." A servant went for the doctor while two of the guards kept Jackson on the couch and tried to slow the bleeding.

"Son of a bitch. It hurts like hell. Did you get the bastard?"

"Yes, Mr. Jackson, we did. He's gone to meet his maker and will probably spend a lot of time in a very hot place."

"I guess it is a good sign he is swearing," said Mrs. Jackson. "The last time he was shot, he was pretty quiet, and that was much worse."

The doctor arrived and took over. "You are very lucky, Andy. It is only a flesh wound and should not be a problem after it heals. I'll get you bandaged to stop that bleeding."

"It had better be all right, you old sawbones. I have to campaign for president, and I don't need a bum arm while I'm doing it." They all laughed, and Jackson soon joined them. *Thank God he is going to be all right,* his wife thought.

It was another hot and humid night in Charleston, even though it was late summer. Hiram Middleman was ready to carry out his assignment. There were four guards surrounding the house and two inside. He only needed to pass by two of the guards at the rear of the house. He approached the house from the next street. He had a length of wire with wooden handles he used as his favorite killing instrument. He took out the first guard without a sound. The next guard saw him coming but could not get his hands up fast enough. He was dead in short order. Hiram was enjoying himself. This wasn't work for him. This was fun. He climbed the sturdy vines that grew up the back of the house and entered through an open window. John C. Calhoun was in the next room taking care of some of his personal effects. When the door opened, he looked up and saw the assassin bearing down on him. He calmly lifted the only loaded pistol on his desk and shot Hiram Middleman right between the eyes. The look of surprise on Middleman's face was classic. He dropped like a stone, and the remaining guards converged on the room at the sound of the pistol shot. They were shocked at the scene they found.

"You all are going to catch holy hell from Zeb Cardwell for this. It's a good thing I clean one pistol an evening, or I'd be on this floor."

Morgan arrived home that evening all dirty and smelling of gunpowder. "Where have you been, William?" Lucinda asked.

"I was shooting with some friends, and one of the muskets blew up."

She didn't know whether to believe him or not, but she kept her thoughts to herself. "I saved you some food. Clean up, have something to eat, and come to bed."

Everything had happened so quickly that Morgan didn't see who the attackers were. All he remembered were the Indians bearing down on them after the cannon exploded, and it scared the hell out of him. He panicked and ran. He just wanted to get out of there as fast as he could. He didn't care about Wollstonecraft, Melbourne, the Craft, or any of their plans. He just wanted to stay alive. He went back to Batavia and made up the story he would tell Lucinda when he got to his house. What an awful mess. His main worry was Wollstonecraft. If Wollstonecraft survived the attack, he would come after him. He doubted anyone could have survived, though. Those who weren't killed by the exploding cannon were cut down by the Indians. The attackers had become the attacked. This was not part of the plan, and Melbourne would be furious. Well, to hell with Melbourne. He had a job to do now, and that was to get the damned book published and his family far from Batavia.

Zeb and his men reached Fort Niagara late that night. The survivors from Wollstonecraft's group were taken to the infirmary and then put in the stockade. Zeb met with Seth and made arrangements for the transfer of the survivors after they were able to travel.

CHAPTER 46

MATT WENT TO BATAVIA AND soon found that Morgan, David Miller, and the book on the Masonry were the talk of the village. Someone had set fire to the newspaper office, and Morgan was in jail on charges of not paying his bills. Matt went to see Lucinda. She told him William had been working to finish the book, and he wanted to leave Batavia as soon as it was finished. She was afraid he would be killed before the book was ever published. He was in jail for an unpaid debt, and she feared something would happen to him. She was trying to have him transferred to Canandaigua, which had a larger and more secure jail. She had some friends working on the transfer who told her it would probably happen in a few days. Matt told her he would see what he could do.

Several days later, Morgan was transferred to the jail in Canandaigua. When Matt went to talk to David Miller about getting Morgan released, Miller laughed. "He will be released, all right, from what I have heard, but not how you would expect." He told Matt about the plans he discovered. The Masons were going to take Morgan from the jail to Fort Niagara and make him disappear. This gave Matt an idea, and he went to the inn in Caledonia where Zeb, Richards, and Phillips were waiting for him. They discussed the idea and soon managed to change it to a plan that could work.

Zeb needed to make a few arrangements first, and then they would be ready.

It was nearly dark, and the jail's most famous person was very worried. William Morgan paced from wall to wall in his cell and kicked the dirty straw that covered the floor. There were a few flickering candles in the corridor, and the light moved in waves across the bars in his cell, sometimes providing illumination, but mostly providing very little light. Morgan was still scared. When they transferred him, there were men outside the jail who told him he was a disgrace to the Masons, and death was too good for him. There was a shadow in the corridor, and the jailor, his ring of keys held in front of him, came to Morgan's cell and opened the door. "Get the hell out of here. I have some official paperwork ordering your transfer to Rochester. They say it is for your own safety, and they are doing it for your wife and children. If I were you, I'd get my ass moving and go with them. I can't promise to keep you alive here if any trouble starts." That was enough for Morgan. He left the cell and followed the jailer.

When Morgan and the jailer entered the front of the jail, both were seized immediately. The jailor was tied securely and a rag stuffed in his mouth. The same was done to Morgan, and a bag was pulled over his head. He was so scared that he almost lost control of his bowels. He was dragged from the jail, kicking and squirming, and shoved into a waiting coach. The coach was similar to those used by undertakers, but larger. It was black and pulled by four strong horses. Three men climbed into the coach with Morgan, and the driver cracked a whip over the top of the horses. They moved quickly away from the jail. No one said anything until they were well beyond Canandaigua and heading north for the ridge road that went from Rochester to Lewiston.

David Miller's information proved to be correct. The coach traveled to Victor and then Rochester, with stops to change horses. When it reached a secluded stretch of road north of Lockport, the driver was forced to stop. A large tree with a thick tangle of branches blocked the road. Suddenly, four masked and armed men appeared. "Everyone get out of the coach—and fast. Keep your hands where we can see them." They grabbed Morgan and shoved him back in the coach.

The first man out of the coach said, "What the hell is this? Don't you know who that man is?"

"No, and we don't give a damn. Now shut up and do what you are told. Drop your valuables in this sack. We want your pocketbooks, money, watches, anything of value. If you hold out on us, you're dead." They men reluctantly complied. "Now take off your clothes and throw them by the side of the coach. You can leave your underwear on." After the men took off their clothes, the bandits tied their hands behind their backs and sat them down at the side of the road. Then they tied their feet together. Next, the armed men moved the tree out of the way.

"Don't you know who this man is? This is the man who has revealed the secrets of our secret order, the Masons. Give us our clothes, and let us deal with him as we had planned. We won't tell anyone about this."

One of the bandits laughed. "I told you to shut up. Gag them all, and let's get out of here." He turned toward the helpless Masons. "Once you get the ropes off, you can get dressed and walk home. Your passenger will come with us." One man climbed into the driver's seat, and the other three got in the coach with Morgan. They continued in the same direction—west.

"William, it is all right. We are not Masons, and we don't want to kill you for publishing that book of yours. Even though you are my uncle, I cannot forgive you for the treachery you have participated in. We are taking you for a much different reason than for writing your book. You see, we know who you really are. Your real name is Andrew Fletcher, and you lived in England for a number of years before returning to your native Virginia. We also know you worked as an agent for the British and are still helping them. We know about Machiavelli, Melbourne, and the work you have been doing for him." They removed the gag but left his hands restrained.

Morgan was so shocked that he could not speak. When he managed to collect his thoughts, the first thing he could say was, "You are my nephew, Matthew—my blood relative. I also considered you a friend during the war."

"Yes, I was your friend during the war and continued to be until I recently discovered who you really are and what you have done. Now I just want to see you punished."

"You should have left me with those Masons. They would have killed me eventually."

"I suppose that is possible, but I don't think it would have happened. Yes, they are angry with you and David Miller, and they don't want the book published, but the local Masons aren't killers."

"Don't be so sure about that. I have faced some pretty angry people these last few weeks." Morgan began to think he might be able to find a way out of this.

Zeb spoke to Morgan. "You don't know me, Morgan, but we have been looking for you for quite some time. Matthew has helped us find you, and now you are going on a little trip."

Richards and Phillips took turns driving the coach, while Matthew and Zeb kept watch on Morgan. Many people saw the coach that night, but none of the men in the coach had any idea what stories would be told about the abduction of William Morgan and his fate. Zeb didn't really care. All he wanted to do was bring Morgan to Washington, where he would have a military trial that would determine his fate. The only people he felt truly guilty about were Morgan's wife and family. He and Matt would never be able to tell her what had happened to her husband, or anyone else, for that matter. Whatever stories or events came from his disappearance must be allowed to play out. President Adams had been very clear about that. The coach continued on into the night and eventually reached Fort Niagara just before dawn. Morgan was locked in a well-guarded storeroom until the next night when he would start a journey that would take him by ship from Lake Ontario into the St. Lawrence River and then to the Atlantic. Eventually, he would arrive in Baltimore and be taken to Washington. It was a long trip, but Zeb wanted to be sure Morgan was far away from western New York and anyone looking for him as quickly as possible.

Zeb needed to talk to Seth. He found him asleep in his bedroom and gently woke him. "Jesus, Zeb. What the hell is going on? This fort hasn't been this busy since the last time the English attacked." Seth rolled out of bed and put on a long dressing robe. They went into the sitting room, and Seth poured both of them a good measure of brandy.

After they had sipped for a few seconds, Zeb started to explain what was going on. "Seth, I need your word on something."

"Of course, Zeb. You have it."

"We just brought a man here named William Morgan. He will be gone after dark tonight. I have arranged for a ship to pick him up and take him to Washington by the long water route. There may be some people looking for this man. You don't know a William Morgan, you have never heard of him, and you have no idea where he is."

"I get your point, Zeb. Don't worry; no one here will say a thing. I'll make sure of it."

"Thank you, Seth. I'll talk to you more tomorrow. Go back to bed and get some rest."

"Are you going on the ship with Morgan?"

"No. I have some unfinished business in New York."

"All right. I'll see you after the sun comes up."

Zeb returned to the room where the others waited. They were enjoying some cider and celebrating Morgan's capture. Zeb looked at them and smiled. "You have all done well. This has been a difficult mission, but before any of you decide to go to bed, I need to tell you we are not completely finished. Morgan will be on his way soon, but there is one more task we need to take care of. Richards and Phillips don't have any choice in this. They will be going with me, but you, Matt, do have a choice. You have completed your charge by helping us find and capture Morgan. You are free to go back to Boston and resume your life. I've noticed that leg of yours has been bothering you lately, and I don't want you to take any more chances or put yourself in danger any longer."

"You know, Zeb, I would love to go back to Boston eventually, but before I do, tell me what this task is, and let me decide if I want to come along."

"Fair enough. Melbourne has gone into hiding. We are pretty sure he has not left the country, and I want to find the son of a bitch and make sure he is punished for his part in the plot. Hopefully we will get him to talk and implicate the others. I think Melbourne is a coward and will tell us anything we want to know if we give him the proper incentive."

"In that case, count me in."

"Dan and a few other men are in New York looking for him. We'll join them as soon as we get there."

CHAPTER 47

SEPTEMBER WAS A GOOD TIME of year in New York. Summer still maintained a hold on the city, and autumn was not far away with the prospect of leaves changing color along the Hudson, clear days, and cool, star-filled nights. This particular day, however, was quite warm for September, and the stevedores and other men working at the docks were sweating like it was July or August. The British ship *Orion* was taking on provisions and cargo for its voyage to England. The captain had been told he would have two very important passengers and not to sail until they were on the ship. He hoped they would be able to clear the harbor early the next morning. It was getting late in the day, and the men had not yet appeared. The captain was paid to bring his cargo in on time, and he was getting impatient. He did not want to waste time waiting for some upper-class dandies who were probably related to some wealthy lord with too much influence. The captain shrugged in resignation and continued supervising the loading of the ship.

Zeb, Matt, Richards, and Phillips waited for Dan in the Lion and Eagle. When Dan walked in, he was surprised to see all of them sitting at the same table. He thought it would be just Zeb and Matthew, but he was glad the others were there, as well. He had some pretty good news, and Zeb could tell from the look on his face that he had something to tell them.

"Hello, Dan. It is good to see you. Why don't you tell us what you have found out before you burst?" They all laughed.

"Am I that easy to read? Yes, I guess I am. Well, I do have good news. I know where Melbourne is hiding, but let me ask you something before I tell you. Considering his character and interests, where do you think he would choose to hide?" He received blank looks from everyone except Zeb.

"Of course, the lecher must be at Mrs. Medley's fine establishment, drinking his fill of wine and having his way with the girls. How long has he been there?"

"I talked to Lydia, and she told me he has been there ever since he found out the attack on Governor Clinton failed. It must be about two weeks. She also told me he is getting ready to leave New York by ship. He hasn't told anyone which one, but that won't be hard to find out. All we have to do is follow him when he leaves."

"That's fine, Dan, but how will we know when he leaves? And when he does, who is going to tell us?"

"I have that worked out. The girls all hate Melbourne and cannot wait for him to be gone. They will tell Lydia as soon as they find out. Lydia will send a message here for Jim, and then he will pass on the information to us. The timing will probably be very close, but I think it is the best we can do."

"Well done, Dan, but I think we need to have someone watching Mrs. Medley's, and I know just who the two men are." He looked at Richards and Phillips. They nodded and left the tavern. They already knew how to contact Zeb, and with any luck, they would be able to capture Melbourne before he made it to his ship. "Dan, you stay here and wait for the message from Lydia. Jim will take good care of you. Matt, you come with me. We are going to check with the harbormaster on ships sailing for England."

They found two ships scheduled to sail for England over the next two days. They were both at the same wharf. They went to the wharf and kept a watch on both ships. When Dan arrived just before dark, he told them Melbourne was leaving Mrs. Medley's at midnight. He wanted to board the ship before dawn in order to be less conspicuous in case anyone was watching for him.

After a few hours of watching and waiting while the air became cooler and fog formed on the water, they heard the sound of approaching carriage wheels. Zeb could see two riders several yards behind the carriage. It was Phillips and Richards. They had put rags on their horses' hooves to deaden the sound. The carriage stopped about twenty yards from the gangplank of the *Orion*, and two men got out. Phillips and Richards grabbed the first man, and just as Zeb and Dan were about to grab the second man, a shot rang out. Zeb fell to the ground. The second man ran to the gangplank, someone helped him aboard, and the gangplank was quickly pulled on board. Dan dragged Zeb away from the ship so they could take a look at the wound. "God damn it, leave me alone. It's only a flesh wound. I'll be fine."

"Sure you will," Phillips said. "For a flesh wound, it's bleeding pretty well. Let's get him to Jim's and have a doctor take a look at him."

"Before you take me anywhere, who do we have, and who was the one that got away?"

Richards answered, "We have Melbourne, but we don't know who the other one was. Melbourne's not talking."

"You know where to take Melbourne. Go there now and make sure you have enough guards to keep an eye on him. Get me up. I think I can walk on this leg."

They gently lifted Zeb to his feet, and he tested the leg that Richards had field bandaged. He could put weight on it but needed to have the bullet out if it was still there. Matt and Dan took Zeb back to the Lion and Eagle, and Phillips and Richards took Melbourne to prison.

Sir Geoffrey was angry that he had nearly been captured. He had put his trust in Melbourne and then had seen the entire plan go balls-up. Now he had to return to England and report on this failure. He did not look forward to that. They would have to think of a better plan.

Melbourne was put in a cell. There was straw on the stone floor and a slop bucket for his bodily functions. It was certainly a far cry from the comforts found at Mrs. Medley's. At least Sir Geoffrey had escaped capture. Melbourne had little hope for his own fate. He was certain he would be executed, but before that, they would interrogate him for information. He needed to be strong and not tell them anything. Time would tell.

The doctor finished examining Zeb's wound. Zeb had been right; it was only a flesh wound. The ball had passed through the muscle and nicked some blood vessels during its passage. The doctor had bandaged the leg and given instructions for Zeb's care. He told Zeb he should be fine in a few weeks, but he needed to rest for several days to let the wound heal.

After the doctor left, Zeb told Matthew and Dan what to do next. "Melbourne is sitting in his cell thinking he is probably going to be tortured and then executed. Let's let him keep thinking that. We used the Seneca herb mixture on him once, so let's do it again. We still have enough left, and the chemist knows how to mix it with the other ingredients. We can put it in his food and wait for it to take effect. He probably won't remember anything."

CHAPTER 48

MELBOURNE WAS BEGINNING TO HATE the smell of his cell. The slop bucket was nearly full, and there were bugs in his mattress that were quickly migrating to his body. He had never felt so filthy. The jailer brought him food that was tolerable, considering the circumstances. The jailor's helper took the slop bucket to be emptied and then brought it back. That was a relief, at least for a few hours. Melbourne ate his meal and then began to feel sleepy. In spite of the bugs, he curled up on his bed and went to sleep. A few moments later, the cell door opened, and Zeb hobbled in, along with Phillips. They checked Melbourne and made sure he was asleep, but not too deeply. They were fortunate. As soon as they began asking him questions, he started to talk.

Zeb asked him some simple questions first and then moved to the more serious ones. He wanted to know when Melbourne found out the plot on DeWitt Clinton had failed and what he did after he found out. Melbourne told them he learned of the failure two weeks ago and had immediately gone to Mrs. Medley's. She was a good friend and gave him shelter with no questions asked. Of course, the money he gave her helped ensure her silence. Zeb asked where Wollstonecraft was, and Melbourne became agitated. "I hope that son of a whore rots in hell. He never could do anything right. I blame myself for continuing to trust him to finally get it all right. If I ever find him, I'll personally kill him."

"So much for British loyalty," quipped Phillips in a low voice. Zeb smiled and then asked a key question. "Who was the man with you when you were boarding the ship?"

Melbourne remained quiet for a few seconds, and they thought the drug was wearing off. Then he began speaking. "The man is Sir Geoffrey Bournewith, one of the key leaders of our organization. He was waiting for the news, just as I was. When I told him about the failure of the attack, as well as the survival of the targeted American leaders, he told me to find somewhere to hide for several days, and he would get word to me. He sent a message to me at Mrs. Medley's telling me to meet him at the consulate. When I did, he said I had to return to England with him. He had to tell the others, and my role was over for now. I needed to leave before I was apprehended."

Zeb continued, "Who were the other men involved in the plot?"

"I don't know any of the men in England, but there were several here in America." Melbourne gave their names and where they lived. Zeb was amazed. They were all wealthy men, and Masons, as well. They would be taken care of in due time.

They finished the questioning and left Melbourne sleeping. When Melbourne awoke later that evening, he had that same familiar feeling that something important had happened, but he could not remember what it could possibly be. He rolled over and went back to sleep after slapping at a few of the bugs crawling under his shirt.

Zeb and Phillips returned to the Lion and Eagle and met with the other men. They discussed Melbourne's fate and those of the other men involved in the plot. Their biggest worry was Wollstonecraft. He had disappeared, and no one knew where he was. Zeb told Matt that President Adams wanted to speak with him before he returned to Boston. In fact, he wanted to speak with both of them. Zeb said he had some personal business to take care of here in New York before they returned to Washington. Eyebrows were raised, and Zeb stared them down and told them it was none of their business. He left with Phillips and Richards.

When her maid announced a visitor, in fact three visitors, Abby knew it must be Zeb. She composed herself but could not hide a look of distress when she saw him. Zeb hobbled over to her on crutches. She looked at the two men and then back at Zeb. He smiled. "It's not as bad as it looks. I injured my leg in a fall, but the doctor tells me it will be fine in a couple of weeks. Anyway, let me introduce my friends who will be leaving in a few minutes." Phillips and Richards smiled. Zeb made the introductions. As they were leaving, Phillips said, "Take good care of him, and make sure he gets some rest."

"Oh, I know all about Mr. Cardwell. I'll make sure he rests."

Abby looked at Zeb. He was tired and thinner than last spring. She knew better than to ask too many questions. "I'll have my doctor look at you tomorrow, Zeb Cardwell. In the meantime, let's have a look at that leg. It seems like I am always tending to your injuries, and don't give me any more stories about a fall. Somebody probably shot or stabbed you."

"Abby, I can't deny it. You will see for yourself soon enough. I can only stay for a few days, and then I have to be in Washington to see President Adams. This time, I promise to come back right after that." From the look in his eyes, Abby knew he was telling the truth. She would find out more of the details about what he had been up to soon enough after she attended to his leg.

Zeb had told Matt to wait in New York a few days and that he would contact him. Matt sent a message to Sarah in Lockport and told her he would be there by the end of October if all went well with his business interests.

Dan returned to Mrs. Medley's that night. Lydia took him upstairs to her room without saying a word. She undressed him quickly and shed her own clothes as fast as she could. They went to bed and stayed there until they could see the first rays of the sun under her door. They had managed to talk a bit during the night between episodes of lovemaking.

"Daniel Sherman, you have been up to something. You did not have that scar on your shoulder the last time I saw you. It looks like a bullet wound to me. Are you going to tell me how it happened?"

"I'll tell you someday, Lydia, but right now we are leaving here, and you are never coming back."

"Dan, I don't care where we go as long as I can get out of here and be with you."

"We are not only leaving, Lydia, we are going to get married, if you will have me."

"Oh, Dan, you know my answer. Of course I'll marry you. I knew that the first night I saw you. You looked so uncomfortable—I had to rescue you." They both laughed.

"Lydia, let's get dressed and leave. A friend of mine has made arrangements for a carriage to take us into New York and rooms to stay in for a few days until we are ready to travel to Washington." They dressed quickly and went to the waiting carriage.

CHAPTER 49

PRESIDENT JOHN QUINCY ADAMS WAS concerned about the uproar the kidnapping of William Morgan had caused. Anti-Masonic feeling spread around the country, and the Masons were accused of killing Morgan. He would like nothing better than to reveal what really happened, but this was not possible. In fact, Zeb Cardwell and Matthew Prescott were waiting for their meeting with him that very moment. President Adams told his secretary to show them in.

Zeb's leg was healing nicely, and he needed only one crutch. Abby's doctor had taken good care of him, and Abby was an excellent nurse. President Adams stood when they came into his office and walked around his desk to shake hands with them. "I want to congratulate you, Zeb, for a fine job, and you, Matthew, for your role in this. Your country and your president are very proud of you."

"Thank you, Mr. President. I couldn't have done it without my men, and Matt has proven to be more than we ever expected."

"Yes, I understand he has, and I am most grateful. I know we had some uncomfortable moments in April when I charged him with helping in this affair, but I think we both understand each other."

"Mr. President, I have had a very busy and challenging several months with Zeb and the others since our meeting in April, and I wouldn't trade it for all the tea in China."

"Well said, Matthew. Zeb, what is the news about Mr. Morgan? The newspapers all over the country have him dead at the hands of the Masons."

"Yes, I have been following the stories. Mr. Morgan is now on a ship bound for Washington. It is nearly the end of October. I expect to hear something from the captain in a few days. They will need to stop and take on provisions before docking in Baltimore."

The president spoke next. "Good. What about Mr. Melbourne and Mr. Wollstonecraft, Zeb?"

"Mr. Melbourne is still in our prison in New York, and Wollstonecraft is still missing."

"What about the men involved in Machiavelli? They are all prominent businessmen and Masons. I suppose with the current state of feelings in the country, we could let the press know who they are, and the anti-Masonic mob would take care of them, but that is just my wishful thinking. I don't suppose there is much we can do. We don't have any evidence against them except for the word of Melbourne, which is not worth very much."

"We are watching them, Mr. President. It may not come to anything, but if they do try to meet or correspond, we will find out."

"Good. Well, I have a meeting in a few minutes. I just wanted to personally thank both of you for what you have done for your country. Matthew, I understand you are considering expanding your shipping business into the area west of Buffalo. I have made arrangements for all the necessary documents and permissions to be granted. This is the least I am able to do as a most grateful president for your role in this endeavor."

"Thank you, Mr. President."

Zeb and Matt left the mansion and went to the Constitutional Tavern for lunch and sat in the same room where it all began a few months ago. They drank a toast to success. Both men realized they had become friends and had come to respect each other.

"Well, Matt, now that this is all over, what is next for you?"

"I'm leaving tomorrow for Lockport to see Sarah. I need to figure out how to take advantage of the canal and the trading opportunities that will develop. I think Buffalo will grow fast and trade along with it. I'll take Sarah back to Boston, and we'll be married there. Then I need to decide who will take care of the shipping business in Buffalo. Sarah and I will live in Boston, but who knows? Maybe we will move west to Buffalo as the country expands, as I'm certain it will."

"Matt, I need to tell you something. It wasn't my idea to have you help us. I gave the information to President Adams, but with a request that we not involve you. He made the final decision to include you in the group. But I admit I was wrong. You have been of immense help in stopping the attack on DeWitt Clinton and especially in helping find Morgan. One suggestion. Stay away from Batavia when you travel to Lockport. If anyone has figured out what really happened, you could be in real danger."

"Don't worry, Zeb. As much as I feel sorry for Lucinda Morgan, I know she has friends who will help her. I just need to see Sarah and get back to Boston."

"Good. Make sure I receive an invitation to the wedding. Also, don't get too comfortable. I may need you to help us again sometime."

That same evening, Melbourne was asleep in his cell. The guards had been drugged. He never heard the noise of his cell door opening. The footsteps were what awakened him. "What the devil!"

"Shut up, you fool." Wollstonecraft pulled him from his bed and tied his arms and legs securely. He carved a Masonic symbol on Melbourne's chest as he screamed in pain. "This is what happens to those who fail the Craft." A sharp knife ripped Melbourne's body from his sternum to his groin. Wollstonecraft made another cut horizontally, and Melbourne watched in horror as his intestines dropped to the floor. He continued screaming as Wollstonecraft left. He was found the next morning, lying in his own offal with his mouth wide open in a final, silent scream. There was something carved into the right side of his chest that looked like the letter *A* over the letter *V*.

Chapter 50

THE STORM WAS GETTING WORSE, and the ship was taking on water. The Atlantic could be a son of a bitch in early fall, and this night was no exception. The hurricane season was supposed to be almost over, but this storm sure seemed like one. The captain had twenty years of experience in the navy and did not want to lose his ship, especially the passenger he was carrying. Zeb had been quite clear on that point.

The pitching and rolling of the ship was making Morgan even sicker. He was not good on ships, and this was no exception. One of his greatest fears was drowning, and now it appeared to be more than a likely possibility. When the storm became more intense, they stopped bringing him food and emptying his slop bucket. Morgan and his cell were a mess.

The captain told the helmsman to keep steering into the wind. They had stripped as much sail as they dared and were now just riding out the storm. The waves were huge, and if the storm continued much longer, they were dead men. If they made it to daybreak, they might have a chance. The storm continued to batter the ship, but the ship held together. By morning, the wind began to subside, and the waves became smaller. The captain breathed a sigh of relief. They would sail to Boston and take on supplies before continuing to their final destination. He had the crew bring Morgan on deck, and they poured buckets of water over him to clean him off. The cell was cleaned, and Morgan was shackled to the bulkhead once again.

The ship took on provisions in Boston with no one being the wiser concerning the now famous passenger on board. They sailed into Baltimore and handed Morgan over to four of Zeb's men, who would bring the spy to Washington. There would be no trial, no publicity, and no defense attorney. His fate would be determined by a secret tribunal.

Epilogue

Wollstonecraft eluded Zeb's men and found passage to England. He became the gamekeeper on Sir Geoffrey's estate, plus other duties that Sir Geoffrey gave him to carry out for the Craft.

The storekeeper in Plain Brook disappeared in November and was never seen again. The village drunk swore he saw Indians take him away, but no one believed him. Stories eventually began to circulate around the area that he was seen in Canada. Others claimed his ghost had appeared to several people in the nearby swamps. No one was ever able to confirm these stories. If anyone had asked Francis Smith about the storekeeper, they might have learned something about what actually happened. As far as Francis was concerned, he was glad the man was gone and didn't care where.

Matthew Prescott and Sarah Reynolds were married in Boston in May of 1827 after a nearly proper courtship. It was a beautiful spring day with clear skies and seasonal flowers. The announcements in the Boston newspapers informed the public that the couple would honeymoon in the Caribbean and then return to Boston. Of course, the newspapers did not know they were expecting their first child or that they planned to move to Buffalo so Matthew could personally supervise his new shipping venture on the Great Lakes. The guests included several people that were not known to Boston society. The most surprising guests were two Seneca Indians everyone was talking about. They all wanted to find out how the Indians knew Matthew Prescott.

Zeb and Abby were married in New York in a small, private ceremony in July of 1827, officiated by a minister and a rabbi. Mr. and Mrs. Matthew Prescott, Mr. and Mrs. Daniel Sherman, and several of Zeb's men attended, as well as the same two Seneca Indians who were in Boston in May. The Boston society matrons would really have something to talk about if they ever found out someone of Abby's status had married a Jew. Rabbi Solomon read a letter of congratulations from President John Quincy Adams at the ceremony.

John C. Calhoun became very superstitious about his dueling pistols and continued to clean them on a regular basis. They were always nearby when he was alone.

Sir Geoffrey Bournewith may have escaped to England, but he was not forgotten. President Adams told Zeb to find him and execute him. He had been sentenced by the same tribunal as Morgan. The president told Zeb that he might want to encourage Matthew Prescott to help him. The president was convinced Matthew brought them good luck.

William Morgan wanted to work with stone again. He got his wish to practice his craft, but only to help build the prison he would remain in for the rest of his life. Even if he managed to escape, he would have to swim a hundred miles to the nearest mainland. Morgan's only consolation was that his disappearance had caused more damage to the Masons than the publication of his book of secrets ever would. However, the Craft still looked for him.